Deadly Prayers

"How did you get the scratch on the back of your hand?" my partner Peters asked.

Reverend Brodie looked at it. "We've been doing a lot of yard work around the church," he said. "It happened the other day when we were pruning."

A car pulled up just then. A man and three women got out. "We're having a prayer session right now," the Reverend explained, backing away from Peters and me. "We're praying for the murderer's immortal soul. It's our way of turning the other cheek."

The purpose of the prayer meeting stuck in my craw. I would have preferred the prayers be for Angel or even her mother, Suzanne. I didn't think the scumbag who murdered Angel deserved any prayers. I didn't then, and I don't now.

UNTIL PROVEN GUILTY

J.A. JANCE

AVON BOOKS ◢ NEW YORK

UNTIL PROVEN GUILTY is an original publication of Avon Books. This work has never before appeared in book form. This work is a novel. Any similarity to actual persons or events is purely coincidental.

AVON BOOKS
A division of
The Hearst Corporation
105 Madison Avenue
New York, New York 10016

Copyright © 1985 by J. A. Jance
Published by arrangement with the author
Library of Congress Catalog Card Number: 84-91265
ISBN: 0-380-89638-9

First Avon Books Printing: July 1985

To Jay, Jeanne, and Josh,
and bargain matinees everywhere.

Chapter 1

SHE was probably a cute kid once, four maybe five years old. It was hard to tell that now. She was dead. The murder weapon was a pink Holly Hobbie gown. What little was left of it was still twisted around her neck. It wasn't pretty, but murder never is.

Her body had rolled thirty feet down a steep embankment from the roadway, tossed out like so much garbage. She was still tangled in a clump of blackberry bushes when we got there. As far as I could see, there was no sign of a struggle. It looked to me as though she had been dead several hours, but a final determination on that would have to wait for the experts.

My name is Beaumont. I've been around homicide for fifteen years, but that doesn't mean I didn't want to puke. I was careful not to think about my own kids right then. You can't afford to. If you do, you crack up.

My partner, Ron Peters, was the new man on the squad. He had only been up from burglary a couple of months. He was still at the stage where he was long on homicide theory and short on homicide practice. This was his first dead kid, and he wasn't taking it too well. He hadn't come to terms with the idea of a dead child as evidence. That takes time and experience. His face was a pasty shade of gray. I sent him up to the road to talk to the truck driver who had called 911, while I prowled the crime scene along with a small army of arriving officers.

After the pictures, after the measurements, it took the boys from the medical examiner's office a good little while to drag her loose from the blackberry bushes. If you've ever tried picking blackberries, you know it's easy enough to get in but hell on wheels to get back out. By the time they brought out the body bag, I was convinced we weren't going to find anything. We slipped and slid on the steep hillside, without finding so much as a gum wrapper or an old beer can.

I climbed back up and found to my relief that I had waited long enough. The swarm of killer bees that calls itself Seattle's press corps had disappeared with the coroner's wagon. I like reporters almost as much as I like killers, and the less I have to do with them, the better off I am.

Peters' color was a little better than it had been. He was talking with a man named Otis Walker, who was built like an Alaskan grizzly. In the old days people would have said Walker drove a sewage truck. These are the days of sanitary engineers and environmentalists, so Walker told us he drove a sludge truck for the Westside Treatment Center. That may sound like a high-class detox joint, but it isn't. A rose by any other name may smell as sweet, but if it looks like a sewage plant and smells like a sewage plant, that's what I call it.

However, Otis Walker had a heavy, square jaw and a nose that showed signs of more than one serious break. His biceps resembled half-grown trees. I chose not to debate his job title. Despite his fearsome appearance, he was having a tough time talking to Peters. The words stuck in his throat, threatening to choke him.

"You gonna catch that SOB?" he asked me when I appeared over Peters' shoulder. I nodded. "I got a kid of my own at home, you know," he continued, "almost her age. Wears the same kind of gown. Shit!" He stopped and swiped at his face with the back of one meaty paw.

"That's our job," I told him. I wondered what kind of murder this was. The easiest ones to solve are the hardest ones to understand, the husbands and lovers and wives and parents who murder people they ought to cherish instead of kill. The random killers, the ones who pick out a victim at a football game or a grocery store, are easier to comprehend and harder to catch. That's the problem with homicide.

I turned to Peters. "You about done here?"

He nodded. "Pretty much."

Walker pulled himself together. "You guys through with me?"

"For right now," Peters told him, "but don't go out of town without letting us know where to find you. With all this timely-trial crap from the Supreme Court, we may need to get ahold of you in a hurry.''

Walker looked dolefully at the blackberry clump halfway down the hill. He shook his head. "I wish I never saw her," he said. "I wish I'da just driven past and never knew she was down there, know what I mean?" He climbed back into the huge blue tractor-trailer and started it, waving halfheartedly as he eased past where Peters and I were standing.

"What now?" Peters asked.

"Not much doing here as far as I can tell. Let's go get something to eat and come back for another look later." The call had come in about eleven in the morning. It was now well after three. I'm one of those guys who has to have breakfast, lunch, and dinner, or I begin to foam at the mouth. I was getting close.

Peters gave me a reproachful look. "How can you think about food? Where are her parents? The medical examiner says she died sometime around nine or nine-thirty. Someone should have come looking for her by now."

"Somebody will come," I assured him. "With any kind of luck it will be after we finish eating." As it turned out, they found us before we even got out of the car in the parking lot at G.G.'s. A marked patrol car pulled up beside ours. The officer rolled down his window. His name was Sanders. I had seen him around the Public Safety Building on occasion.

"What have you got?" I asked him.

"Missing child," he replied. "A girl. Five years old."

"Brown hair, in braids?" I asked him. "Holly Hobbie nightgown, pink?"

He nodded. "The call came in a little over half an hour ago. I went to check it out before calling you guys in. It could have been someone who forgot to come home for lunch."

"She missed lunch, all right," I told him. "And it looks as though we will too. What's the address?"

"Gay Avenue," he answered. "Forty-five forty-three. I'll lead you there."

Peters wheeled out of the parking lot behind the patrol car. "Why the hell didn't someone call us right away?" he muttered. "We could have been there a long time ago."

Peters sometimes reminds me of an Irish Setter—tall, reddish hair, good-looking, loose-jointed, not too bright at times. "Calling us on the radio would have been as good as taking out a full-page ad in the *Post-Intelligencer*," I told him. "We just got rid of that mob of reporters, remember?"

Peters' jawline hardened, but he said nothing. Our partnership was still new and relatively uneasy. We drove through Magnolia without the fanfare of lights and sirens.

Magnolia is set apart from the rest of Seattle by a combination of waterways and railroad tracks. On this warm day in late April, flowers in well-manicured lawns were just coming into their own. Magnolia is mostly an older, settled, residential neighborhood. Some of the houses are stately mansions with white columns and vast expanses of red brick. I think I had a preconceived notion of the kind of house we were going to, but I was in for a rude awakening. Gay Avenue was anything but gay in every sense of the word.

The patrol car led us to a hidden pocket of poverty just off Government Way a few blocks east of the entrance to Discovery Park. The house at 4543 Gay Avenue was a ramshackle two-story job that had formerly been someone's pride and joy. It had fallen on hard times. Once-white shingles had deteriorated to a grubby gray. Here and there a missing one gaped like a jagged, broken tooth. Two giant stubs of trees gave mute testimony that there had once been a front yard. Yellowed newspapers and old tires littered the weedy grass. It was a perfect example of low-rent squalor plunked down in an otherwise acceptable neighborhood. If I had been one of the neighbors, I would have considered suing whoever owned that eyesore.

At the sound of the cars a band of barefoot, ragtag kids came racing around the house. One pressed a runny nose against Peters' window and stared in at us as though we were gorillas in a zoo. Peters turned to me. "Well?" he asked. "Are we getting out, or are we going to sit here all day?"

I'd rather take a beating than knock on a door and tell some poor unsuspecting soul his kid is dead. I always think about how I'd feel if someone were telling me about Scott or Kelly. There's no way to soften a blow like that. "Don't rush me," I growled. "It's the worst part of this job." I got out and slammed the door.

Sanders came up just then. "What's the name?" I asked him.

"Barstogi. Mother's name is Suzanne. Kid's name is Angela, but they call her Angel."

"Father?"

"I didn't see one. There's some kind of meeting going on in there. Probably ten or twelve people."

Peters ambled up. He glanced at his watch. "What time did you say the call came in?"

"About two forty-five," Sanders answered.

"Five hours after she's dead, somebody finally notices she's missing." Peters' voice was grim.

I pushed open a gate that dangled precariously on one rusty hinge. Gingerly I threaded my way through the debris and climbed some rickety wooden steps. The bottom one was gone altogether. Most of the others were on borrowed time. We stood on a tiny porch with those kids silently staring up at us. None of them said a word. It struck me as odd. I would have expected a barrage of questions from a group like that.

"Don't these kids talk?" I asked Sanders.

He stopped with his hand poised, ready to knock. "Not to me and probably not to you either. I meant to tell you. It seems to be some kind of religious cult. The kids aren't allowed to talk to anyone without permission. Same thing goes for the adults."

He knocked then. Through a broken windowpane in the door we could hear the low murmur of voices inside, but it was a long time before anyone answered.

The woman who opened the door was in her mid to late twenties. She was about five-six or so, solidly built. She had long dishwater-blonde hair that was parted in the middle and pulled back into a long, thick braid that hung halfway to her hips. With a little makeup, a haircut, and some decent clothes she might have been reasonably attractive. As it was, she was a very plain Jane. She looked very worried.

"Did you find her?" she asked.

Sanders didn't answer. Instead he motioned to me. "This is Detective Beaumont, ma'am, and Detective Peters. They'll be the ones helping you now." He backed away from the door as though from the entrance of a cave full of rattlers. He didn't want to be the one to tell her. Peters hovered in the background as well, leaving the ball in my court.

"May we come in, Mrs. Barstogi?" I asked.

She glanced uneasily over her shoulder. She looked as happy to have us on her doorstep as we were to be there. "Well, I don't know. . . ," she began hesitantly, stopping abruptly as someone came up behind the partially opened door.

"I thought I told you to get rid of them, Sister Suzanne." The unseen speaker was a man. His words and tone held the promise of threat.

"I did," she said meekly. "I sent the first one away like you said. There are two more." Before she had looked worried. Now she seemed genuinely frightened.

"Your faith is being tested," he continued severely. "You are failing. Jesus is watching over Angel. You have no need to call on anyone else. Jesus wants you to trust in Him completely. Haven't you learned that yet? Are you still leaning on your own understanding?"

She shrank from the door at his words. I think she would have slammed it in our faces if I hadn't used my old Fuller Brush training and stuck my foot in the way. "We need to talk to you, Mrs. Barstogi. Is there someplace where we can be alone?"

I moved inside and Peters followed. The man who had been standing just out of our line of vision was a heavy-faced, once-muscular man in his late forties who was well on his way to going to seed. He was a little shorter than I am, maybe six-one or so. He was wearing one of those Kmart special leisure suits that went out of style years ago. On his chest hung a gold chain with a heavy gold cross dangling from it. The suit was electric blue. So were his eyes, glinting with the dangerous glitter of someone just barely under control.

He placed himself belligerently between Suzanne and me. "We're all family here," he said. "No one has anything to hide from anyone else. Privacy and pride are Satan's own tools."

"Are you Angela's father?" I asked him.

"Of course not!" he blustered.

"Then I have nothing to say to you." I looked around. The living room was furnished with several period pieces in the Goodwill-reject style. There was an assortment of degenerate chairs and worn couches. The gray carpet was mottled with stains and soil. Seated around the room was a group of women. They could have been sardines from the same can for all you could tell them apart. None of them spoke. All eyes were riveted on the man who stood between Suzanne Barstogi and me.

"Is your husband here, Mrs. Barstogi? Where can we reach him?"

She glanced surreptitiously at the man's face before answering, as if expecting him to tell her what to say or whether or not she should answer at all. "I don't have a husband," she said finally, looking at the floor.

The four of us had been standing in a muddy vestibule, just inside the door. Now Peters moved swiftly around me. He took Suzanne Barstogi's elbow. Before anyone could object, he led her out onto the porch. The man made as if to follow, but I barred his way.

"We are going to talk to her alone," I told him. "If you don't want to end up in jail, you'll stay right here while we do it." I turned and left him there, closing the door behind me.

The children, standing in an ominously quiet group, were still watching. Peters was attempting to shoo them away as I came out the door. He maintained a firm grip on Suzanne's arm. I think he figured she might try to dash back into the house if he let her go.

"Mrs. Barstogi," I said. "When is the last time you saw your daughter?"

"When I put her to bed." Her eyes were wide with fear as she answered. I couldn't tell if it was fear for her daughter or fear of the consequences that would greet her when she returned to the house.

"What time was that?" This, unsurprisingly, was from Peters. I never met anyone so concerned about time.

Suzanne paused uncertainly. "It must have been between three and four."

"In the morning?" Peters asked incredulously.

She nodded. "She fell asleep at church. I carried her in from the car and put her to bed." She spoke as though there were nothing out of the ordinary in the hour.

"What was she wearing?"

"I told the other man all this. Do we have to go over it again?"

"Yes," I answered. "I'm afraid we do."

"She was wearing a pink nightgown, one she got for Christmas last year."

"We'll need you to come downtown," Peters said.

"Now?" she asked.

"Yes, now," I told her. Peters propelled her off the porch. He opened the door and helped her into the car, motioning for me to follow. "I'll drive," he said.

It figured. If he drove, I would have to tell her. I'm not the kind to keep score or hold grudges, but about then I figured Peters owed me one.

I followed her into the backseat. She scrambled as far as she could to the opposite side of the car. She looked like a cornered animal. "Who is that man in the house?" I asked as Peters turned on the ignition. "Is he a relative of yours?"

She shook her head. "That's Pastor Michael Brodie. He's the pastor of our church, Faith Tabernacle. I called him when I couldn't find Angel. He said the best thing for us to do would be to turn it over to the Lord. He brought the others over, and we've been praying ever since. Wherever two or more are gathered together—"

"What time was that?" Peters interrupted. He was beginning to sound like a broken record.

"I got up about eleven and they got here a little before noon," she said. Peters made a sound under his breath. I couldn't hear, but I don't think it was too nice.

"Angel does that," Suzanne continued. "She wakes up before I do. She'll have breakfast and watch TV." She stopped suddenly as though something was just beginning to penetrate. "Why are we going downtown?" It was the moment I had been dreading. There was no way to postpone it further.

"I believe we've found your daughter," I said gently.

"Where is she? Is something the matter?"

"A little girl was found in Discovery Park earlier this morning. I'm afraid it may be Angel. We have to be certain. We need you to identify her."

"Is she dead?" she asked.

I nodded. I deliberately didn't tell her about the gown. I didn't want to dash all hope at once. She needed some time for adjustment. I expected tears, screaming, or wailing. Instead, Suzanne Barstogi heard the words in stunned silence. She closed her eyes and bowed her head.

"It's my fault," she whispered. "It's because I called you. Pastor Michael is right. I'm being punished for my lack of faith."

We were at a stoplight. Peters turned and looked at her. "She was dead long before you called us," he said bluntly. "Your lack of faith had nothing to do with it." The light changed, and we went on.

Suzanne gave no indication that she had heard what Peters said. "I disobeyed, too," she continued. "I snuck upstairs to use the phone so no one would know." She lapsed into silence. We left her to her own thoughts. It seemed the decent thing to do.

By the time we led her up to the slab in the morgue, Suzanne Barstogi was a study in absolute composure. When the attendant pulled back the sheet, she nodded. "I killed her, didn't I?" she said softly to no one in particular. She turned to me. "I'm ready to go home now."

Chapter 2

WHEN we brought Suzanne back to Gay Avenue, the place was crawling with people. It seemed to me there were even more Faith Tabernacle people than earlier in the day. Evidence technicians had gone over the house thoroughly, searching for trace evidence, dusting for fingerprints, looking for signs of forced entry or struggle. Everything pointed to the conclusion that Angel Barstogi had left the house willingly, wandering off maybe with someone she knew.

So who did she know? I looked around the room. All these folks, certainly, including Pastor Michael Brodie himself, who was holding court in the living room. He was very angry. His parishioners were walking on eggs for fear of annoying him further, abjectly catering to his every need.

Sergeant Watkins brought us up to speed on the situation. Police procedures notwithstanding, Brodie was accustomed to being in charge. He didn't want anyone talking to his people outside his presence. It was only after Watkins threatened to jail him for obstruction of justice that he finally knuckled under. He sat by the door, still silently intimidating those who filed past him. One by one our detectives took people to separate rooms to record their statements. They were not eager to talk. It was like pulling teeth. We could have used some laughing gas.

Peters and I took our turn in the barrel. The other officers had pretty well finished up with the adults and were going to work on the grungy kids. I took one of the boys, the one who had pressed his nose against the car as Peters and I drove up the first time. We had to walk past Pastor Michael. He shot a withering glance at the kid. The boy seemed to cower under its intensity.

"What's your name?" I asked as we went up the stairs.

"Jeremiah."

"You scared of him?"

He nodded. We went into a bedroom and closed the door. The bed was unmade. I straightened a place for us to sit on the bed, then took a small tape recorder from my pocket.

"Do you know what we're going to do?" He shook his head. "I'm going to ask you some questions and record both the questions and the answers."

"Are you sure it's okay? I mean, we're not supposed to talk to people."

"Why?"

"Pastor Michael says that people on the outside are tools of the devil and that we can catch it from them. It's like chicken pox."

"You won't catch anything from me, Jeremiah. I promise." I switched on the recorder. "My name is Detective J. P. Beaumont. It's five twenty-five p.m. on Thursday, April twenty-eighth. This statement is being taken in reference to Angel Barstogi, deceased. What is your name, please?"

"Jeremiah Mason."

"And are you giving this statement willingly?"

He nodded his head. "You'll have to give your answers aloud," I told him.

"Yes," he whispered.

"Did you know Angel, Angela Barstogi?"

"Yes." His answer was so muted that I didn't know whether or not my recorder would pick it up.

"You'll have to speak a little louder, Jeremiah."

"Yes," he said again.

"When is the last time you saw her?"

"Last night at church. We were playing tag."

"Was there anything unusual about her last night?"

He thought for a moment, then shook his head. "No," he said, remembering the recorder.

"How long have you known Angel?"

"Long time," he replied.

"Were you friends?"

He made a face. "Angel's a girl," he said. Obviously being a girl precluded her being a friend. "Besides," he added, "she's just a little kid."

"Do you know why we're here asking questions?"

"Somebody said it's because Angel's dead."

"That's true. And we're trying to find out who did it. That's my job."

"Pastor Michael says God did it because Angel wouldn't obey the rules."

"What rules?"

"She was all the time talking to people. Even when Pastor Michael got after her, she still did it."

"He got after her?"

"He gave her a licking in church. That's what he always does, but Angel never cried no matter what he did. The other kids knew that if they'd cry he'd stop. Angel wouldn't cry. That made him real mad."

"I'll just bet it did," I said. "And what about you? Did you ever get a licking in church?"

He nodded. "Once for stealing some food from the kitchen after dinner and once for running away."

"Are you afraid you'll get in trouble?"

He nodded again. "Pastor's mad that we're all talking to you."

"How old are you, Jeremiah?"

"Eight." As we spoke, I had noticed a bruise on top of his wrist. A small part of it was visible at the bottom of his sleeve. I pushed the shirt sleeve up, revealing five distinct marks on his arm, a thumb and four fingers.

"How did that happen?"

He shrugged and looked sheepish. "I fell down," he said.

"Where do you live?"

"In Ballard, not far from the church."

"With your parents?"

"With my mom and my stepfather."

"And how does he treat you, your stepfather?"

"All right, I guess."

I could see I had gone beyond what he would tell me. It was one thing to talk about Angela Barstogi. It was quite another to talk about Jeremiah Mason. He could still feel pain. Angel couldn't. "Is there anything you'd like to add?"

He considered. "I'm going to miss Angel," he said, "even if she was a girl."

I reached into my pocket and pulled out a business card with my name and telephone number on it. "If anyone gets after you about today, I want you to call me, understand?" He nodded.

I started toward the door but Jeremiah stopped me. He reached behind a broken-down dresser and pulled out a cup, a child's cup with the ABC's around the top and bottom. The name Angela was written in bright red letters on one side. Gingerly he handed it to me.

"It was hers," he said. "Pastor Michael told her to get rid of it, but she didn't. We hid it." He stopped and stood looking at the cup, shifting uneasily from foot to foot. "Do you think I could keep it?"

Nodding, I returned it to his grubby hand. "I think Angel would like that."

As soon as he had once more concealed the cup, I walked Jeremiah back downstairs. Brodie glared at him as we came past, but he refrained from comment. I guess Sergeant Watkins' threat of jail had carried some weight with Brodie. He had all the earmarks of a bully and a coward, someone who would lord it over those who were weaker than he. I wondered about his frustration at being faced with a tough little kid who refused to cry. I wondered if, by not crying, Angel Barstogi had signed her own death warrant. It was a possibility.

As a homicide detective, however, I'm not allowed to act on mere hunches. I can move only when I have solid evidence that points me in a certain direction. I had a feeling about Michael Brodie, but nothing substantial. Jeremiah's revelations about the "lickings" in Faith Tabernacle gave us a basis for making inquiries, but nothing more.

Slowly the crowd in the house diminished as people filtered out. At last there were only Peters and Brodie and Suzanne and me. We took them into separate rooms.

Suzanne's original numbness was beginning to wear off, but she had a hard time following my questions, to say nothing of answering them. Some things, like the date of her divorce, escaped her completely. She claimed she simply could not remember.

That bothered me. Cops learn to listen to what's said as well as to what isn't; then they combine the two in order to get at the truth. Suzanne was under a lot of stress, but nonetheless there was a lot she wasn't saying. I didn't know why. She was hiding something, that much was certain, but I didn't know what or who she might be protecting. Did Pastor Michael Brodie exert such influence that he could coerce a mother into concealing her own child's murderer? It was a chilling thought, even for someone who has been in this business as long as I have.

We left Gay Avenue around ten o'clock that night. I was starved. It had been a long time since breakfast. We went to the Doghouse, a lowbrow place in my neighborhood that stays open all hours and has fed me more meals than I care to count.

Peters and I don't exactly see eye to eye on food. Peters is an enzyme nut. He eats sprouts and seeds, which may be okay for rabbits, but in my opinion that stuff is hardly fit for human consumption. He avoids sugar and salt. He consumes little red meat and can declaim for hours on the evils of caffeine. In other words, there are times when he can be a real pain in the butt. I don't mind eating with him, but I've thought of carrying earplugs for when he gets on his soapbox.

I, on the other hand, thrive on ordinary, garden-variety, all-American junk food. Karen got the barbecue in the divorce settlement. It went with the house. Since that was the only piece of cooking equipment I had mastered and since barbecuing was unavailable in my downtown high-rise, I converted to restaurants. Other than the department, the Doghouse is my home away from home.

It's at Seventh and Bell, a few blocks from where I live. It's one of those twenty-four-hour places frequented by cops, cabbies, reporters, and other folks who live their lives while most people are asleep. The waitresses wouldn't win beauty pageants but the service is exceptional. The food is plain and plentiful, without an enzyme in sight. Connie, a grandmotherly type with boundless energy, tapped her pencil impatiently as Peters groused about the available selections. She finally pacified him with an order of unbuttered whole wheat toast and some herb tea.

I wolfed down a chili burger with lots of onions and cheese while Peters morosely stirred his tea. "What do you think?" I asked eventually.

"It's got to be some kind of brainwashing," he said. "He's got her hiding something. The question is, what?"

"Beats me." On the way across town we had exchanged information as much as possible. Afterward Peters had become strangely quiet and withdrawn. That's the tough part about breaking in a new partner. There's so much to learn before you can function as a team. Ray Johnson and I had worked together for almost eleven years before he bailed out to become chief of police in Pasco. I had become accustomed to his habits, his way of thinking. It was hard to tell where Ray's ideas left off and mine began.

With Peters it was different. He had a guarded way about him. I was still very much outside the perimeter. After two months of working together I knew almost nothing about his personal life other than the fact that he was divorced. For that matter, he didn't know much about my personal life, either. It's a two-way street.

Peters gave me a long, searching look. "You ever have anything to do with a cult before?" he asked. The question was evidently the tip of an iceberg. There was a lot more lurking beneath the surface than was apparent in his words.

"No," I replied. "First time."

"Lucky for you," he said, returning to his studious examination of the bottom of his teacup. I waited a moment to see if he would continue. He didn't. At last I gave up and changed the subject.

"What's the agenda for tomorrow?"

Before he could answer, a noisy group meandered out of the bar in a flurry of activity. I caught sight of Maxwell Cole at the same time he saw me. He extricated himself from the group and came to our booth. Max is a hulking brute of a man whose handlebar mustache and ponderous girth give him the appearance of an overfed walrus. "Damned if it isn't old J. P." he said, holding out his hand. "Fancy meeting a brother in a dive like this."

I ignored his hand, knowing it would go away. Max's reference was to our fraternity days at the University of Washington. There was no love lost then and even less now. Then we had been rivals for Karen Moffit's affections. I won that round. Karen Moffit became Karen Beaumont, and Maxwell Cole got his nose out of joint. It's ironic that five years after Karen divorced me, I'm still stuck with Maxwell Cole. I'm a bad habit he can't seem to break.

These days he's a columnist for Seattle's morning daily, the *Post-Intelligencer*. His column, "City Beat," serves as a pulpit for Maxwell Cole, self-professed righter of wrongs. He doesn't pretend to be unbiased. He's one of those liberals who always roots for the underdog whether or not it has rabies.

I could handle this self-righteous, pontificating son-of-a-bitch a little better if I hadn't spotted old Maxey Baby down on First Avenue a couple of times, hanging around the porno flicks. I don't think he was down there doing movie reviews. He looked at home there, a regular customer, like me in the Mc-Donald's at Third and Pine.

Cole likes to take on the Seattle Police Department, casting all cops in the role of heavies. I've lost more than one case after he has tried it in the press, noisily waving the flag of the First Amendment all the while. One of his success stories, Harvey Cahill, killed somebody else within a month after Max got him acquitted. By then nobody remembered Cole's bleeding heart. They went gunning for someone to blame. Yours truly took a little gas.

"Still packing a grudge, I see," Max said, carelessly reaching across our table to flick a drooping ash into an unused ashtray. He was oblivious to the fact that he was intruding. I'm sure the idea never crossed his mind.

"I'd say it's a little more serious than a grudge," I allowed slowly. "Antipathy would be closer to the mark."

He turned from me to give Peters a nearsighted once-over, blinking through thick horn-rimmed glasses. "This your new partner? What happened to Ray?"

"Ask the public information officer," I said. "He gets paid for answering your questions. I don't."

Max looked pained. "You know, it doesn't pay to deliberately offend the press. You might need our help someday."

"It's a risk I'm willing to take."

Connie brought the coffeepot and shouldered Max out of the way. She glared meaningfully at his cigarette and removed the offending ashtray. There didn't seem to be any love lost between Connie and Maxwell Cole, either.

"Come on, Max," someone called from the door. "We're waiting on you."

Max paused as if reluctant to abandon the confrontation. He finally sauntered away. Once the door closed behind him, Connie turned back to me. "He writes mean stuff about you," she said, "and he don't tip too good, either."

That made me laugh. "Maybe I'll get even by doing some

writing of my own one day," I told her. I had no idea the opportunity would present itself so soon.

Once she left the table, I turned back to Peters. "What the hell does J. P. stand for?" Peters asked.

"Don't ask."

"That bad?"

I nodded. He had the good sense to drop it. Jonas Piedmont Beaumont was my mother's little joke on the world and me too, naming me after her two grandfathers. I first shortened it to initials and then settled for Beau. The initials had stuck with people who'd met me during my university days. I wanted to punch Max in the nose for bringing it up. He once had a nickname too. Maybe I could return the favor.

"Now, what's the next move?" I asked, returning our focus to the business at hand.

Peters looked at his watch. "It's only eleven. What say we go back to the office and sift through whatever statements have been transcribed. That'll tell us who we should hit up tomorrow."

"Maybe we'll have a preliminary medical examiner's report by then too, with any kind of luck."

We went back to the office. For another four hours we pored over the Gay Avenue transcripts. Sergeant Watkins must have moved heaven and earth to have them typed that fast. The pattern was fairly obvious. The adults were noticeably vague about details prior to five or six months ago, although two of them indicated they had previously lived in Chicago. They all gave similar accounts of the last few days leading up to Angel's death. I paid particular attention to the statement from Jeremiah's stepfather, Benjamin Mason. The handprint bruise on that kid's arm hadn't come from a fall. No way. Like Jeremiah, all the children gave every evidence of being scared silly. In his own way, Jeremiah was just as plucky as Angel Barstogi. I hoped he wouldn't have to pay the same kind of price.

We finally called it quits about four a.m., so tired we couldn't make our eyes work anymore. I invited Peters to stay over with me, but he wanted to go on home to Kirkland, out in the suburbs across Lake Washington. He in turn offered me a ride home, but I wanted to walk.

"It'll settle me down so I can sleep."

I walked down Fourth. Most city dwellers avoid deserted

streets late at night. They're afraid of being mugged; but then, most people don't pack a loaded .38 Smith and Wesson under their jacket.

Seattle is a deep-water port situated on Elliott Bay in Puget Sound. Huge container and grain ships ply the waters just off the ends of piers that jut out at the foot of steep hills. Although the water isn't more than five blocks from where I live, I seldom smell the ocean. That morning, though, the wind was blowing a storm in across the sound, and the pungent odor of saltwater permeated the air.

I walked with hands shoved in pockets against suddenly chill air. Maxwell Cole came to mind as I walked. He's had it in for me ever since I beat him out with Karen, and for the last twenty-five years of my life it seems like he's always been around, always there to ding me. He was the reporter who covered the shooting when I was just a rookie.

A crazy kid holed up with a gun, and I had to shoot him. He was the only man I ever killed, a boy really, eighteen years old. It tore me up. For weeks afterward I couldn't eat or sleep. All the while my good ole buddy Max, my fraternity brother Max, was playing it to the hilt, interviewing the boy's widowed mother, distraught girlfriend, stunned neighbors, making me sound like a bloodthirsty monster. A departmental review officially exonerated me, but exonerations don't capture headlines. His coverage of that one incident created a killer-cop legend that twenty years of quality police work hasn't dented.

My relationship with Maxwell Cole is anything but cordial, yet, whenever I encounter him in public, he always acts like an old pal has just snubbed him. Old pal hell! As far as I'm concerned, it always takes a monumental effort at self-control just to keep from decking him. I walked into the lobby of my condo, the Royal Crest, feeling some elation that once more I hadn't hit him and given him more fuel for the fire.

The walk had done me good. I was glad to open my apartment door. My place is tiny, a little over eight hundred square feet, with a view that overlooks the city. Lights from Seattle's skyline suffuse my living room with a golden glow, so much so that I often leave the lights off and just sit. Friends have told me it's great light for thinking or screwing. I've done a whole lot more of the former in that room than I have the latter.

Thinking was what I wanted to do right then. I undressed,

pulled on a frayed flannel robe, and settled into my easy chair, a tall old-fashioned leather one that I managed to salvage from the debris when I moved out of the house in Sumner.

A sense of quiet settled over me as I gazed out the window. I thought about Angela Barstogi. Angel. Probably was one now. Yesterday morning she had been a living, breathing five-year-old. This morning she was dead. What had made the difference? What had turned her into a homicide statistic?

I thought about the people I had met during the day, turning them over in my mind one by one, trying to get a clear picture of who was involved. I thought about the men whose statements I had read, from Brodie to Jeremiah's stepfather, Benjamin, to Thomas, Amos, and Ezra. They all seemed like dregs to me, seedy characters you'd expect to find living in a halfway house somewhere. They got my hackles up, made me wary.

Thinking about the people involved, assessing them, trying to sort out the relationship—that's how I get on track with a case. And in my mind that's exactly what this was. The beginning of a case, just like any other. What I couldn't have known that morning as the sun began to color the cloud cover outside my living room window was how much Angel Barstogi's murder would change my life.

I thought that after I found her killer, everything would continue as it had before. That was not to be. After poor little Angela Barstogi, nothing would ever be the same.

Chapter 3

I DRAGGED myself out of the house at seven-twenty and walked to work, propping my eyes open with a cup of muscle-bound coffee from the McDonald's at Third and Pine. The restaurant mirrors the flavor of the street, and Third Avenue in downtown Seattle is an absolute cross section of life in this country. I love it and hate it.

I feel the same way about the fifth floor of the Seattle Police Department. That's the homicide squad. I've worked homicide for almost fifteen years. I came to the fifth floor with all my illusions intact. I was convinced that murderers were the worst of the bad guys and that capturing killers was the highest calling a police officer could have. It took me a long time to lose that illusion, to figure out that murder isn't the worst crime one human can inflict on another. Maybe part of my disillusionment was just getting older and wiser. I don't know when I stopped viewing it as a sacred charge and started seeing it as a job. I wouldn't be surprised to find that it happened about the time Karen left me. Most of my life went sour about then.

But it also had something to do with the ambitious new cops showing up on the squad, the ones who see homicide as a ticket to bigger and better things, who are more concerned with how their exploits will read in the morning paper than they are about doing the job right. They are plugged full of university credits in law enforcement theory taught by professors who have never dirtied their hands with real blood. I don't like the finished product that shows up on the force or the ones that filter up to the fifth floor, either. I think the feeling is mutual.

All this goes to say that I don't care for too many of the guys there these days. Ray and I had been a breed apart from the

26

others, and it was only after he left that I looked around the
floor and found out what was there. Peters is young, but from
my observation, he's probably the best of the lot. That is not to
be taken as high praise, however, and even now we still hadn't
settled into a solid working relationship. Peters arrived a few
minutes after I did that morning and dropped a file folder on my
desk. It was a preliminary report from the medical examiner's
office.

He said nothing when he tossed it in front of me. He stalked
away, hands stuffed in his pockets. I didn't have to look at the
report to know what was coming. I didn't need a coroner's text-
book terms to tell me that Angel Barstogi's last few minutes on
this earth were brutal testimony to man's inhumanity to man. If
anything, the technical phraseology only made it worse, more
dehumanizing.

It said that cause of death was strangulation and that the murder weapon had indeed been the twisted nightgown around her
neck. Analysis of stomach contents revealed that she had eaten
a hamburger within an hour of time of death. It detailed other
injuries—broken bones, bruises, cuts. The medical examiner
had removed bits of human tissue and other substances from beneath her fingernails. Surprisingly, she had not been raped. At
least she had been spared that indignity. It was a blessing, a
very small blessing.

Peters came back and threw a newspaper down in front of
me. I don't take a newspaper. It's a personal protest against
people like Maxwell Cole. Consequently I hadn't seen the lurid
headlines above Angel Barstogi's baby-toothed smile. One
thing about newspapers, they never disappoint me. I always expect the worst. I consistently get it.

The preliminary report was still warm in my hand, yet I could
have read the same information on the front page and not bothered to go to the office at all. My phone rang before I could say
anything to Peters. It was Arlo Hamilton, the public information officer, wanting to know if I had anything for his nine a.m.
press briefing.

"Are you shitting me?" I asked him. "Those assholes know
everything we do. Maybe they should be giving us the briefing."

"Don't growl at me, Beau. I'm just trying to do my job."

"Me too," I responded, and slammed the receiver down in

his ear. "Let's get the hell out of here," I said to Peters, grabbing up both the paper and the file. "This case has just become a media event."

I was pissed off as we headed for the elevator, pissed and looking for somebody to blame. Peters happened to be close at hand.

"What'd you do?" I asked sarcastically. "Pick up the report on the way home and drop it by the newspaper just for fun?"

Peters stopped in midstride and glared at me. "I thought maybe you did. Maxwell Cole isn't an old fraternity buddy of mine."

I looked at the paper again. The byline was indeed Maxwell Cole's. Somehow he had managed to worm his column onto the front page. He's always there, just when I least need him.

I backed off. "If you didn't leak it, and I didn't leak it, then somebody in the medical examiner's office has a big mouth."

Peters looked somewhat mollified, but not totally so.

The Public Safety Building has what are reputed to be the slowest elevators in Seattle, possibly in the Western Hemisphere. We were still in the lobby when Sergeant Watkins nailed us. "Where are you two running off to?" he asked.

He was carrying a folded newspaper under his arm. "You've already read that?" I asked.

"I've read it, Powell's read it, the chief's reading it even as we speak. You'd better come back and brief the captain before you take off. The press is going to be all over this place today."

Captain Powell's office is as private as a glass fishbowl can be. We gave Sergeant Watkins and Powell a verbal rundown of what we knew, including what Jeremiah had told me about Faith Tabernacle and the good Pastor Michael Brodie. Powell took our copy of the preliminary report and read it through. "What was this Brodie character wearing yesterday when you saw him?" Powell asked.

"Blue suit, white shirt, no tie."

"Long sleeves?"

I nodded. The captain continued. "According to this, there were fragments of flesh under her fingernails. If he's our man, there should be scratches showing." You don't get to be captain because you're dumb. Powell rubbed his chin thoughtfully. "Then there's the hamburger, too. Where do you get a hamburger that early in the morning?"

We theorized awhile longer before we finally made our get-away from the fifth floor and picked up a car from the motor pool. The motor pool is run on a strictly first-come, first-served basis. We were a long way from first served. The television shows that have the detectives driving the same high-powered vehicle week after week crack me up. They don't live in the real world of city budgets. It must be nice. I've grown immune to cars. All that's important to me is whether or not they run and have enough leg room. This one ran all right, but the leg room was sorely lacking. That happens a lot when you're six-three.

Peters drove, but not far. We stopped for breakfast. I washed down bacon and eggs with coffee while Peters told me about the dangers of cholesterol and the nitrate preservatives in bacon. I enjoyed the food, not the accompanying lecture. I missed Ray. He and I shared much the same vices as far as food was concerned.

Over breakfast we decided to tackle the leak in the medical examiner's office. A blabbermouth there or in the state crime laboratory could blow up a case before it ever hit prosecution. We drove up to Harborview Hospital on Capitol Hill and parked behind a car with a bumper sticker that said, "Have you hugged your medical examiner today?"

Dr. Ralph Baker is in charge. He is a full-fledged physicain and also an elected official. His jurisdiction covers all of King County and includes the city of Seattle. He glanced balefully up from some papers and looked at his watch as we were ushered into his cluttered office. "You're late," he growled. "I expected you half an hour ago."

"We stopped for breakfast."

He grunted. He reached over and picked up a manila folder. Inside was a folded clipping of the Angel Barstogi article. It had a series of red markings on it. He sighed. "Some of this is almost verbatim," he said wearily.

"Any ideas?" I asked.

He shrugged. "Two people were on duty last night. Lillian Roberts and Dan Royden."

"So which one runs off at the mouth?" I asked.

Baker looked at Peters, then nodded in my direction. "That's one of the things I like about Detective Beaumont. He has such a way with words." He paused briefly. "You ever hear of the Equal Employment Opportunity Commission?" he asked.

I nodded. Baker picked up a stray paper clip from his desk and lobbed it across the room, where it fell expertly into a chipped clear-glass vase that sat on a bookshelf near the window. From the number of paper clips in it and the few scattered in close proximity, I guessed catching paper clips was the vase's sole reason for existence.

The chief medical examiner is a florid Scandinavian with a shock of white hair. His face flushed a little more violently than usual. "You ever have an EEOC grievance filed against you?"

I shook my head. He tossed another paper clip into the vase. "I have," he said. "In this state that's tantamount to political suicide. I don't see this job as the end of the line, you know."

As a matter of fact, the thought had never occurred to me. I thought once a medical examiner, always a medical examiner, but that shows how much I know. On the other hand, I suppose it's a short jump from performing autopsies to political office. At least you'd have some preparation for handling the stench of corruption.

I said, "In other words, Lillian Roberts is Deep Throat."

"Maybe she talks in her sleep," he replied. "I'm not making any official accusations, mind you."

Peters had been pretty much left out of the conversation, but now he put two and two together. "You mean Lillian Roberts and Maxwell Cole?"

Another paper clip clinked into the vase. Baker said nothing.

Peters was outraged. "I'd fire her ass."

Baker studied Peters for a moment the way a small child might examine an ant before deliberately crushing it into the sidewalk. "You probably would," he said, "but then, you don't want to be King County Executive, either. Of course," he added, "I'll deny everything if any of this hits the street."

There was no point in sticking around. I had to give Baker credit for letting us know the lay of the land. He could have left us fumbling around in the dark. Besides, I wanted to get Peters out of there before he said something we would both regret. I was afraid his combination of temper and mouth would end up getting us both in trouble. I helped myself to one of Baker's paper clips and made a pretty respectable shot, considering I'd never tried it before. "See you at the polls," I said over my shoulder.

I hurried Peters out the door. He was still blustering in the outer office, but I shushed him until we were outside and climbing into the car.

"Do we let him get away with that?" Peters exploded when I finally let him talk.

"We don't have a whole hell of a lot of choice."

"It's . . ." Peters stopped, totally at a loss for words.

"It's the way it is," I finished for him, "and nothing you or I do is going to change it. We just have to work around it, that's all."

The drive from Capitol Hill to Magnolia was hair-raising. It's common knowledge that police forces are stocked with frustrated juvenile delinquents who have grown up and gone straight, driving like hot rodders and justifying it in their minds because they are finally on the right side of the law. We didn't talk as we drove. I was too busy considering whether or not my Last Will and Testament was up-to-date.

We wheeled onto Gay Avenue. "Oh-oh," I said when I saw Maxwell Cole's rust-colored Volvo parked in front of Suzanne Barstogi's house. Max, Suzanne, and Michael Brodie were huddled on the front porch, deep in conversation. They broke it off as soon as soon as we pulled up behind the Volvo. Peters didn't recognize the car, but he swore under his breath when he recognized Maxwell's walruslike visage.

Max hurried down the steps toward us as though some trace of the conversation might linger in the ethers of the front porch. He checked his speed and sauntered up to the gate.

"Fancy meeting you here," I said before he had a chance. "What did they do, yank your column back onto the police beat?"

He reddened slightly. "I'm working on the column right now, as a matter of fact."

Suzanne Barstogi came down from the porch and stood near the dangling gate. I ignored her and spoke directly to Maxwell for Suzanne's benefit. "I hope you warned these nice folks that you don't always quote people verbatim." The good pastor came down to stand protectively, or maybe defensively, behind Suzanne.

"Knock it off," Maxwell muttered.

"They know you're the one who plastered Angela all over the front page this morning? I'll bet they think you're a really nice man. You tell 'em what kind of movies you like to watch?''

"I said knock it off!"

"You know," I said, focusing on the bulbous nose supporting his sagging glasses, "I'd like nothing better than to knock it off." Maxwell got my subtle message.

He grabbed open the gate with such force that he wrested it from its last frail hinge. For a long moment he stood there holding the gate in his hand. I think he considered throwing it at me. Instead, he slammed it down and pushed his way past me to clamber into the Volvo. He drove off, leaving a trail of rubber on the asphalt.

"I'll give you that one," Peters grinned.

We turned our attention to Pastor Michael and Suzanne. I've already mentioned that I put in some time as a Fuller Brush salesman. In fact, that's how I worked my way through the University of Washington. I learned a lot about life from a sales manager there. He had a list of trite sayings he would spew with little or no provocation. One that I particularly remember is, "Men change but seldom do they." Those words flashed through my mind as Pastor Michael cordially extended his hand. "I suppose you have some more questions."

My partner shot me a wondering glance. "We certainly do," Peters said.

Brodie gave Suzanne a gentle tap on the shoulder. "Why don't you run along inside with the others." His smile was benevolent. "They can talk to you later if they need to."

Suzanne backed away from him as though she, too, was wary of his change in demeanor. Unconcerned, Brodie picked up the fallen gate and appeared to study the possibility of reattaching it to the fence. There was a long scrape across the back of his hand. Peters saw it the same time I did.

"Will you be conducting the funeral?" I asked, looking for an opening.

"The services," he corrected gently. "In Faith Tabernacle we don't have funerals. Even though the circumstances in this case appear tragic, it is always an occasion for thanksgiving when one of the True Believers is called home to be with our Maker."

"I see," I said unnecessarily. I was trying to reconcile this seemingly soft-spoken, considerate man with the explosively tempered one I had seen the day before. It was inconceivable that the two could be one and the same. Yesterday he had been out of control. Today he was the picture of unctuous self-confidence.

"The Thanksgiving Service will be Sunday at two up on top of Queen Anne. You're welcome to come, if you'd like," he added.

Inconsequential small talk quickly exhausted Peters' patience. "How long have you known Suzanne Barstogi?" he interjected.

There was a slight but definite pause. "Eight or nine years, I suppose," Brodie replied.

"You've known her since before Angel was born?"

Brodie nodded, and Peters continued. "What became of her husband?"

Brodie shook his head sadly. "Andrew slipped away from our flock of True Believers."

"That's why Suzanne divorced him?" I asked.

"Yes." Again there was an almost imperceptible pause. "There can be no marriage with someone outside the Faith."

"Do you have any idea where he is?"

"No, I don't. When someone leaves us, we believe they have died and gone to perdition. No contact with any one of the True Believers is allowed."

"Will anyone try to let him know about Angel? After all, he is her father. He would probably want to be here," Peters suggested.

Brodie looked at Peters as though the detective was a little dense and hadn't quite grasped the finer points of the conversation. "It would be very difficult for someone who is already dead to attend someone else's Thanksgiving Service."

"I see what you mean," I said. Peters' temper was on an upswing again. Maybe control comes with age. I fervently wished Peters could age ten years in about as many minutes.

"How'd you get the scratch on the back of your hand?" Peters asked.

Brodie looked at it. "We've been doing a lot of yard work around the church," he said. "It happened the other day when we were pruning."

A car pulled up just then. A man and three women got out. They walked past us, nodding to Brodie as they picked their way into the house. "We're having a prayer session right now," Brodie explained, backing away from Peters and me. "We're praying for the murderer's immortal soul. It's our way of turning the other cheek."

"Is the whole congregation coming?" Peters asked.

"The ones who aren't working."

"Speaking of working," I said, "what about Benjamin Mason. Does he work?"

Brodie's face went slightly brittle. "He does yard work."

"You know where he is now?"

The pastor shook his head and I handed him a card. "You have him call me when you see him." Brodie took the card without looking at it, then excused himself to go deal with his flock. The purpose of the prayer meeting stuck in my craw. I would have preferred the prayers be for Angel Barstogi or even Suzanne. I didn't think the scumbag who murdered Angela deserved any prayers. I didn't then, and I don't now.

Chapter 4

WE were standing with the doors open, ready to climb into the car when a voice hailed us. "Yoo-hoo," a woman called. "Over here."

Gay Avenue looks as though it started out to be an alley for another set of streets. Everyone, except the builder of 4543, seemed to understand that. Suzanne Barstogi's house was the only one that fronted on Gay Avenue. All the rest showed reasonably well-kept back doors and backyards. It was one of those backyards, across the street and down one house, to which we were summoned.

A five-foot cedar fence provided an incongruous foundation for a massive wild blackberry bramble. The bush and the fence were like two drunks holding one another up, the resulting wall totally impenetrable. "Over here." It was a quavery, old woman's voice. At the far corner of the fence, the bramble had been cut back enough to allow a wooden gate to open ever so slightly "You are the cops, aren't you?" she asked.

"Yes ma'am," Peters answered. The gate opened a little further, wide enough for us to ease into the opening, but not without picking up a couple of thorny jabs in the process.

Inside, we found ourselves in a weedy yard, facing a diminutive old lady with bright red hair and a spry way about her. She wore old-fashioned glasses with white harlequin frames and narrow lenses. She gave the heavy wooden gate a surprisingly swift shove and padlocked it in one easy motion. "Go on, go on," she said impatiently, motioning us up an overgrown path toward her back door. Peters gave me a slight shrug, then led the way.

"You certainly took long enough over there," she muttered

accusingly as we climbed a flight of steps. "I didn't enjoy a single one of my TV programs today because I was watching for you. I was afraid I'd miss you when you left."

We entered through the kitchen. A large gray cat, standing in the sink lapping water from a leaky tap, eyed us speculatively. Our hostess made no effort to chase him out of the sink. "That's Henry, Henry Aldrich. He doesn't talk much but he's good company."

She directed us into a living room. On a blaring black-and-white television set an announcer was gearing up for another episode of "General Hospital." So she had been willing to risk missing her soaps in order to catch us. I gave her credit for making a considerable personal sacrifice.

She settled into an ancient rocking chair, while we attempted to sit on an overstuffed and lumpy couch that had been built with no regard for human anatomy. "Since you're not wearing uniforms, I suppose you young men must be detectives. I'm Sophia Czirski," she announced, "but you can call me Sophie. What can I do for you?"

Peters looked at me helplessly. It was time for him to earn his keep. I shrugged and said nothing. Peters cleared his throat. "I don't know, Mrs. Czirski . . . Sophie. . . . You invited us."

"Oh, that's right. How stupid of me." She wore ill-fitting dentures that rattled and clicked when she spoke. I was afraid they might fall out altogether. Bright red hair gave the illusion that she was much younger than she was in actual fact. Upon close inspection I would have guessed she was pushing the upper end of her seventies. She was tough as old leather, though, and any lapses in thought were only temporary.

"Did you arrest her?"

"Arrest who?" Peters asked.

"Well, Suzanne Barstogi, of course. Her and that phony preacher friend of hers."

"No ma'am," Peters said carefully. "We haven't arrested anyone. This is Detective Beaumont, and I'm Detective Peters."

"Well," she sniffed, "I'm glad you have enough good manners to introduce yourself. What about your friend—Beauchamp, did you say? Can't he talk?"

Peters looked at me and grinned. "Beaumont," he corrected.

"No, he's really shy around women. I usually have to do most of the talking."

"You go ahead and ask me anything you like then, Detective Peters. Your friend there can take notes." Obligingly I got out a notebook and a stub of a pencil. Somehow I knew I'd get even; I just didn't know when.

Sophie Czirski didn't require any prompting. "I saw that child outside in February. February, mind you! Without so much as a jacket or a pair of shoes! I could see her, you know." She indicated the living room window, which, from her chair before the television set, offered an unobstructed view of Barstogi's front yard. "I can see everything that goes on there, people coming and going all hours of the day and night. All that stuff about prayer meetings and fellowship. I don't believe it, not for one minute."

"Excuse me for interrupting," said Peters, "but you asked if we had arrested Suzanne Barstogi. Is there some reason you feel she should be under suspicion?"

"Goodness, yes. People who would mistreat a child like they have wouldn't hesitate to kill her. And all the time they pretend to be so holier-than-thou. But they don't fool me, not for a minute."

The gray cat meandered in from the kitchen. He favored us with an insolent look, then leaped to the back of the couch. Once there he stretched out, languidly settling himself directly between Peters and me. I wondered how much gray cat hair would be on my brown jacket and trousers when I stood up. Sophie focused on the cat for a moment, then jumped to her feet.

"Good gracious, talk about manners, now I'm forgetting mine. I haven't even offered you coffee or tea."

I thought about the cat in the sink. "No thanks," I said. "I'm fine."

"I'll have some tea," Peters said agreeably, "but I like the water boiling."

"Absolutely," Sophie said, hurrying into the kitchen. "Tea doesn't steep properly if the water's only lukewarm."

I didn't trust myself to say anything to Peters in her absence. What I did do was check the notes I had taken from the previous day's statements. There was no mention of Sophie Czirski.

She returned a few minutes later with a tray and three chipped but dainty cups and saucers. If she had heard my polite refusal, she ignored it. She passed me a cup and saucer without asking. Peters winked at me behind her back as she placed it in my hand. There was a cat hair floating on the surface of my tea. I discreetly removed it with my spoon once her back was turned.

She settled comfortably into the rocking chair with her own cup. "Now then, what was I saying? Oh yes, I called Child Protective Services right then, that very day. I'm sure they thought I was just a nosy old biddy, although they said they'd look into it. I don't think they ever did, at least not then.

"About a week later I was just finishing watching "Good Morning America" when she came wandering down the street. Henry was outside. She went up to try to pet him, but he doesn't like children. When he wouldn't let her touch him I could see it almost broke her heart. She didn't cry, though. I never did see her cry. She looked so lonesome that I just couldn't help myself. I went to the door, my back door, the one you came in by, and asked her if she'd like to have some cookies and milk.

"She did. She marched right in as if she owned the place." Sophie stopped, put down her cup, and wiped her eyes with a lacy handkerchief. "She talked a blue streak. She called me Soapy." Sophie sniffed noisily and wiped her eyes again. "She loved to talk. She talked about that church her mother goes to, meetings every night until the wee hours. She came to see me every morning for almost two weeks, but she was always careful to be back home before her mother woke up. Can you imagine a mother sleeping until eleven or twelve every single day and leaving that poor little tyke on her own?"

"Did she ever say anything about her father?"

Sophie wrinkled her forehead in thought. "No, she never did. She talked about her mother, and an Uncle Charlie, and that minister fellow. I don't know this Uncle Charlie."

"She talked about Brodie?" Peters asked.

Sophie nodded. "Yes, a lot. She was afraid of him."

"I can't say that I blame her," Peters said.

"One day he drove up while Angela was still here. I never called her Angel. I think that's a terrible name to pin on a little girl. Anyway, she tried to run home, but he caught her coming through the gate. He grabbed her and dragged her home by one arm. The next day she had a cast on it."

"You mean he broke her arm?"

"That's not what they told Child Protective Services. Some young investigator, a snot-nosed kid still wet behind the ears, came out then to look into it. I talked to him, told him what I had seen, but it didn't make any difference. He insisted Angela said she had fallen down. He didn't care that I had seen a handprint on her face or bruises on her arms."

I had been taking notes the whole time. "You said she talked about Uncle Charlie. Who's he?"

Sophie glowered. "How should I know? He's probably from that group. She never came back again after that, wouldn't even wave to me from the yard! I know they killed her though; I'm just as sure of it as I can be. And you can write that down, young man!" Sophie Czirski put down her teacup and wept into her handkerchief.

We sat and waited for her to finish crying. "If only Child Protective Services had listened to me, she wouldn't be dead right now. I have half a mind to call the governor's office and complain."

That seemed like a splendid idea to me. "We had officers in the neighborhood last night, asking questions. I didn't see your name on any of the reports."

"Oh no," she said. "Thursday I have my doctor's appointment; then I go to Bainbridge on the ferry and stay overnight with my son and his family. That's the one night a week I babysit my grandchildren."

We asked more questions, but she could add no more details, at least not then. The doctor's appointment had prevented her from seeing any unusual vehicles the day of the murder. I couldn't help but marvel that so far Maxwell Cole had overlooked Sophie. I hoped that would continue to be the case, but I didn't want to trust to luck.

"Did you happen to notice the Volvo that was at Barstogi's house when we drove up?" I asked as we were getting ready to leave.

"A what? Oh, the brown car. I haven't seen it before."

"It belongs to a reporter. His name is Maxwell Cole."

"Is he the one who wrote the article this morning?"

She was a sharp old dame. Nothing much got past her.

"Yes," I answered. "He was over there talking with Suzanne Barstogi and Brodie when we drove up. If he comes nosing around asking questions, I'd appreciate it if you wouldn't say anything to him. I'd especially like it if he didn't learn any of what you've told us."

For the first time she looked at me as though I might possibly be a member of the human race. "You mean you think this might be important?"

"I'm sure it's important, and I don't want the papers to get ahold of it until after we have a chance to check it out." Unexpectedly, Sophie Czirski started crying again. They seemed to be tears of gratitude that at last someone was taking her seriously, paying attention. I was grateful we had gotten to her first.

"I wouldn't give him the time of day," she said determinedly when the third bout of tears finally abated. She pulled herself together long enough to let us out. We heard her padlock the gate behind us.

It was getting on toward afternoon. The storm that had been hinted on the breeze the night before finally drifted in off the Pacific, kicking up the wind and bringing with it a drenching downpour. Seattle is used to the kind of gentle drizzle that lets people walk in the rain for blocks without an umbrella and without getting wet. This was not that kind of storm. The wind would have gutted any umbrella we had tried to use. We were glad to retreat to the car.

We had barely gotten inside when Peters picked up the preliminary report that had been carelessly dropped in the backseat. He studied it for a few minutes, then handed it to me, pointing at a paragraph close to the bottom. It was something we had missed the first time, and Maxwell Cole evidently hadn't given it any notice either. In her death struggle, Angela's Barstogi's left arm had been broken. Actually a recent fracture had been rebroken. In addition, X rays revealed an old break in her right arm and one on her left leg.

"Must have been a really accident-prone kid," I said sarcastically.

"Right," Peters replied. He was looking at Suzanne Barstogi's house. Like me, he was probably thinking about the living room full of kneeling supplicants. "I'll just bet that asshole's our man."

"Could be," I said. "Sounds more plausible all the time.'

"And Suzanne Barstogi's an accessory!" Peters ran his hand

over his forehead and hair in a gesture of hopelessness. For a time he was quiet, waging an internal war.

"You ever hear of Broken Springs, Oregon?" he asked at last. It was an off-the-wall question. I thought for a minute, then shook my head without making any connection. He continued. "It's a little place in central Oregon south of The Dalles that's been taken over by a cult. The peons eat long-grain rice and go without, while the swami or whatever the hell he is rides around in one of his thirty or so Cadillacs. My ex-wife and kids are there."

He stopped. For a space there was no sound in the car but the rain slapping the windshield and the roof. I had worked with Peters for the better part of two months without a hint that something like that was in his background. Now he had dropped the whole load at once.

"I'm sorry," I said.

"Me too," he responded bleakly. "I can't understand how it happens, how people put themselves totally under someone else's control. That's the way it is with Suzanne Barstogi. She probably stood right there and watched, maybe even helped." It was a chilling, sobering possibility.

Once more the sound of the rain filled the car. Peters sat hunched over the steering wheel saying nothing, gripping it with such force that his knuckles turned white. The hurt and pain were so thick in the front seat you could almost touch them. "I'll ask Powell to pull you off the case. I think your objectivity is shot to shit."

That jarred him out of his introspection. He sat up and glared at me. "If you so much as try to get me pulled, I'll kick your ass till Sunday, J. P. Beaumont."

"That's fair enough." I could handle him pissed a whole lot better than I could handle him grieving. "Now let's get the hell out of here. I want to go take a look at Faith Tabernacle."

Peters straightened his shoulders and started the car. I wouldn't be surprised if that's not about the time we started being real partners. At least we had taken the gloves off. It was about time.

Chapter 5

It was still raining Saturday morning, so I grabbed a bus to the Public Safety Building. The lady Metro driver winked at me. I don't think getting hit on by a lady bus driver is exactly dignified. Besides, I spent too many years with a ring around my finger to know how to handle a pass when I meet one. I consider myself a relatively cool customer. That's why I got off the bus by the back door.

There was a whole stack of messages on my desk. I returned what calls I could. One was from a Tom Stahl. When I tried his number, I discovered it was the telephone company business office. It was closed until Monday. I've had calls from Ma Bell before. It usually means I've neglected to pay my phone bill. I looked in my checkbook. Sure enough, no check showed in April for the March bill. It was nice of Mr. Stahl to remind me! Karen used to handle that. I wadded up the message and pitched it, making a mental note to pay all my bills.

I went over the Sophie material. Who was Uncle Charlie? I pored over the list of Faith Tabernacle members. No Charles or Charlie there, only those quaint biblical names that sounded like they'd just stepped out of the Old Testament. I fed the names into the computer, looking for driver's licenses, vehicle registrations, unpaid traffic fines. There was nothing on any of the names in the state of Washington, except for Brodie. He was the registered owner of a total of five vehicles. Not finding any information is enough to arouse any good detective's suspicions. Who the hell were these people? I fired off another inquiry, this one to Illinois.

Afterward I waited, drumming my fingers on the desk, wondering about Uncle Charlie. No one in Faith Tabernacle had mentioned him. Whoever he was, in or out of the group, he had been important to Angela Barstogi. She had mentioned him to Sophie Czirski when she hadn't mentioned her own father.

I looked up to find Captain Powell perched on the corner of my desk. "How's it going?" he asked.

I guess Powell's all right. He's probably thirty-seven or thirty-eight. He's what I call a young Turk, one of those guys who's on a fast track and plans to make it all the way to the top in a hurry. The best way to handle people like that is to stay out of their way. Their ambition has a way of clobbering anyone who isn't pushing and shoving in the same direction.

"We're plugging," I replied noncommittally.

"What are you finding?"

"We spent a good part of yesterday afternoon around Faith Tabernacle over in Ballard. We didn't get inside. No one was there. The doors were locked, but we spent lots of time with the neighbors."

"And?"

"Pastor Michael Brodie is not well thought of in that neck of the woods. People say odd things go on in Faith Tabernacle, that they sometimes hear children crying."

"Have there been complaints?"

"Peters is checking that out right now. No one has ever been able to get close enough to the kids to talk to them."

Powell rubbed his chin. I'm always about half-suspicious of chin rubbers. It's the same way with deliberate tappers and cleaners of expensive, hand-carved pipes. The gestures are calculated distractions, serving to divert attention from the current topic of discussion.

"Speaking of Peters, how's he working out?"

"He's okay."

"You knew there was some difficulty downstairs. We had to shift him out of property. It was either send him to homicide or bounce him back to walking a beat."

"No, I didn't know that." I might have added that I was outside the departmental gossip mills, but I let it go.

"Captain Howard down there specifically asked for you to be his partner."

"Oh," I said.

"And you think he can handle this case without a problem?"

"Absolutely," I replied. I wasn't about to let on that Peters had told me anything about Broken Springs, Oregon, and losing his family to a cult. I didn't want to risk giving Powell any ammunition about Peters' impartiality. Powell is the kind who might use it. He ambled away from my desk then, no wiser, I hoped, than when he had arrived. I was a little wiser, though. Peters was on our squad without Powell's wanting him there. If the captain was looking for an excuse to bump the newcomer, he wouldn't get any help from me.

Peters showed up a few minutes later. He had checked through 911 records for any complaints from the Ballard area around Faith Tabernacle and come up empty-handed. He looked a little worse for wear, as though he hadn't slept more than a couple of hours.

"You tie one on last night?" I asked.

"No."

"Maybe you should have," I told him.

He didn't take kindly to my remark. "What's the program today?" he asked.

"Let's go downstairs and talk to the crime lab folks. They might have something for us."

The Washington State crime lab is on the second floor of the Public Safety Building. They work for all the law enforcement agencies in Washington, with a number of labs scattered throughout the state. There's a backlog of work, but murder gets priority treatment. Angela Barstogi deserved at least that much. Janice Morraine offered us some acrid coffee that Peters had the good sense to refuse. I didn't. I'm a dog for punishment.

Janice lit a cigarette, and Peters grimaced. I was surprised he didn't launch into an antismoking lecture on the spot. Jan took a long drag on her cigarette, ignoring Peters' pointed disapproval. "What can I do for you?" she asked.

"Have you come up with anything on Angela Barstogi?"

"She had a Big Mac for breakfast, if that's any help."

"As in McDonald's?" Peters asked.

Janice nodded. "She had mustard with whatever she ate. There were traces of mustard under her thumbnails like you'd get from opening one of those little individual packages. You can collect samples, but it'll probably only separate Burger King from McDonald's."

She flicked an ash into an ashtray. Her tone was matter-of-fact. Evidence is evidence. People in this business can't afford to look beyond the evidence to the human suffering involved. If they do, they crack up.

"Did you find anything in her room or in the house?"

"Nothing that appears to be important at the moment. Fingerprints from the room are mostly the girl's and the mother's. There are a few that belong to other children, but no adult prints."

"What makes you say McDonald's?" Peters asked.

"It may not be McDonald's, but it was one of those fast-food joints. Hamburger aside, Baker's office says she was generally malnourished, had been for some time."

Janice reached across me to the end of the table and picked up a folded newspaper. She opened it to the editorial section. "I read this coming in on the bus this morning." She handed me the paper, open to Maxwell Cole's "City Beat" column.

I skimmed through an emotional portrayal of Suzanne Barstogi as a woman of unshakable faith and courage, one who was walking through a time of personal trial supported by her beliefs and the willing help of fellow church members. It spoke eloquently of the group's communal sharing of food and heartbreak. It told in heartrending prose how the congregation as a whole had spent the previous afternoon on its knees praying for the murderer's immortal soul.

Murderers are always the first victims in Maxwell Cole's book, unless the person pulling the trigger happens to be a cop.

I finished reading the column and handed the paper to Peters. "They sound like wonderful people, don't they?" Janice said with just a hint of sarcasm tinging her voice. "Just the kind of people you'd expect to systematically abuse a child for years. The broken bones she had would be consistent with a highly abusive environment. Kids that age don't break bones. They have too much cartilage. Are there other kids stuck in that mess?"

I thought about Jeremiah and how afraid he had been. His fear was not unfounded. I was convinced the bruise on his forearm was not an unusual occurrence. Janice finished her cigarette and rose, dismissing us. "I don't have anything else right now, but I'll call if anything turns up."

"So what now, coach?" Peters asked as we waited in the elevator lobby.

"I vote we go back to Ballard. This time we'll get inside Faith Tabernacle if we have to have a search warrant to do it."

Ballard is a predominantly Scandinavian enclave about five miles from downtown Seattle. It sits across Salmon Bay from Magnolia. You get there by crossing the Ballard Bridge, a drawbridge used to let through sleek sailing vessels as well as stodgy, loaded barges on their way to Alaska. If Magnolia is highbrow, Ballard is lowbrow. If Magnolia is known for its upwardly mobile professionals, Ballard is known for its sturdy blue-collar folks who march along, never quite getting ahead but never falling very far behind either. Ballard is pretty much middle America at its best or worst, depending on your point of view.

Faith Tabernacle was a respectable-enough-looking place situated on the corner of Twenty-fourth and Eightieth N. W. in the Loyal Heights area. It was an older church that gave evidence of some recent renovations, the most jarring of which was a neon sign. New gray shingles sparkled, and surrounding trees had been pruned back with a vengeance. Double doors, new but cheap, stood wide open.

The day before, neighbors had told us that it had originally been a Lutheran church. A steady decline in enrollment and a consolidation of congregations had left it vacant for a number of years until purchase by Michael Brodie's group some six or seven months earlier. Two similarly shaped, parallel buildings had been connected at either end. Half the building was used as a church and half as a parsonage.

The interior of the sanctuary reminded me of a barren medieval church. I'm not a regular visitor of churches, but the ones I have encountered usually have some of the amenities like heat, carpeting, reasonably comfortable pews, that sort of thing. Walking into Faith Tabernacle, the first sensation was one of bone-numbing chill. There was no heat, and the barren concrete floor retained the damp cold from the previous late-spring night. Two banks of rickety benches formed the seating arrangements, with a center aisle between them leading to a raised altar. The benches had no backs on them. If Angel Barstogi had fallen asleep during church, where had Suzanne put her, on a bench or on the cold, bare floor?

At first we thought we were alone, but then a woman emerged from behind a makeshift pulpit. Armed with a scrub brush and a bucket of soapy water, she crawled across the cold surface on hands and knees, diligently scrubbing every inch of the altar, like a buck private preparing for a major inspection.

Peters approached the woman and asked her where we might find Brodie. She motioned with her hand, indicating that she was unable to talk but that we should go through the door on the right of the altar. It led us through a darkened, closetlike room. In the dim light from the doorway behind us we could see a wooden kneeling frame with an open Bible on a stand before it. Other than those two items, the room was empty.

Another door barred the way. I knocked. Beneath my knuckles I found the deep sound of a solid wooden door, not the hollow laminate of the church's front doors. Pastor Michael himself answered my knock. If he was startled to see us, he certainly covered it well. "Come in," he said, stepping back and holding the door. "I was just preparing for this afternoon's service," he said.

I doubt Peters was surprised by what we found there. I wasn't. The room could hardly have been called sumptuous, but it was a long way from the grim, unadorned rooms through which we had entered. The contrast was striking. The place was immaculate. There was none of the dirty clutter of Suzanne Barstogi's house. A well-padded deep brown carpet covered the floor. The two walls that weren't covered with bookshelves were papered in a tasteful grass cloth. A stately mahogany desk with a brass study lamp dominated the room. An open Bible lay in a halo of light the lamp cast on gleaming wood. Pastor Michael snapped the Bible shut as I approached the desk.

"Won't you sit down?" he offered.

We sat. I looked at Peters, grim faced and tense. I wondered how this office compared with the Cadillac-driving swami of Broken Springs, Oregon. Peters was holding himself in check, but just barely. "We wanted to see your church," I said before Peters had a chance to open his mouth. "We thought seeing it might give us some ideas about Angel's death."

Brodie's defenses came up instantly. "Surely you don't think someone in the church had anything to do with it."

"We haven't ruled out anyone so far," Peters commented stiffly, glancing at Brodie's hand. Brodie covered the scratched hand with the other one in a pious and, I thought, highly suspicious, manner. Peters noticed it too.

"How long have you been here?" I asked.

There was the pause—slight, but enough to be noticeable. "Oh, a little over six months, I guess. Before that we met in private homes."

"I see," I said.

"Would you like to see the rest of it?" he asked, rising suddenly. "We have a fellowship hall and a kitchen in addition to my little apartment."

"What's the room we just came through," Peters put in, "the one with the Bible stand in it?"

There was another pause, as if Brodie wanted to consider his words carefully before answering. "That's our Penitent's Room. It's where people can spend time in prayer when they have strayed."

He hustled us out of the study through his apartment, as if anxious to leave the area and the subject matter behind. The apartment was something less than luxurious, but obviously Brodie didn't believe in living in the same kind of squalor deemed appropriate for his flock.

We followed him through the rest of the building. What little of the upstairs that wasn't devoted to parsonage contained several small Sunday School rooms. Downstairs we found a commercial-style kitchen off the fellowship hall. The equipment was polished to a high gloss. The Faith Tabernacle women evidently spent far more time maintaining church facilities than they did their own homes. The fellowship hall was outfitted in the same barren style as the sanctuary. Its only furnishings consisted of two sets of splintery redwood picnic tables pushed together to form two long banks of tables.

When the tour was over, Brodie ushered us back to the Penitent's Room in the best bum's-rush tradition. "I need to go outside to greet people now," he said. "Once the service starts, you will have to leave." He gave a rueful smile lest we think him rude or inhospitable. "It's like a Mormon temple. No one who isn't a True Believer is allowed inside during services."

The lady with the scrub brush was kneeling in front of the little altar in the Penitent's Room, her bucket of soapy water still beside her. She was totally immersed in prayer. We stopped nearby but she never looked up. We went back through the sanctuary under our own steam.

Outside, a little flock of True Believers waited patiently for their shepherd to welcome them to worship. The women, their hair covered with either scarves or hats of some kind, dropped their eyes demurely as we passed. The men nodded without speaking, while the children maintained the same eerie silence we had noticed the day Angel Barstogi died. It was not a joyful gathering.

Jeremiah stood next to a beefy man with a full red beard. He had to be Benjamin Mason. He was a big man who looked like he had spent some time on the working end of a shovel. I walked up to Jeremiah and nodded at him without speaking. There was no sense in getting him in more hot water.

"Are you Mr. Mason?" I asked.

"Yes," he answered, his tone wary, uneasy.

"I'm Detective Beaumont. Did you get a message to call me?"

"Didn't have a phone," he mumbled.

"Mind if we talk to you for a minute?" Reluctantly, he followed us to our car. I thumbed through some notes I'd made from the transcripts. "Brodie says you were working Friday morning?"

He nodded. "That's right."

"And you do yard work. Can you give us a list of places you worked Friday morning?"

"Wait just a minute." Suddenly he came to life. "You've got no right—"

Peters' hand shot out, catching Mason's arm just above the elbow. "You wait a minute, pal. He asked you a civil question. You can answer it here, or we can take you downtown."

"Viewmont," he said. "I was working some houses up at the north end of Viewmont over on Magnolia."

"Anybody see you?"

"Dunno. Usually nobody's home." He mumbled the addresses and I wrote them down.

"Got any I.D. on you?"

His hand shook as he fumbled his wallet out of his hip pocket. When he dragged the battered piece of plastic out of its holder, the license turned out to be an Illinois one, several years out of date. The name on it was C. D. Jason. I felt a jab of excitement.

"What's the *C* stand for?" I asked.

"Clinton," he answered shortly.

Not Charles, not Chuck, not Charlie, but Clinton. The picture matched, but the names were different. Peters took it from me and examined it. He put it in his pocket. "We'll just take this with us," he said easily.

"But I need it to drive," Mason protested, reaching for it.

"You'd best get yourself a Washington license. Meantime, what did you do to the backs of your hands?"

Mason withdrew his hands and stuffed them in his pockets. Not before I noticed that the backs matched Brodie's, scratch for scratch.

"Let me guess," Peters said. "I'll bet you got those scratches trimming hedges."

"That's right," Mason said. "How'd you know that?"

"Psychic," Peters replied.

Mason or whoever he was scurried into the church like a scared rabbit. Peters said nothing until Mason was out of earshot. He turned to look at the church. "I'd love to get a stick of dynamite and blow this whole pile of shit to kingdom come."

"You'd best not let Powell hear you talk like that. Powell might be looking for an excuse to bust you back to the gang."

Peters gave me a searching look. "You know something I don't know?"

"I don't know anything. I have a suspicious nature."

We spent a couple of hours touring arterials, collecting sample packets of mustard from every fast-food joint we could find that seemed to be within a reasonably close geographical area. It would be strictly blind luck if we happened to get a match, but that sort of thing does happen occasionally. I believe the psychologists call it intermittent reinforcement. It's what keeps bloodhounds like me on the trail. Every once in a while we hit the jackpot. It happens often enough that it keeps us from giving up. We just keep at it.

We carried a picture of Angela Barstogi with us, the one that had been in the newspaper. We asked all the clerks, all the busboys, if anyone remembered a little girl in a pink Holly Hobbie gown. Nobody did.

With the mustard sacked and labeled, we drove over to the Westside Treatment Center. The receptionist was off for the weekend, but we managed to get a list of employees, their schedules, and their phone numbers from a supervisor. We spent the remainder of the afternoon on telephones working our way through the list to no avail. It wasn't that people were uncooperative or reluctant to help. It was just that no one had seen anything. We finally called it a day around seven Saturday night. We were getting nowhere fast.

Peters offered to drive me over to Kirkland and back, to take me to a wonderful health food restaurant he knew. I appreciated the offer, but I was beat. I wanted to be home in my own little apartment with my own little stereo and my own little self. ''I'll take a rain check,'' I told him.

I declined the offer of a ride, too. I didn't want Peters to know that I was going to stop and pick up a Big Mac and an order of fries at the McDonald's at Third and Pine. He had made enough sarcastic remarks about junk food while we were gathering the mustard. I wasn't about to let him know that I am a regular customer at the local Big Mac outlet, that the clerks know me by name and order. It's not that I'm ashamed. It's just that I didn't want to give Peters any more ammunition.

As I stood waiting for my order, I looked around at the stray slice of humanity sitting in those four walls munching Big Macs. There was a genuine bag lady with her multilayered coats. There was a group of young toughs arguing loudly in one corner. In another a couple of long-legged hookers daintily dipped Chicken McNuggets under the watchful eye of a well-dressed pimp.

The clerks took the orders and the money, shoving the food back across the counter with studied disinterest. It was business as usual as far as they were concerned. With all the weirdos hanging around, it was hardly surprising no one had noticed a kid in a nightgown eating a hamburger for breakfast at eight o'clock in the morning.

I went home and let myself into the peace and quiet of my apartment. I mixed myself a generous MacNaughton's. Then I set the table with a place mat and a matching linen napkin. I may like McDonald's, but I won't eat on paper plates in my own home, either. I arranged the hamburger and fries tastefully on the brown-bordered stoneware plate the decorator had assured me was very chic and very masculine. Then I dragged a Tupperware container of radishes and celery out of the fridge.

Those mealtime amenities may seem silly at times, but for three months after I moved out of the house, I ate on nothing but paper plates with plastic forks, knives, and spoons. I was sure

Karen would come to her senses and take me back. I was living in a world of miserable, not blissful, ignorance. I kept thinking Karen had divorced me on my own merits, believed that what she said about being a cop's wife was the truth. I hadn't known about the accountant then, the accountant for an egg conglomerate who had come to town looking for an egg-ranch site near Kent or Puyallup. I hadn't known this jerk had walked into the real estate office where Karen had just started working and swept her off her feet.

The day after the divorce was final she married him, and I hired an interior decorator. That's almost five years ago now. He moved Karen, Kelly, and Scott to Cucamonga, California. I guess he's an all-right guy. The kids have never complained to me, and Kelly told me last Christmas that he (his name is Dave) has them put the child support money I send in a special savings account for college. He may be all right, but I hate him, and I eat on real plates with real napkins because I want Karen to know my world didn't end just because she left. At least, it didn't end completely.

I ate, cleared the table, and put the dishes in the dishwasher. I run the diswasher once a week on Sunday morning whether I need to or not. I made a fresh drink and went to stand on the balcony. It was a chill spring evening, tending more toward winter than summer. Across the street at the Cinerama the ticket holders' line for the nine o'clock show disappeared behind the Fourth and Blanchard Building, a tall, pointed, black glass monstrosity called the Darth Vader Building by locals. For a while I stood there watching and listening, hearing little snatches of conversation and laughter that wafted up to my eleventh-floor perch. Periodically a juggler appeared to entertain those waiting in line. Some people will do anything for money.

I was tempted to mix another drink and stay home to lick my wounds, to bring up all that old family stuff and beat myself over the head with it. It occurred to me, however, that it wouldn't be healthy. At eight fifty-five I put my glass in the sink and rode the elevator downstairs. The ride down was longer than the walk across the street. The last of the line had entered the theater by the time I bought my ticket. I didn't bother to ask what was showing.

It wasn't a good decision. The wife in the movie was getting it on with every Tom, Dick, and Harry in town. Instead of cheering me up, the story rekindled my anger over losing my family.

When I came home, I took myself and a bottle of MacNoughton's to the recliner in my darkened living room, and I didn't quit until we were both gone.

Chapter 6

SUNDAY morning dawned clear and cold. I woke up, still sitting in my chair, nursing a terrific hangover.

Friday and Saturday's storm had blown itself out. The cloud cover that usually keeps Seattle temperatures moderate was missing. The sun had barely come up when banks of fog rolled in. Once the fog burned off, the sun's rays offered no warmth.

Hindsight is so simple. I should have had some premonition my life would change that day. If I had called old Dave, Karen's new husband, and asked him to spare me a few chicken entrails, maybe I could have gotten a seer to give me some advance warning. I wouldn't have been caught quite so off guard. Unfortunately—or perhaps fortunately—Dave and I don't have that kind of relationship. As it was, the morning appeared routine, ordinary, once I'd swallowed enough aspirin to quiet the pounding in my head.

I made breakfast, hoping that food would help. I have mastered the art of microwave bacon and soft-boiled eggs. Then I ran my weekly load of dishes and washed my weekly load of clothes. Anything that has to be ironed goes across the street to the cleaners and laundry. By then I was feeling half human.

After I finished my chores, the week's collection of crossword puzzles was waiting in the hall outside my door. Ida, my next-door neighbor, knows I hate newspapers and love crossword puzzles. She saves them for me all week. On Sunday morning she leaves a little stack outside my door after she finishes with her own paper. I've come to regard the weekly stack of puzzles as a variation on the Easter Bunny theme. It's almost as magical.

Peters has season tickets to the Mariners' games. That particular Sunday, the Yankees were in town. We had decided the day before that I would pull the funeral duty. It's a part of the job that I don't relish, but season tickets are season tickets.

I suppose I should explain why cops go to murder victims' funerals. They go to see who shows up and who doesn't. Statistically most people are murdered by someone they know. Oftentimes a murderer will attend the funeral for fear his not being there will throw suspicion in his direction. Sometimes it works the other way too. The killer is a complete stranger who goes to the funeral because it gives him a feeling of power to be there without anyone knowing who he is, so homicide detectives go to funerals. It comes with the territory.

Brodie had told me that Angela's Thanksgiving Service would be held at Mount Pleasant Cemetery on top of Queen Anne Hill. It struck me as being a little odd. I would have expected them to have a hellfire-and-brimstone sermon in Faith Tabernacle itself. It seemed self-effacing, as though they didn't want to draw attention to the church itself.

I decided to walk to the cemetery. I suppose I could have gone down to the department and checked out a car, but I didn't feel like going anywhere near the department, not even as close as the motor pool.

I got over being a suburban type all at once. I sold my car when I moved to the city. I got my apartment cheap because it didn't come with a parking place. Later I found out why it was cheap. Parking in downtown Seattle costs a fortune. I did the only sensible thing—I learned to love the bus.

Gone were the days of the fifty-five-minute commute. All commuting ever got me was an ulcer, hemorrhoids, and a divorce. Walking isn't all that bad except that having dates without a car has proved to be something of a challenge. The upshot is that I've virtually given up dating except for those rare cliff-dwelling creatures like myself who aren't insulted by an offer of dinner or a movie contingent upon walking to and from. There aren't too many women like that, so my sex life has dwindled. I chum around with some of the lavender-haired ladies from the Royal Crest who are glad to have my friendship but don't make demands on my body or my schedule. Like me, they mostly don't have cars. It's a lifestyle that suits me.

The two-and-a-half-mile trek to Mount Pleasant Cemetery, much of it almost perpendicular, felt good. It finished the job of clearing my head. A chill wind was blowing off Puget Sound, and a few clouds scudded across the sky ahead of the wind. Seattle wouldn't be the Emerald City if it didn't rain on a fairly regular basis.

It wasn't necessary to stop and ask directions at the cemetery office. I could see a little knot of people gathering just over the crest of the bluff. I stationed myself a little apart with my back to a suddenly gray Lake Union. I checked off the arriving players against Brodie's roster.

The True Believers arrived first. It was clear they had been instructed to speak to no one. They came as a group, huddled together near the coffin as a group, and knelt to pray as a group. Suzanne Barstogi, kneeling stoically in the middle of the second row, was accorded no special recognition or position of honor as the mother of the slain child. This was a group Thanksgiving Service, I reminded myself, and Pastor Michael Brodie would not tolerate any individual outpourings of grief that might crack the shell of his little facade.

I had called Brodie earlier and jotted down the names of those he expected to be in attendance. Looking at his flock now, I was able to put some names with faces. Jeremiah, of course, Benjamin Mason/Jason, Ezra, Thomas. There was one more man, but I couldn't recall his name. Other than Suzanne, the women eluded me. They were so drab and so alike, it was impossible to sort them out.

Sophie Czirski was there, her ramrod thinness totally at odds with the pudgy Faith Tabernacle women. She planted herself firmly at the foot of the coffin and glared at the kneeling pastor with open defiance, daring him to question her right to be there. The wind, blowing at her back, periodically made her red hair stand on end. It gave her a wild appearance. If I had been Brodie, I would have thought twice about picking a fight with her.

Maxwell Cole turned up with a long-haired photographer in tow. At Cole's insistence, pictures of the kneeling congregation were taken from every possible angle. His taste is all in his mouth. Sophie watched the proceedings with a malevolent glare. When Cole unwisely asked her to move over so they could get one more picture, she told him in no uncertain words and with considerable volume what he could do with both the photographer and his camera. She didn't budge an inch.

Scattered here and there were a few hangers-on, people who

make a habit out of going to funerals, ones who get a kick out of watching as other people's emotions go through a wringer. I looked at them closely, wondering if any of them were named Charlie. After the service I would request a copy of the guest register.

The service itself was just getting under way. The Faith Tabernacle group began singing a tuneless little hymn that no one else seemed to recognize. I moved closer so I could hear what was being said, taking up a position just to Sophie's right at the end of the coffin.

I don't know why I looked up, probably nothing more than good old-fashioned male instinct. Had I paid attention, I would have seen every man in the group staring unabashedly in the same direction. The most beautiful woman I had ever seen stepped over the crest of the hill and strode without hesitation toward Angela Barstogi's coffin.

Even now, thinking about that moment is enough to take my breath away. She was a slender woman, of indeterminate age, wearing a brilliant red dress topped by a short but magnificent fur jacket. Her hair fell in dark, lustrous waves that flowed and blended into the dark fur on her shoulders. Her finely chisled features might have been carved from tawny marble. Her eyes, gray in the changing sunlight, flashed with an interior storm. For all her beauty, it was plain to see she was very angry. She walked quickly, covering the ground with a long, well-booted gait. She stopped less than two feet from Sophie and bowed her head.

If she was aware of the sensation her appearance caused, she gave no indication of it. She seemed to lose herself completely in the proceedings. Unchecked tears rolled down her cheeks and lost themselves in the deep pile of her coat. In one hand she held a single red rose, not a dark red one, but a bright red one that matched the striking hue of her dress.

I noticed Maxwell Cole sidling toward her. When she raised her head and opened her eyes, he would be at her side. That offended me but I didn't have much room to talk. I was fighting the urge to follow suit. Instead I contented myself with observing her from a distance of several feet. The sun had slipped behind a cloud. When it moved away, her hair came alive with burnished highlights. She was exquisite, beautiful beyond anything I had ever imagined.

Pastor Michael Brodie was just getting into the swing of his message. I looked at him, only to find he too was riveted, his mouth moving mechanically as his eyes devoured every inch and curve of the newcomer's body. I felt an almost uncontrollable urge to leap in front of her and shield her from his gaze. For him to be able to look at her seemed an unbearable violation. The impulse startled me even as it occurred. I am not someone who imagines bedding every piece of desirable flesh that passes in my direction. I'm a healthy, middle-aged, well-adjusted, reasonably disciplined, heterosexual male. This woman's presence rang all my bells.

Brodie droned on and on without my hearing a word of what he said. I thought he would never finish. On the other hand I dreaded the service coming to an end. That would mean she would leave, march back up over the hill and out of my life. My mind scrambled wildly, trying to think of what I could say to delay her, to make her stop so I could at least hear the sound of her voice.

Suddenly there was a chorus of amens. The casket began sinking slowly from view. With the fluid grace of a dancer, the slender woman glided forward and tossed her single rose onto the descending casket. Only then did she brush away the tears that had fallen silently throughout the service.

She turned to find Maxwell Cole directly in her path. The photographer hovered at his elbow. "Excuse me," Max said, "I don't believe we've been introduced."

"No," she replied coldly, looking at his press badge. "I'm sure we haven't. I see no reason to remedy that now."

She stepped to one side as if to walk past him, but he placed himself in her way once more. "I'm a columnist for the *Post-Intelligencer,*" he said lamely. "Would you mind telling me what brought you here?"

"I would mind very much." Her voice was sharp, impatient. Uninvited, I moved swiftly to her side.

"I believe the lady has made it quite clear that she doesn't want to talk to you, Maxey. If I were you I'd beat it." Maxwell Cole looked as though he wanted to throttle me, not only for interfering, but also for bringing up a long-despised college nickname. He looked around, checking to see if anyone else had heard. There was too much potential for ridicule in the situation for him to want to hang around. He backed away, taking

the photographer with him. Finally, he turned and followed the
True Believers, who were trudging up the hill in a dreary single
file that somehow reminded me of the seven dwarfs. All they
needed were picks on their shoulders to complete the air of joy-
less drudgery.

The woman turned to me than. "Thank you," she said, ex-
tending her hand. "We certainly haven't been introduced. My
name is Anne Corley." She smiled. I was entranced by the
sound of her voice, low and vibrant. I almost forgot to take her
hand. When I remembered myself and did, I was startled to find
her grip surprisingly firm and sure.

"My name is Beaumont, Detective J. P. Beaumont. My
friends call me Beau."

"I'm glad to meet you, Detective Beaumont."

"I'm assigned to this case." I continued motioning vaguely
in the direction of Angela Barstogi's grave. Some people are repulsed when they find out you're a homicide detective. I more
than half expected her to turn away from me in disgust. Instead
she gave me a glorious smile.

Sophie Czirski appeared at my elbow. She allowed herself to
examine Anne Corley in minute detail before she spoke. "I certainly gave that Maxwell Cole fellow a piece of my mind."

"That you did," I said. "Thank you."

Another smile played around the corners of Anne Corley's
lips. "Who, Maxey? I gave him a piece of my mind too. Don't
I get any thanks?"

"Yes, of course you do," I said. "Thank you." And then
the three of us stood there laughing uproariously as though we
had just shared some outrageous joke. When we stopped laughing, Anne Corley introduced herself to Sophie.

"Were you a friend of Angela's too?" Sophie asked, her
eyes suddenly filling with tears.

"No," Anne replied. "I never met her. I had a sister who
died when I was eight. My mother wouldn't let me attend the
funeral. She thought it would upset me. To this day I go to the
services whenever I hear of a child dying under unusual circumstances. I always cry. Part of me cries for the child who's gone
now, and part of me still cries for Patty."

Sophie took Anne's hand and held it for a moment, her
rheumy old eyes behind cat's-eye glasses studying Anne Corley's young gray ones. "There were so few flowers," Sophie

said. "Your rose was beautiful and so are you." Sophie turned
and walked away with surprising speed for someone her age,
her back stiffly unbowed as she climbed the steep hillside.

Anne Corley moved slightly downwind. For the first time I
was aware of the delicate scent of her perfume, expensive and
intoxicating. She stood next to me, saying nothing but driving
my heightened senses into overload.

"Are you still on duty, Mr. Beaumont?" she asked.

I glanced around, dumbfounded to find that the entire funeral
party had disappeared. Only Anne Corley and I remained on the
windswept hillside. "I guess not, except I need to stop by the
cemetery office to pick up a copy of the guest register."

"Do you mind if I tag along? I have a feeling that Maxey
may very well be waiting for me in the parking lot."

I looked down at her in absolute amazement. "No," I managed. "I don't mind at all." She took my arm with the calm as-
surance of someone used to getting whatever she wants. I'd like
to pretend that I had the presence of mind to offer my arm to
her, but that's not the case. She reached out and rested a feath-
erweight hand on my forearm; then the two of us walked up the
hill through the Mount Pleasant Cemetery as though it were the
most natural thing in the whole world.

It's ironic to think that Maxwell Cole, a man who had been
the bane of my existence for some twenty-odd years, was the
catalyst that caused her hand to take my arm. I have a lot to
thank Maxwell Cole for. Maybe someday I'll get around to telling him.

Chapter 7

ANNE Corley stood quietly near the door while an attendant photocopied the guest register for me. I tried not to stare at her while I waited. She smiled as I returned with the copy in hand. "Should I have signed that too?" she asked.

"Shouldn't be necessary," I told her. "I already know you were here."

"What about you? Why are you here?" she demanded.

I explained briefly how killers often present themselves at the funerals of their victims.

"And do you think that's true in this case?"

I shrugged. I thought of Pastor Michael Brodie piously intoning biblical passages over a small casket, of Benjamin Mason/Jason kneeling with his hands clasped in prayer under the flowing beard. "It could be," I answered.

"Oh," she said under her breath. Quickly I folded the piece of paper the attendant had given me and stuffed it into an inside jacket pocket. Out of sight is out of mind.

Back outside, walking toward the tiny parking lot, I noticed a rust-colored Volvo still very much in evidence. Maxwell Cole was observing us over the roof of it. I couldn't help but feel just a little smug. "Where's your car?" I asked Anne.

She nodded in the direction of a bright red Porsche parked at the far end of the lot. "What about yours?"

"I don't have a car," I said, suddenly feeling embarrassed about it. "I walked."

"I probably should have," she said unexpectedly, "but these boots aren't built for walking. Why don't I give you a lift?" The invitation caught me off guard, but not so much that I didn't accept.

We reached her car. She unlocked the door, and I opened it for her. Maxwell Cole followed us at a wary distance. He was approaching the driver's side, jotting down the numbers from the temporary license in the back window. The Porsche was evidently brand-new.

Anne saw him out of the corner of her eye as she turned to ease her way into the leather interior. She smiled again. ''Well? Are you coming or not?''

I closed the door behind her and hurried to the rider's side. I came around behind the car, walking directly in front of Maxwell Cole, and climbed into the rider's seat. Max was still standing there, a little to one side, when Anne fired up the powerful engine and rammed the car into reverse. He must have executed a pretty quick sidestep to be sure he was out of the way. I didn't wave to him as we drove by, but I sure as hell wanted to.

I liked this lady, liked her instincts about people and her ability to handle them. She was a lot more than a pretty box of candy.

Anne Corley held the powerful Porsche well in check as she maneuvered the grades, curves, and angles that make Queen Anne Hill an incomprehensible maze for most outsiders. It's a course lots of sports car drivers regard as a Grand Prix training ground. She drove with a confident skill that was careful but hardly sedate.

The fire that had made her gray eyes smolder as she approached Angela Barstogi's grave site had been banked. When she paused at a stop sign and looked at me, they sparkled with intelligence and humor. ''Where to?'' she asked.

''I live downtown,'' I said. ''Corner of Third and Lenora. How about you?''

''I'm just visiting. I'm staying at the Four Seasons Olympic.'' That put me in my place. The Four Seasons is absolutely first-class, but then so was the lady.

''Do you have to go home?'' she asked after a pause. ''Wife and kiddies, or major league baseball on television?''

''Wrong on all counts,'' I replied. ''No wife and kiddies at home. I've got a twelve-inch black and white that I only use to keep tabs on how the media gets things ass-backward. I don't like baseball. I wouldn't go to a live game, to say nothing of watching one on TV.''

''You sound like an endangered species to me,'' she grinned, and we both laughed. "Then what you're saying is that you don't have any pressing reason to go straight home?"

"No."

Her face darkened slightly. I might not have noticed it if my eyes hadn't been glued to her face, drinking in her finely carved profile that could easily have graced the cover of any fashion magazine. A slight frown creased her forehead, then disappeared in far less time than it takes to tell.

"They had a huge potluck after Patty's funeral," she said somberly. "I couldn't go to that, either, so whenever I attend a funeral in Patty's honor, I always treat myself afterward. Care to join me?"

"Sure."

"Where, then?" she asked.

How do you answer that question when you've just met someone and haven't the slightest idea of their likes or dislikes? "I don't know. Where do you want to go?"

She looked at me and laughed. I felt stupid, inadequate, as though I had somehow failed to measure up to her expectations. "I'll tell you what," she said. "I'll choose this time and you choose next time, deal?"

I nodded but I didn't feel any better. My wires were all crossed. I was a gawky kid on his first blind date, which turns out to be with the head cheerleader. I wanted to impress her, although there was nothing to indicate she was in need of being impressed. Like someone who has always lusted after fine china, once he is faced with a Wedgwood plate, does he eat off it or put it away on a shelf? Here I was in a Porsche with the most beautiful woman I had ever seen, and I didn't know what to say or what to do with my hands and feet. I hadn't been that ill at ease in a long time.

She hit Lower Queen Anne, turned left at Mercer, and headed for the freeway, driving easily but purposefully. I didn't ask where we were going. She bypassed downtown and took the exit that put us on Interstate 90. There had been a long silence in the car. I was content to leave it at that.

She had tossed her jacket carelessly in the half-baked backseat they put in Porsches to evade sports car insurance premiums. Her dress was made from some soft fabric that clung to the gentle curves of her body. The neckline, a long V, accentuated her slenderness. In the hollow of her throat lay a pendant, a single jewel suspended on a delicate gold chain. I'm not much of an expert, but real diamonds, especially ones that size, have a way of letting you know they're not fake.

Despite the diamond, despite the fur jacket, despite the car, gradually I stopped being so self-conscious and started enjoying myself.

First Seattle, then the suburban sprawl of Bellevue disappeared behind us. Forested hills rolled by as we climbed toward the Cascades. "Washington is really beautiful," she said while the car sped effortlessly up the wide, curving roadway. We had been quiet for so many minutes that the sound of her voice startled me.

"Have you been here long?" I queried.

"No," she answered. "Not long at all. I just flew into town yesterday."

"I'm not surprised," I laughed. "You couldn't have been around Seattle very long without my knowing it."

She took the Fall City exit and shot me a sidelong glance. "I take that to be a compliment?"

"That's how it was intended."

She said nothing. Somehow I seemed to have offended her. I reverted to adolescence and kept my mouth shut. I was still wondering how to make amends when we pulled into the parking lot at Snoqualmie Falls. Spring runoff was well under way. A thunderous roar of cascading water assailed our ears as we got out of the car.

"This is one of my favorite places," she said. She set off in her long-legged stride toward the viewpoint that overlooks the water, while I followed at a distance.

Snoqualmie in spring is spectacular. Rushing water surges over a sheer basalt cliff into a swirling pool nearly three hundred feet below. The plunging torrent sends a cloud of misty spray back up the wall of the canyon. Mist settled around Anne Corley as she stood on the observation deck. It seemed to bathe her in an otherworldly essence.

The viewpoint was filled with Sunday afternoon tourists, the bermuda-shorted, knobby-kneed, see-America-first variety. The hesitant sunshine of that spring afternoon had brought them out in droves. I didn't miss the contrast between Anne Corley and them, nor did I miss the appreciative men and the covertly wary women. Her delicate beauty swathed in the flowing red dress commanded attention, although she was too engrossed in the water to be aware of it.

When she finally turned away from the falls, she seemed almost surprised to find me standing at her side, as though she had forgotten my existence in her total concentration on the water. She recovered quickly. "Let's eat," she said. "I'm starved."

We followed a flower-lined pathway up to the lodge. Snoqualmie Lodge boasts a fine restaurant, and I certainly couldn't quarrel with the choice. The place does land-office business, however. When I saw the jammed tables and crowded entry, I was sure we would have a long wait. Purposefully, Anne made her way through the crowd and spoke quietly to the hostess. "Why certainly, Mrs. Corley. It will only take a moment," the hostess said.

I stationed myself near the door, hoping we could spend part of the enforced wait outside rather than in the crowded vestibule. Anne made her way back through the crowd. I marveled at the grace and clarity of her movement. People simply melted out of her way. Heads turned to follow her progress. If she had noticed it, acknowledged it, I probably wouldn't have been so impressed, but she was oblivious.

She reached me, took my arm, and guided us back through the crush. By the time we reached the cashier's desk, the hostess was waiting for us, menus in hand. "Right this way, Mrs. Corley."

"How'd you do that?" I asked in whispered admiration as we followed the hostess to a corner table set for two. Her answer was a shrug that told me nothing. Once seated, I pursued it. "Look here, I heard some of the men talking out there. You have to have reservations three weeks in advance to get in this place."

"I do," she said simply. "I called from Phoenix when I knew I'd be coming up for a few weeks. I ate here with friends when I was here a few years ago and fell in love with it. I plan to have dinner here every Sunday afternoon as long as I'm in the area. It's possible to have a standing reservation, you know, if the price is right."

It was my turn to be offended. At least I did an adequate job of faking it. "In other words, when you asked me to choose where I wanted to eat, it was a put-up deal."

"That's right," she agreed mildly just as the waitress arrived with the menu. "Although, if you'd come up with a brilliant suggestion, we could have canceled. Look at that line. I don't think they'd fine me."

Anne ordered a glass of white wine with ice and I ordered MacNaughton's and water. Anne picked up her menu, clasping it with long, well-manicured fingers. She wore scarlet nail polish that matched her dress. She gave the menu a cursory glance, then lay it back down.

"You already know what you want?"

"Yes," she said.

"Why don't you order for both of us then."

She did. Prime rib, baked potatoes, steamed broccoli, and carrots julienne. The food was served elegantly, and it was masterfully prepared. Anne ate with a gusto that seemed at odds with her trim figure. I spent the entire salad course trying to think of something intelligent to say. If I'd had any illusions of turning this into a romantic conversation, she squelched them completely when she asked, "Just who was Angela Barstogi?"

The question stunned me. The pleasure of Anne Corley's company had removed all thought of the dead child, of the case, of time itself. It took me a moment to pull my scrambled thoughts together. "Just a kid who ended up living in the wrong time and place," I said lamely.

Anne leveled serious gray eyes on mine, looking at me with the unblinking steadiness of a skilled inquisitor. "Tell me about her," she said.

"You ask that in a very professional manner," I responded. "Are you a reporter?"

"Well, of sorts. I'm a sociologist. I'm working on a book about young victims of violent crimes. I'm not interested in them from the criminological or sensational point of view. I study them in terms of psychosocial considerations."

She was a far cry from the mousy, passive image of a sociologist that I'd formed, more from fiction than from experience. She was like a breath of fresh air. I guessed rich people could decide to do anything they damned well pleased with their lives. She sure didn't live on a sociologist's salary.

I started out to tell her only a little of the Angela Barstogi story, but somehow it all rolled out, from Sophie Czirski's unproved allegations to a Jesus Loves Me poster that had hung above Angela's bed. I hadn't talked about a case that way since Karen left, and never to someone I didn't know. It was a serious breach of discipline in the loose-lips-sink-ships tradition, yet I was unable to check myself. Anne Corley listened quietly, nodding encouragement from time to time.

I finished. We were sipping coffee. She stirred the strong black liquid thoughtfully. "If that's what she had to live with, no matter how she died, she's probably better off."

I don't know what I had expected Anne to say, but that wasn't it. She'd lost her professional demeanor and seemed to be weeping inwardly for Angela Barstogi. Her sadness didn't seem weak, however. There was strength and resilience under Anne Corley's veneer of graceful beauty. It was like finding real wood when you expected particle board.

We left the restaurant within minutes after that. There was no question of lingering over a conversational after-dinner drink. Once more I felt oddly responsible for her abrupt change of mood. It was somehow my fault. That wasn't the only thing that made me uncomfortable. Anne Corley bought my dinner. That had never happened to me before, and I wasn't sure I liked it.

We drove back to Seattle in a subdued mood. I wanted to redeem the evening, but it was obviously beyond recall. She had moved away from me, was grieving for a child she'd never met. No banter, no small talk could bring her back. I congratulated myself for being a social failure. Who goes to dinner with a gorgeous woman and squanders the conversation on murder, child abuse, and other such scintillating stuff? J. P. Beaumont, that's who.

When Anne stopped to let me out in front of the Royal Crest, I halfheartedly asked her up for a drink. She gave me a wilted smile and said, "Some other time," in a voice totally empty of enthusiasm. Dejectedly I watched her drive away. It was clear that whatever interest I had held for her was gone. There was no sense in calling the Four Seasons. I had had one shot at her, and missed. Whatever it was I had lost, it was something I suspected I wanted.

Chapter 8

THE phone was ringing as I stepped off the elevator. I didn't rush to answer it. I figured whoever it was would call back later. It was still yelling at me after I unlocked the door and turned on the lights.

"Where the hell have you been?" Peters growled before I had a chance to say hello.

"It's none of your goddamned business, actually. It is Sunday, you know."

"I've been trying to get you for a couple of hours. I'll pick you up in ten minutes."

"I don't want to be picked up. I want to go to bed and sulk."

"You're going to the airport. We're meeting someone."

"All right, Peters. Cut the crap. Who are we meeting?"

"A fellow by the name of Andrew Carstogi."

"You mean Barstogi."

"Barstogi is an alias. Andrew Carstogi is Angela's father."

"I'll meet you downstairs," I said.

Peters picked me up in a departmental car, explaining to me as we drove that Carstogi had called in during the funeral. No one could find me, but they had finally located Peters after he came home from watching the Yankees strangle the Mariners.

"How was the funeral?" Peters asked.

The funeral was light-years away. I had gone to the funeral without knowing Anne Corley, and now, five hours later, I had met her and lost her. It had to be some kind of indoor world record for short-lived romance. I shrugged. "Michael Brodie gave quite a performance," I said.

"Faith Tabernacle people were out in force?"

I nodded. "They arrived as a group and left as a group."

"The inquiry came back from Illinois. Drew a blank on everybody—except Brodie and Jason. They show that old license on Clinton Jason, but that's all. I asked them to check him further and to keep looking for the others."

We drove down the Alaskan Way Viaduct, along the waterfront with its trundling ferries and acres of container shipyards punctuated by the red skeletons of upraised cranes. We sped down a canyon of railroad freight cars that towered on either side of the road. The long springtime evening of gray sky and gray sea matched my own dreary outlook. I tried to get Anne Corley off my mind, to focus on Angela Barstogi, the case, anything but a lady driving out of my life in a bright red Porsche.

"Tell me about Angela's father," I said. "What brought him out of the woodwork?"

"There's not much to tell so far. He called the department between two-thirty and three. He had just heard. I don't know how. He raised hell with whoever answered the phone. Said he knew it would happen, that he had tried to stop it. When he said he was catching the next plane out, it sounded like he intended to do bodily harm to Brodie and Suzanne as well. The brass thought we ought to intercept him. Powell wants us to park him someplace downtown where we can keep an eye on him. I had to beat up the airlines to find out what flight he's on."

"I think doing bodily harm to Pastor Michael Brodie is a wonderful idea. What say we miss the plane?"

"Orders are orders," Peters replied.

We rode the automated underground people mover to the United Airlines terminal. We didn't have to wonder who Andrew Carstogi was. An angry young man stumbled through the gate, shedding flight attendants like a wet dog shakes off excess water. He was drunk and spoiling for a fight. I'm sure Carstogi didn't enjoy walking into the welcoming arms of two waiting homicide detectives. The feeling was mutual. It's never fun to be put on the baby-sitting detail, especially when you're dealing with a grieving parent.

Peters and I fell into step on either side of Carstogi. Peters flashed his badge. I thought Carstogi was going to coldcock Peters on the spot.

"What're you guys after me for?" he demanded sluggishly. "My kid is dead. I just got to town."

I thought I'd deflect a little of the anger, calm the troubled waters. "Take it easy. We're here to help."

"You can help me, all right. Just tell me where that asshole Brodie is, that's what you can do." He turned to me with a swaying leer and shook a clenched fist under my nose. "You know where he is? I'll take care of that son-of-a-bitch myself."

Carstogi allowed himself to be guided onto the subway. The security guard eyed us suspiciously as we led him, ranting and raving, through the gate. He hadn't brought any luggage. "Don' need any luggage," he mumbled. "Only came to town to smash his fucking face."

Carstogi balked at the car. "Hey, where're you takin' me? I got my rights. I wanna lawyer."

Peters was losing patience. "Shut up," he said. "You're not under arrest. We're going to try to sober you up."

"Oh," Carstogi replied.

We went to the Doghouse. They have a sign in there that shows all roads leading to the Doghouse the same as signs all over the world tell the distance to that godforsaken end of nowhere called Wall Drug in South Dakota. Connie put us in a corner of the back dining room even though it was closed. She brought me coffee and Peters tea, then asked what Carstogi wanted. He wanted beer. He didn't get it. Peters ordered him bacon and eggs and whole wheat toast served up with a full complement of questions. I thought it commendable that Peters put aside his own personal prejudices and ordered some decent food for Carstogi.

It took a while for food and exhaustion to do their work. When we finally dug under the bluster and bullshit, what we found was a twenty-eight-year-old guy in a world of hurt, a man who lost his wife once and his child twice, all to the same man, he figured, Pastor Michael Brodie.

The story came out slowly. First there had been a series of tent meetings to save souls, of miracles performed before wondering sinners who were prepared to follow the miracle worker to the ends of the earth. Except the miracle worker turned out to have feet of clay. He was into weird stuff like multiple wives and physical punishment for redemption of sins. Anyone who tried to stop him was liable to find himself smitten by the right hand of God. God's right hand turned out to have a mean right hook.

Andrew Carstogi had come to his senses one morning with the crap beaten out of him. It had made a big impression. He had crossed Brodie on the righteousness of physical punishment, on Brodie's requirement that all wives belonged to God's Chosen Prophet first and their husbands second. Brodie hadn't quit until Carstogi was unconscious. If Carstogi had left it at that, it wouldn't have been so bad, but Andrew Carstogi didn't take kindly to being beaten up or losing his wife. He called in the cops and the press.

Chicago is a pretty tolerant place, but once the charges had been made, even though Carstogi had been unable to substantiate them, Faith Tabernacle was held up to ridicule. Experience tells me that the Pastor Michael Brodies of the world can handle almost anything but ridicule.

Carstogi was Disavowed. It's worse than it sounds. In the world of Faith Tabernacle, he ceased to exist. Not only was he no longer a member, he was no longer a husband or father either. He tried to get a court order for custody of Angela. Unfortunately, Suzanne was neither a prostitute nor a drug addict. Later, when Brodie made a killing in a real estate deal on some property the church owned, the whole congregation folded their tents and stole away in the middle of the night. Once they left Chicago the group had as good as fallen off the edge of the earth until a cousin of Carstogi's, a guy in the navy in Bremerton, put two and two together and came up with the connection.

Carstogi finished his story and looked from Peters to me as if we should understand. I still felt there were big chunks missing. "Why do you say he killed her?" I asked.

"He almost killed me," he replied. He had sobered up enough that his words no longer slurred together.

"That's two men going at it. It's a long way from killing a defenseless child."

"You been in the church?" he asked.

"We've been there," Peters replied.

"But during a service?" Carstogi continued doggedly. "Have you been there during a service? If I just coulda gotten that judge to go to a service he woulda given me custody."

"Tell us about the service," Peters suggested.

"You probably won't believe it. Nobody else does."

"Try us," I offered.

He looked at us doubtfully. The sobering process made him

more reluctant to talk. "It's like he owns them body and soul. Like it's a contest to see how far they'll jump if he tells them."

"For instance," Peters said.

"If he told them to eat dog shit they'd do it." He said it quickly, with a ring of falsehood.

"That's not really what you're talking about, is it?" Peters' face was a mask that I had a hard time reading myself. Carstogi gave him an appraising look, then shook his head.

Peters followed up on the opening he had made. "You're afraid to tell us for fear you'll end up being prosecuted too, aren't you?"

"It's scary," Carstogi admitted. "I didn't realize until after I got out. You just do what he tells you, what everyone else is doing. It doesn't seem so bad at the time. You don't think that you're hurting someone. The whole time Brodie is there telling you that suffering is the only way those sinners are going to heaven, that you are the chosen instrument of God."

"Shit." Peters got up and left the table. He went into the bar and came back a few minutes later. A distinct odor of gin came with him. Maybe the juniper berries in gin had been promoted to health food status. Because I knew about Broken Springs, Oregon, and Peters' own situation, I could feel for him, but to leave in the middle of an interrogation was inexcusable, to say nothing of drinking on duty.

I made a mental note to climb his frame about it later. I don't like personal considerations to get in the way of doing the job. If you're a professional, that kind of thing doesn't happen. Objectivity is the name of the game. While I was making that little set of mental notes, I should have remembered something they used to say in Sunday School about taking the beam out of your own eye before you start worrying about the mote in somebody else's. But then, I was still very much the professional. J. P. Beaumont hadn't reached his own breaking point yet. It was coming.

Carstogi was exhausted. We put him up in the Warwick, which happens to be at Fourth and Lenora, a half block cornerwise from where I live. It made dropping him off and tucking him in a simple matter. He seemed more than happy for us to stick him in a hotel room and tell him we'd come get him in the morning.

Peters came with me to my apartment. I got out my Mac-

Naughton's and located a dusty gin bottle with enough dregs for a reasonable drink or two. We tried to plan for morning, which by now was already upon us.

"You think he's telling the truth?" I asked Peters.

He nodded. "Sounds like it to me, as far as it goes. He's scared some of the shit is going to roll downhill and he'll end up with charges lodged against him. I'm afraid he'll rabbit on us before we can get him into court."

I had to agree with Peters' assessment. If we went strictly with Carstogi, we would be leaning on a bent reed. "Do you suppose we can use him to bring Suzanne around?"

Peters considered for a moment. "It would be worth a try, although I doubt it'll work. Even considering what she's been through, she won't squeal on that Brodie bastard. That's the mystifying part about brainwashing. She may know he's a killer, but she'll stick to him like glue."

"You could be right," I allowed, "but we have the element of surprise on our side. She has no way of knowing that Andrew Carstogi is in town. Maybe if we brought him over and dumped him on her, it would jar her into slipping. After all, they were together almost ten years. She probably still has some feelings for him."

"It's worth a try," Peters agreed.

We made arrangements to meet at the Warwick at eight. We'd take Carstogi with us to breakfast and then head for Gay Avenue. We'd try to get there before Suzanne had a backup group from Faith Tabernacle. Our best bet was to catch her alone.

Peters left. In the quiet of my apartment, Anne Corley returned to tantalize me. I had managed to keep thoughts of her at a distance while Peters was there, while I was doing my job, but now her presence—or rather the lack of it—filled the place. Considering she had never set foot in my apartment, it seemed odd that it should feel empty without her. Considering I had never laid a glove on her, it was even odder that I should want her so much.

I leaned back in the leather chair and closed my eyes. I must have dozed off. In a dream I opened my door, and she was standing in the hall. She was wearing a filmy red gown, one of those Frederick's of Hollywood jobs with a split up the side. I reached out to draw her into the room. She came close enough to kiss me on the cheek, then slipped out of my grasp and disappeared around the corner of the hall. The hall became a maze. I followed her, turning one corner after another. Every once in a while I caught a fleeting glimpse of the red gown. She stayed elusively out of reach, but all the while I could hear her laughing.

I woke up in a cold sweat. It was just after three. I stumbled off to bed telling myself that there's no fool like an old fool—an old fool with delusions of adequacy.

Chapter 9

WE were at 4543 Gay Avenue by nine-thirty the next morning. During breakfast we had attempted to explain to Carstogi the importance of bringing Suzanne around. He wasn't wild about seeing her. He still wanted us to take him to Brodie, but sober, he wasn't quite as anxious for a confrontation as he had been the night before.

No one answered our knock, although the doorknob turned in my hand when I tried it. The house was empty. No dirty dishes filled the sink. The beds were made. Someone had gone to a good deal of trouble to clean the place up. We got back in the car and drove to Faith Tabernacle.

Carstogi's reluctance surfaced as we climbed the steps to go inside. Pastor Michael Brodie wielded some residual power that made the younger man, if not downright scared, at least more than a little wary. It's the old talk-is-cheap routine.

The church proper was open but empty. We found Suzanne in the Penitent's Room, kneeling on the stand before the open Bible. Peters and I dropped back while Carstogi approached her.

"Sue?" he asked tentatively. "I'm sorry about Angel. I just heard."

Suzanne didn't so much as look up. There was no sign of recognition or acknowledgment. He stood over her, clenching and unclenching his fists in a combination of nervousness and frustration. A range of emotions played over his face—grief, anger, rejection. He knelt beside her and touched her arm. Her body tensed at the touch but still she didn't look up. "Please, Sue," he pleaded gently. "Come back with me. Let's start over again, away from here, away from all this."

75

The door to the study swung open and Pastor Michael Brodie charged into the room. He grabbed Carstogi by the collar and hauled him to his feet, shoving him off-balance and away in the same powerful motion.

"Satan is speaking to you through the voice of a devil, Sister! Pray on. Your immortal soul is hanging in the balance."

Carstogi recovered and came back swinging, his face a mask of fury. He was pretty well built in his own right, with the broad shoulders and thick forearms of a construction hand, but Brodie outclassed him all the way around. With the ease of a trained fighter, Brodie fended off first one blow and then another before sending Carstogi crashing against the opposite wall. By then Peters and I moved between them. Peters helped Carstogi to his feet and bodily restrained him. The younger man's nose and lip were bleeding. Brodie may have looked like he had gone to seed, but looks can be deceiving. Carstogi was no match for him.

Brodie turned on me. "Get out," he snarled. "You've no right to bring an infidel into a place of worship."

"She's his wife," I said.

"She's his widow!" he shot back. Brodie lunged toward Suzanne. For a moment I thought he was going to hit her. Instead he knelt in front of her, his face inches from hers. "Do not be tempted to leave off your cleansing. These apparitions are Satan's own instruments, sent to tempt you from the True Way. Shut them out, Sister! Pray without ceasing." He rose, turned on his heel, and returned to the study, locking the door behind him.

Carstogi struggled free from Peters' grasp and rushed toward the door just as it slammed shut in his face. He leaned against it, his shoulders heaving with impotent sobs. Carstogi was no lightweight in the physical department, yet Brodie had disposed of the younger man so easily, he might have been a child. A lot of the power Brodie wielded over the True Believers had to do with sheer brute strength and fear. Fear so strong that he could walk away from a kneeling Suzanne and know she would refuse to speak to us even with her spiritual master out of earshot.

Carstogi swung away from the door and went back to Suzanne. He too knelt before her, cradling her face in his hands. "How could you let him do it? How can you let him get away with it?"

Suzanne Barstogi's eyes were blank. She might have been struck blind. When he let her go, she dropped to the floor like a limp rag doll.

"Come on," Peters said, placing his hand on Carstogi's shoulder. "Let's go. This isn't doing any good."

Carstogi rose to his feet like a sleepwalker. Peters led him outside. A thin mist was falling, and I welcomed it. There was a sense of reality in the rain's touch that was lacking inside the barren waste of Faith Tabernacle.

"You did what you could," Peters was saying to Carstogi.

"I shoulda brought a gun," Carstogi mumbled. "I shoulda brought a goddamned gun."

"It's a good thing you didn't," Peters replied. "Airport security would never have let you out of O'Hare. We need your help. Are you in?"

Carstogi nodded grimly. "What do I do?"

"For one thing, tell us everything you know about what goes on in Faith Tabernacle."

We spirited him back to the Warwick. No way were we going to take him down to the department. The last thing we needed was to give the press a shot at him.

Peters picked up a paper on our way through the lobby. Maxwell Cole's article and picture were the lead items of the local section. The headlines read, SLAIN CHILD BURIED. There was a close-up of Suzanne Barstogi kneeling stoically during Angela's service. According to Max's story, Pastor Michael Brodie was a man of God with enough courage and faith to say hallelujah when one of his flock made off for the Promised Land. Suzanne Barstogi's face reflected total agreement with Brodie's words.

Peters read the article first, then handed it to me. Our charge went into the bathroom. "According to that, Brodie's some kind of latter-day prophet," Peters said.

"I picked up on that too. I can hear our case getting picked apart on page one, can't you?"

Carstogi returned to the room and read the article without comment.

"What was Suzanne doing at church this morning?" I asked.

"It's the start of a Purification Ceremony," he said as he studied the picture. "Did she talk to the cops when it happened?"

I nodded.

"That's why, then," he continued. "True Believers are never supposed to talk to outsiders, especially cops. That's why he threw me out."

"Why doesn't he throw her out?"

Carstogi looked at me incredulously. "Are you kidding? If he kicks a woman out, he loses food stamps, welfare, and medicaid, to say nothing of part of the harem."

"Welfare fraud and sex?" Peters asked. "Is that what all this is about?"

Carstogi flashed with anger. "Of course, you asshole. Did you think this was all salvation and jubilee? I couldn't make that judge back home see it either."

I took the newspaper from Carstogi's hand. "With the likes of Maxwell Cole working for the opposition, we'll be lucky to get anyone to believe it here, either," I said. "What do you know about the good pastor?"

"Brodie's a fighter."

"We picked up on that," Peters observed dryly.

"No, I mean he really was a fighter. Middle heavyweight in Chicago. Local stuff. Never made a national name for himself, but he never lost the moves. The only time I think I can whip him is when I'm juiced." He rubbed his bruised chin ruefully. It occurred to me then that maybe Carstogi was growing on me.

He continued. "When Sue and I started going to Faith Tabernacle, we were having troubles. Too much drinking and not enough money. Not only that, we wanted kids and couldn't seem to have any. Sue went first and then she dragged me along. There were probably fifteen to twenty couples then."

"There aren't that many now," I said.

"No. Most of the men get lopped off one way or another. One of them wound up dead in an alley in Hammond, Indiana. I always thought Brodie did that too, but nobody ever proved it. At first I was really gung ho, especially when Sue turned up pregnant. I thought it was a miracle. Now I'm not so sure, but I loved Angel just the same. I wanted her out of this."

"So who are the five or so who are left?"

"Kiss-asses. The ones who get the same kind of kicks Brodie does."

"We did some checking with the state of Illinois. None of

the names check out except for the one named Benjamin.'' Peters was studying Carstogi closely.

"I never knew their real names, only the Tabernacle ones. I imagine Brodie changed them all by a letter or two, just like he did Suzanne's. Some of the True Believers have records. I know that much."

"You said kicks a minute ago," I put in. "What kind of kicks?"

Carstogi looked from Peters to me. He shrugged. "Go to the ceremony," he said. "That'll tell you everything you need to know."

"You know they don't let outsiders in. What happens?" I asked.

"Last night she probably made a public confession of sin. Talking to the cops is probably the major one. They took her to that room afterward for her to pray for forgiveness. Tonight they'll decide on her punishment. She could be Disavowed, but I doubt that. They'll think of something else."

"What else?" Peters was pressing him.

"Anything that sadistic motherfucker thinks up. Maybe she'll have to stand naked in a freezing room or get whipped in front of the group. He's got a whole bag of tricks." Carstogi's hands were clenched, his eyes sparking with fury. I wanted to puke. It's a cop's job to keep people safe, but how do you protect them from themselves?

Eventually he continued. "Tonight they'll leave her to pray in the church itself rather than in the Penitent's room. In the morning they'll have a celebration."

Peters got up. He paused by where Carstogi was sitting on the bed. "Do you think Brodie killed Angela? You said that last night, and we thought you were just drunk. What about now that you're sober?"

"If she wouldn't do what he said . . ." Carstogi's voice trailed off.

Peters walked to the door with a new sense of purpose. "We need to go down to the department for a while. Will you be all right if we leave you here?"

Carstogi nodded. "I'll be okay."

I followed Peters out. I was a little disturbed by the way he was giving Carstogi the brush-off. "I thought we were supposed to stick with him like glue until we got him back on a plane for Chicago."

Peters ignored the comment. "You ever done any bugging?" he asked.

I stopped. "You're not my type."

"Bugging, you jerk, not buggering. As in wiretapping, eavesdropping, Watergate."

"Oh," I replied. "As a matter of fact, I haven't done any of that either."

Peters favored me with the first genuine grin I could remember, the ear-to-ear variety. We got in the car and he turned up Fourth Avenue, the opposite direction from the Public Safety Building.

"Just where in the hell are we going?" I asked.

"Kirkland. I've got some equipment at the house we'll need to use."

"I take it this is going to be an illegal wiretap as opposed to the court-ordered variety?"

"You catch on fast, Beaumont."

"And you know how to work this illegal equipment?" I asked.

Peters' response was prefaced by a wry face. "How do you think I got the goods on my own wife's missionary?"

"And where do you propose to install this device?"

"I think I can make it fit right under the pulpit itself."

"How long is the tape?"

"Long enough. It's sound activated, so if nothing's going on, it shuts off. It'll get us just what we want." Peters' face was a picture of self-satisfaction.

It sounded like Peters knew what he was doing, but I decided to do a reality exercise, play devil's advocate. "Of course you realize that nothing we get will be admissible in a court of law?"

"Absolutely," he responded, "but it may tell us where to go looking for solid information."

"As in where the bodies are buried." That's what I said aloud. I was thinking about Angel Barstogi and a man left dead in a Hammond, Indiana, alley. It seemed to me that God wouldn't frown on our using a little ingenuity to even the score. God helps those who help themselves. Besides, there was a certain perverse justice in the idea of dredging the truth out of Pastor Michael Brodie's very own sermon. Somehow that seemed fair.

Chapter 10

IN the final analysis, we weren't able to get it under the pulpit, but we got close enough. Suzanne Barstogi was still in the Penitent's Room when we returned from Kirkland with Peter's tiny sound-activated tape recorder. By this time her knees must have worn out. She was lying prostrate on the floor, sound asleep.

We were alone in the sanctuary. Peters sat down casually on a front bench and attached the recorder under the seat. He handled the equipment with well-practiced competency. As soon as it was concealed, I went past the sleeping Suzanne and knocked on the door to Brodie's study. We had agreed to beard the lion in his den. We wanted to turn up the heat on Pastor Michael Brodie. We could at least give his self-confidence a good shake.

"What are you doing back here?" he demanded in a voice that caused Suzanne to stir and struggle once more to her knees. He looked around, presumably for Carstogi. "What do you want?"

"We want to ask you a few questions about your whereabouts on Thursday morning."

Brodie's florid face twisted. "Are you accusing me . . ." He broke off abruptly. "I was here, at the church, in my study. Are you listening to that heathen's accusations?"

"You mean Carstogi? No, we're just doing our job. Did anyone see you?" I prodded.

"I told you I was here by myself. Nobody saw me. Almighty God is my witness."

"Have you ever been in Hammond, Indiana?" The tone of Peters' question was deceptively mild. He leaned casually, almost insolently, against the entrance to the Penitent's Room.

Brodie's red face went suddenly slack and ashen. He recovered quickly. "What does that have to do with this?"

"Oh, nothing," Peters said. "I was just wondering."

"I know what you're trying to do. Andrew is making trouble. He is a man with a burden of vengeance in his heart. He blames me for his fall from grace. You tell him from me that Jehovah sees into his vile soul. He will rot in hell for his unjust accusations."

"So you claim you were here all Thursday morning, or at least until Suzanne Barstogi called you? Is that right?" I continued.

"That's what I said. Twice." His fists were tight and so was his voice. He was losing control.

"Why did you change her name? Are the others using different names too?"

I could tell that Peters' roundabout questions were having the desired effect. Brodie's eyes shifted uneasily back and forth between Peters and me as if he were watching an invisible tennis ball. We were developing into a team. I liked Peters' way of approaching issues in an off-the-wall manner.

"We're starting new lives with new names," Brodie explained.

"And new wives," Peters added. "What about your name? Did you change yours too, or only the names of your followers?"

"I want you out of here," Brodie ordered. His voice dropped to an ominous whisper. "I want you out of here now!"

Peters uncrossed his legs and stretched. There was no sense of urgency in his movements. He stepped around Suzanne and approached the open Bible, running his finger down the page. "It might be worth your while to go looking for someone who can remember your being here on Thursday morning. Maybe there was a cleaning woman around or a neighbor who saw you."

"Are you threatening me?"

Peters shook his head. "You can call it that if you like. I call it a friendly suggestion."

With that Peters ambled out of the room. I followed, wishing Peters' little recording device had a remote listening capability, because I was sure all hell was going to break loose the moment we were out of earshot.

We made it into the office by one forty-five and found stacks of messages. Tom Stahl had called again. I had left the phone bill payment envelope with the outgoing mail before I left the Royal Crest that morning. I resented his calling me at the office about it, but then, I never was available at home during business hours. I gave the yellow message sheet a toss.

There was a call from Maxwell Cole. I wadded that one up and threw it in the trash along with the first one. Cole had more nerve than a bad tooth to call me for anything. Detectives don't speak to the press. That dubious privilege belongs to the supervisors.

Captain Powell and Sergeant Watkins wanted to talk to Peters or me. We drew straws. Peters lost and took off for Powell's fishbowl. There was one more message, one that intrigued me. It was from a woman who said she would call back around two. There was no name on the message, nor was there a number I could call.

I looked at the clock, drummed my fingers on my desk, then reached for the phone. I had made a mental note of the number on the slip of paper in Anne Corley's back window. I called Motor Vehicles and asked them to get me some information on the Porsche.

Two o'clock was just around the corner. I hauled out a form and started working on a report. I can deal with the creeps. It's the bureaucratic garbage I can't stand. I dictated a brief summary of our activities for the day and put Michael Brodie's and Benjamin Mason/Clinton Jason's names into the FBI hopper. There was an off chance they had a record somewhere, maybe even an outstanding warrant or two. I phoned Hammond, Indiana, to see if Brodie was still under active investigation in the case Carstogi had mentioned.

My phone did not ring at two o'clock. At two-fifteen, though, I looked up to find Anne Corley being led to my desk by Arlo Hamilton, the public information officer, who was grinning like a Cheshire cat. Look what I found, his face seemed to say. Visitors on the fifth floor are kept to a minimum. I think Anne Corley's looks had a whole lot to do with the visitor's badge that was clipped on her jacket. Heads turned in her wake. If there was a grin on Hamilton's face, I'm sure mine mirrored it. No way could I disguise the pleasure and surprise I felt at seeing her again.

"Here you are, Miss Corley," Hamilton was saying as he led her to my desk.

"Thank you very much, Arlo," Anne responded graciously. "I appreciate your help."

"Think nothing of it. The pleasure was all mine." Hamilton looked at me. "I was giving her some information for her book," he explained. "Of course, you know all about that."

"Yes," I said. I did know about the book. "How's it going?" I asked.

She smiled. "Fine. Arlo here has been a world of help."

Anne sat down on a chair beside my desk. For a few moments Hamilton wavered, uncertain whether to go or stay. Finally he made the right choice and left. Anne was wearing a navy blue suit with an innocently ruffled blouse and a daring slit up one side of the skirt. When she crossed her legs, the skirt fell away, revealing a length of well-formed thigh. A few more heads waggled in our direction. The boots she had worn the day before had obscured two of Anne Corley's most notable assets.

"Hello, Beau," she said. Elbows propped on the arms of the chair, she rested her chin on clasped fingers and regarded me with a level, gray-eyed appraisal. "You've been busy."

"Peters and I have had our hands full," I admitted. "Have you had lunch yet?"

She shook her head. I hurried to my feet in hopes I could spirit her out of the building before Peters returned from his debriefing. It didn't work. He caught us in the elevator lobby. There wasn't much I could do but invite him to join us. I'd as soon have bit my tongue, and I could have belted him for not saying a polite no-thank-you. Now I owed him two.

It was still misting out. We walked to a little Italian place in Pioneer Square. Anne was able to talk enzymes knowledgeably enough even though she didn't seem particularly prone to eat them. As a dedicated processor of junk food, I couldn't hold my own in that conversation. She and Peters hit it off, making me more than a little resentful. I was also painfully aware that he was much closer in age to Anne than I was. They chatted amiably and laughed, while I did a slow burn through lunch that had nothing to do with indigestion. Peters was the life of the party. I wanted to choke him.

Toward the end of the meal, he leaned back in his chair and

said, ''Beau says you're working on a book?'' I had made the mistake of mentioning it to him.

Anne gave Peters a clear-eyed look that nonetheless put distance between them. ''I come at this through the eyes of the victims. That's the name of my book, *Victims*. How do children become victims, and what happens to them or their families afterward? I had some personal experiences with that sort of thing in my own family. I've made a lifelong study of it.''

''You make it sound as though you've been working on this book for quite a while.''

''I have,'' Anne said. ''All over the country.''

''Making any money at it?'' Peters asked. There was a classic cut to her clothing, elegant and expensive. They spoke of style as well as money.

Anne laughed, easily, comfortably. ''If I were in it for the money, I'd have quit a long time ago. No, it's strictly a labor of love.'' The laughter disappeared from her face. She regarded Peters seriously. ''Why do you think Angela Barstogi is dead?''

Peters shrugged. ''No logical reason; she just is.''

The light dawned slowly. I'm not a fast learner. Hearing Anne questioning Peters about the case, I realized that I had been nothing more to Anne Corely than part of her pet research project. It was an ego-bruising realization. I reached for the check, ignoring the fact that neither Anne's nor Peters' coffee cup was empty.

I walked too fast, making it difficult for Anne to keep up. Let her dawdle along with Peters, I fumed. She probably had a whole string of questions to ask him. As for me, I had better things to do with my time than answer questions for some half-baked author. I felt suckered, used. I squirmed a little too. I remembered the previous evening's dinnertime topic. I had shot my mouth off royally, all the time thinking Anne Corley was interested in me when in fact she had only been fishing for information. It would have been easier for me to handle if I had been a rookie. No veteran cop should have been so stupid.

Peters and Anne caught up with me in the elevator lobby on the first floor. Peters excused himself because he had to run an errand. I waited for the notoriously slow elevators, fervently wishing one would come quickly so I could escape Anne Corley's quizzical look.

"Are you angry?" she asked, her question unnervingly direct.

"No," I said quickly, defensively. "Of course not. Why should I be?"

"But you are," she replied.

A bell rang and a door opened. People filed into an elevator, but I didn't. "Yes," I admitted at last. "You're right. I am angry."

"Why?" she asked.

"It's a long story," I answered. "I thought you were . . . Well, I mean I . . ."

"Why aren't you listed in the phone book?" she asked. "I changed my mind about the drink after I dropped you off, but there was no way to call you."

"I'm a homicide detective. We don't have listed numbers." I felt a momentary flash of pleasure that she had tried to call me, but then I remembered her subterfuge and was angry all over again. Another elevator showed up, and I made as if to get on it. She put one hand on my wrist. Her touch nailed my feet to the lobby floor.

"I'm not here about the Barstogi case, Beau," she said. "I came because I wanted to see you."

"Come on, Anne, there's no fool like an old fool. I've been saying that to myself all day. If you want to ask questions, do it aboveboard. Don't play games."

"Will you meet me after work?" she asked.

"Do you want me to bring Peters? We're both working the case." I couldn't resist a dig.

She responded in kind. "Bring a chaperone if you want, but that wasn't what I had in mind."

I swallowed the bait like a starving mackerel. "Where?" I asked.

"Meet me in the lobby of the Four Seasons," she said. "We can have a drink there. About five-thirty."

She turned and walked away. I missed the next elevator fair and square. In fact, I might have stood in the lobby for the rest of the afternoon if Peters hadn't come through and dragged me back to the fifth floor.

The phone on my desk was ringing. "Hello, J. P." Maxwell Cole said. "You didn't return my call."

"You noticed," I observed dryly. "You know I can't talk to you directly. Lay off it."

"Who is she? The car is owned by a law firm in Phoenix, Arizona, and they won't tell me anything."

"I won't tell you anything either, Max. You're barking up the wrong tree."

"Come on, give. You left with her."

"It was stricly social, I can assure you. Had nothing to do with the case, if that's what you're getting at."

"If it was strictly social as you say, tell me who she is."

"Go piss up a rope, Maxey," I told him, and I hung up.

The sole advantage of going to lunch at two-fifteen is there's not a whole hell of a lot of day left when you get back. Maxwell Cole had good sources. The Department of Motor Vehicles gave me the same information he had, the name of a law firm in Phoenix. I called and got a chilly reception from the lady who answered the phone. "Mr. Ames handles Mrs. Corley's affairs," she said, "but I have been instructed to give out no information."

"This is a very serious matter," I said. "I'm investigating a homicide."

"Give me your name, then, and Mr. Ames will get back to you."

"Don't you want the number?"

"No. If you really work for the Seattle Police Department, we'll be able to get your number through information.

My phone rang a few minutes later, and a Ralph Ames introduced himself as Anne Corley's attorney. "You'll have to forgive my receptionist, Detective Beaumont," he said. "Yours was the second call on Mrs. Corley we've had this afternoon. The first one didn't check out."

"Was his name Maxwell Cole?"

"As a matter of fact, it was."

"And he tried to pass himself off as a cop?"

"Well, as an investigator of some kind."

"He's a member of the local press."

"I figured as much," Ralph Ames laughed. "Now, what can I do for you?"

"As I told your receptionist, I'm working on a homicide and—"

"Excuse me for interrupting, Detective Beaumont, but let

me guess. You're working on the murder of a young child, and you're trying to figure out why Anne Corley came to the funeral, right?''

"That's exactly right, Mr. Ames.''

"She's working on a book. She's been working on it for several years. I get calls like this all the time.''

"Yes, she told me about the book,'' I said, relieved. "Still, I have to check things out. It's my job.''

"That's quite all right, Detective Beaumont. This is my job too. Is there anything else I can help you with?''

"No. Nothing I can think of. Thanks.''

"Anytime,'' he said. He hung up.

I waited while Peters finished taking a call from Hammond, Indiana. Yes, Brodie had been investigated in the bludgeoning death of one of his parishioners two years earlier, but he had never been indicted. The case was still open.

There wasn't a whole lot more we could do then, so we took off about four-thirty and went by the Warwick to check on Carstogi. He told us he had made plane reservations for the following morning. Peters went down to the lobby for a telephone huddle with Watkins to see what he thought about Carstogi returning to Chicago. While Peters was out of the room, Carstogi told me he planned to go to a movie that night. There are at least six theaters within walking distance of the Warwick, not counting the porno flicks. I didn't see any reason why he shouldn't go.

As I opened the door to let Peters back into the room, he signaled everything was okay. "You'll keep us posted on how to get in touch with you once you get home?'' Peters asked.

"Sure thing,'' Carstogi said agreeably. He seemed to be in good spirits, all things considered. We left him to his own devices. His close encounter with Michael Brodie's fist had pretty much taken the wind out of his sails.

Peters drove off in his Datsun. I hurried to my apartment and put on a clean shirt; then I caught the free bus back up to the Four Seasons. I didn't tell Peters I was going to meet Anne Corley. I was afraid he'd want to tag along.

Chapter 11

WALKING into the Four Seasons was like walking into a foreign country. Each marbled floor, gleaming chandelier, polished brass rail, and overstuffed chair belonged to another time and place. It all spelled money. The best Italian marble. The best Irish wool for the carpet. "Anne must be quite at home here," I said to myself.

I wandered through the spacious lobby into the Garden Court. The tables were occupied either by takers of tea in the English tradition or drinkers of booze in the American tradition. Some tables included both. Late-afternoon sun had breached the cloud cover and sparkled through an expanse of arched windows that formed one entire wall of the massive room. Anne Corley was seated at a tiny table in a far corner, her face framed by a halo of sunlight shining through her hair.

Her eyes met mine as I entered the room. I declined the services of the maître d' and made my way to the table. So what if she only wanted to pump me for information? I was willing to trade information for the chance to be with Anne Corley. On the table before her sat two glasses, one with white wine and ice and the other with MacNaughton's and water. Pump away.

"Been here long?" I asked, taking a seat.

She shook her head. The room was crowded. There was a line of people waiting to be seated. "Did you have reservations here too?"

She smiled and nodded. "Reservations make things simpler." She examined my face. "Have you cooled off?"

"I guess. I'm here."

She laughed. "You don't look too happy about it."

I sipped my drink, disturbingly aware of her eyes studying

my face. I had the strange sensation that she was burrowing into my mind and decoding the romantic delusions I had manufactured around her. It was at once both pleasant and uncomfortable.

"You didn't bring Peters," she observed.

"No, I decided I could handle the assignment on my own. I'm a big boy now."

"What does a girl have to do to show you that she's interested? Hit you over the head? I find you very attractive, Detective J. P. Beaumont. Is that so hard to believe?"

"Look," I said impatiently. "I told you this afternoon, I don't play games. I'll talk to you about the case as long as what I tell you in no way jeopardizes the investigation. You don't have to pretend I'm some latter-day heartthrob to do it."

She smiled again. "Actually, you sound like a maiden aunt who has just been invited up to see some nonexistent etchings. Let me assure you, my intentions are entirely honorable."

I didn't mean to sound quite so self-righteous. I laughed. "That bad, eh?"

She nodded. The waitress came by with offers of fresh drinks, but Anne waved her away. "I've thought about you all day," she said quietly. "You're really quite pleasant to be with. I realized that after I dropped you off last night."

I could feel a flush creeping up the back of my neck. "That was a compliment," she added. "You're supposed to say thank you."

"Thank you," I murmured.

"You're welcome." Her eyes sparkled with humor. For a time we sat without speaking, listening to the sound of talk and laughter, to the tinkling of leaded glassware that filled the room. It was a companionable silence. I appreciated the fact that neither of us grilled the other about their past. It was enough to be together right then. Eventually she emptied her glass and stood up. "Let's go," she said. "I can only sit around for so long without doing something."

I reached for my wallet, but Anne shook her head. "I already took care of it."

She paused in the lobby long enough to remove a pair of battered Nikes from an Adidas carryall. Her navy pumps disappeared into the cavernous bag.

"Where to?" I asked as she stood up.

"Let's just walk," she replied, and we did. It's unusual for someone with a car to get out and walk like that. We covered the whole of downtown, from Freeway Park to the waterfront. She set a brisk pace and maintained it regardless of the steeply pitched inclines. We walked and talked. She asked nothing about Angela Barstogi, nor did we delve into matters personal. The conversation ranged over a world of topics, from politics to religion, from economics to music. Anne Corley was well read and could hold her own on any number of subjects.

Her mood wasn't as mercurial as it had been the day before. She told wry jokes and laughed at her own punch lines. We wound up at a small Greek restaurant halfway up Queen Anne Hill. We finished dinner about ten-thirty. I bought. My ego needed that hit.

As we left the restaurant, we paused outside to admire a full moon rising behind the Space Needle. She slipped her hand under my arm, her touch both casual and electrifying.

"What now?" she asked.

"A nightcap at my place?" I suggested.

"I'd like that," she replied.

We cut through Seattle Center and walked the seven or eight blocks to my building with her hand still resting on my arm. My mind was doing an inventory of my apartment. How much of a mess was it? Had I picked up the scatter of dirty socks and shirts that often litters the living room? For sure the bed wasn't made. It never is.

The Royal Crest isn't quite as luxurious as its name would imply. We entered the lobby. I tried to look at it through the eyes of a lady with a Porsche. Not that bad, I decided, but it could be better. I was grateful none of my lavender-haired cronies were still in the lobby. Some of them watched the closed-circuit channel twenty-four hours a day, however, and they consider it a sacred charge to know who comes and goes. My bringing home a female visitor would keep the gossip mills running for days.

I pushed open the door and let Anne lead the way into 1106. I didn't turn on the lights. She went straight to the window to look at the downtown skyline. I came to the window and stood beside her. A delicate perfume lingered around her, the same scent that had entranced me the day before at the cemetery. She was as transfixed by the view as I was by her. Her skin reflected back the golden glow of the city lights. The play of light and shadow gave her beauty a haunting quality.

The impulse was more than I could resist. I reached up and ran my finger along her jawline. Her skin was smooth and cool. She made no move away from me. Instead, she turned toward the touch, allowing my finger to retrace its path down her cheek. I felt my throat constrict. "Hello there," I said huskily.

"Hello, yourself," she replied. I took her in my arms and kissed her, feeling her mouth moist and welcoming on mine. I crushed her to me, awed by her response, her willingness.

Self-imposed celibacy is fine as far as it goes, but once you break training, months of deprivation take over. Every sensation is heightened. We were frantic for release. Each kiss was more demanding than the one before. Anne didn't shrink before my onslaught. She matched me move for move, her need as deep and overwhelming as my own.

My hands were trembling with urgency as I fumbled with the top button on her blouse. The ruffled material fell away, revealing the deep hollow of her throat. I kissed her there and felt her response in a sharp intake of breath. Two more buttons revealed her breasts, firm and tense with excitement beneath a lacy bra. She pushed my hands away. "Let me do that," she whispered. With swift, deft movements she undid the remaining buttons and slipped off the jacket, blouse, skirt, and bra. She returned to my arms clothed only in the glow from the downtown skyline.

I had removed my tie and jacket, but not the regulation .38 I carry in a shoulder holster under my left arm. She nestled against my chest. Most women, encountering the pistol for the first time, express something—surprise mostly, dismay sometimes, sometimes repulsion. Anne showed none of these. Her fingers strayed easily across the metal handle, then settled on the small of my back. This time her lips sought mine, sought them, found them, made them her own.

I put my hand on her chin and pushed her away from me. "I thought you said your intentions were honorable."

"I thought you said not to play games," she replied matter-of-factly.

I wasn't prepared to argue the point. I kissed her again, letting my tongue explore at will, learning each corner of her, each curve and crevice. I could probably get away with saying I took her there in the living room on the floor, but it wouldn't be the truth. She took me every bit as much as I took her, maybe more. Her body arched to meet mine, her fingers in my back spurred me, goaded me. My need and her need melded into one, and when the climax came, I heard an aching sob escape her lips. I kissed her cheek. It was wet with tears.

I moved away from her and lay on my side, watching her, "I didn't mean to make you cry," I said.

She snuggled against me, nestling her back into the curve of my body, placing my hand so it rested on the sloping fullness of her breast. "I didn't expect it to be that good. It hasn't been that good in a long time."

We lay like that together, letting the aftermath of our lovemaking slowly dissolve around us. She lay so still, I thought she had dozed off. My arm went to sleep. When I tried to move her to one side, she rolled away from me and stood up. "Do you have a robe I could wear?" she asked.

I dragged two of them out of the closet, one for her and one for me. Considering we had just made love, it was silly to be self-conscious, but we both were. The one I gave her was huge when she tied it around her slender frame. She rolled the sleeves up a turn or two so her hands showed. "I offered you a drink," I said. "You want one now?"

All trace of tears was gone. She smiled mischievously. "No thanks, I already have what I came for."

I grabbed her arm and swung her toward me. "Why, you little vixen," I said. "You ought to be ashamed of yourself."

"I'm not," she said. She gave me a glancing kiss, slipping away from me at the same time. I poured a drink for myself and turned on the lights. I watched with some amusement as she padded barefoot around the room, examining my decorator-dictated knickknacks as well as the pictures of Kelly and Scott on the wall in the entryway.

"Your kids?" she asked.

I nodded. "They're both in high school now. They live in California with their mother."

"How long have you been divorced?" she asked.

"Long time. Five years."

"Girlfriends?"

"I'd like to think I've got one now," I said. "What about you?"

She settled cross-legged on the couch, pulling the robe demurely around her. "I'm a widow. My husband died ten years ago." She regarded me seriously. "I've had too much money to be able to tell who my friends are, to say nothing of lovers."

"You're a little young to be a widow."

"I was a lot younger ten years ago." She didn't offer to divulge her age and I didn't ask, although she couldn't have been more than thirty, thirty-two at the outside. She sat there looking off into space. She had a way of mentally going off by herself that I found disconcerting. When she came back to the present she was looking directly into my eyes. "Are you going to ask me to spend the night, or do I have to get dressed and go home?"

I almost choked on a very small sip of MacNaughton's. "Would you like to spend the night?"

"Yes," she replied. She waited for me to finish my drink; then I led her into the bedroom. I squirmed that the bed wasn't made, but she wasn't paying attention to the furniture. She loosened the tie of the robe, letting it fall open. She pulled my hands inside it, wrapping them around her until I could feel the smooth swell of her breasts against my chest.

"Please," she whispered.

We did.

Chapter 12

THROUGH a sleepy haze, I sensed someone touching me. It was soft and teasing. I thought I was having one of my famous Beaumont dreams. Then I smelled her hair and felt warm lips on mine.

"'What are you doing?'' I mumbled.

"I'm getting you up,'' she whispered softly, her lips nibbling my ear.

"I think I am up."

"Ooh. So you are,'' she smiled.

I pulled her onto my chest, settled her on me, our bodies blending comfortably. My hands closed on her slender waist. I watched her face, her lips parting as her body caught fire. Her hunger was almost frightening in its intensity. We each made love as we had never made love before. In the quiet that followed, she wept. This time I didn't question her tears. I was grateful for them. This time I thought I knew what they meant.

She was resting on my chest, our heartbeats just then slowing, when the phone rang. It was Captain Powell. He was frantic. "Get your ass down here."

I struggled to see the clock. It was a little before five. "What's up?" I asked. The phone cord tangled in Anne's hair, and I struggled to untangle it and listen at the same time.

"They're dead. Brodie and the woman are dead! Somebody found them both at the church."

I eased away from Anne. "Both of them? Have you called Peters?"

"Yeah. He's on his way."

"Tell him to meet me at the Warwick. I'll go there to check on Carstogi."

"You'd better have him under wraps, Beaumont."

I looked out the bedroom window and could see the silhouette of the Warwick against a gradually graying sky. "Snug as a bug," I said lightly.

"I hope to God you're right," Powell muttered, "for your sake and mine."

Anne Corley was wide awake by the time I hung up the telephone. Wrapped in the voluminous robe, she looked wonderful, with that special glow a woman's skin has after lovemaking. "Good morning," she said, smiling.

I kissed her on the forehead, barely pausing in my headlong rush to the shower. "I've got to hurry."

"Trouble?" she asked.

I nodded. "Emergency call. I need to be out of here in about ten minutes." I left her standing in the bedroom and hurried into the bathroom. By the time I finished showering and shaving I could smell coffee. A steaming cup was waiting for me on the dresser. Anne Corley was back in bed, propped on a pillow, coffee mug in hand. She watched me thoughtfully as I dressed.

"Can you tell me what happened?" she asked.

"No." I planted a quick kiss on her forehead as I sat on the bed to pull on my shoes. "Thanks for the coffee," I added.

"Consider it payment in kind for services rendered." I looked at her, gray eyes alive with laughter over the top of her cup. She had evidently taken no offense at my not telling her what was going on. I appreciated that. "Do you mind if I stay for a while, or do you want me to leave when you do?" she asked.

"Make yourself at home," I said. "Stay as long as you like."

She lay back on the pillows, luxuriating. "Thanks. Any idea when you'll be done?"

"None whatsoever." I shrugged my way into the shoulder holster and pulled on a jacket. I bent over her. She pulled me down on the bed beside her and gave me a lingering kiss. I wanted to crawl back into bed with her and forget the world, the department, everything.

"Thank you," she whispered.

"You're more than welcome." Reluctantly I pulled myself away. There was no mistaking that what had passed between us had been good for both of us. "You're a very special lady," I said as I straightened up to leave.

Euphoria lasted for a little over three minutes. I rode down the elevator in my building, walked the half block to the Warwick, and rode that elevator up to the seventh floor. I knocked on Carstogi's door to no avail. When he didn't answer the third barrage of hammering, I went looking for a night clerk, who used his passkey to let me into the room. Carstogi wasn't there. The bedspread was rumpled, as though someone had lain on top of it to watch TV for a while, but the bed had not been slept in.

I left the room as I found it and returned to the hall, where the night clerk hovered nervously, wringing his hands. He was anxious about adverse publicity. I assured him that whatever had happened was no reflection on the Warwick. Asking him to keep me informed of any developments, I went downstairs to wait for Peters. I had the sickening feeling that we'd been suckered, that Carstogi had played us for a couple of fools. Peters' Datsun screeched to a stop about the time I hit the plate glass door. He hadn't taken time to go by the department for another car. I gave him a couple of points for that.

"Carstogi's not here," I said, folding my legs into the cramped front seat. "We'd better go straight to Faith Tabernacle."

Two uniformed cops were standing guard when we got there, holding off a horde of media ambulance chasers, to say nothing of neighborhood curiosity seekers. We hadn't discussed it during the drive to Ballard, but I knew that getting the recorder out of Faith Tabernacle undetected was imperative. Whatever was on it would be totally inadmissible as evidence, but it might provide vital information. Information that would lead us to the killer.

We found Suzanne Barstogi near the pulpit at the front of the church. She lay on her left side with one leg half curled beneath her, as though she had been rising and turning toward her assailant when the bullet felled her. She was still wearing the same dowdy dress she had been wearing earlier in the day. It had been ripped from neck to waist. Her bra had been torn in two, exposing overripe breasts. In addition to the bullet hole that punctured her left breast, her upper torso was covered with bloody welts. Before she died, Suzanne Barstogi had been the victim of a brutal beating.

There was little visible impact damage. The bullet had entered cleanly enough, but behind her, where the emerging slug had crashed out of her body, Suzanne Barstogi's lifeblood was splattered and pooled on the pulpit and altar of the Faith Tabernacle.

Peters looked at her for a long time. "He didn't nickel-dime-around, did he?"

No one was in the church with us right then, but they would be soon. Peters quickly retrieved the recorder and put it in his pocket. We found Pastor Michael Brodie in the middle of his study. He was sprawled facedown and naked on the blood-soaked carpet. Peters and I theorized that he had heard noises in the church and come to investigate. Again there was only one bullet hole.

Shooting at such close range doesn't require a tremendous amount of marksmanship, but you've got to be tough. Tough and ruthless. A hand shaking out of control can cause a missed target at even the shortest distance. Then there's always the chance that the victim will make a desperate lunge for the gun and turn it on his attacker. And then there's the mess.

"I would have bet even money that Carstogi wouldn't pull something like this," I said.

"I hate to be the one to break this to you, Beau, but you did bet money. We both did. Our asses are on the line on this one. Your friend Max will see to it. You just hide and watch."

There's an almost religious ceremony in approaching a crime scene. First is the establishment of the scene parameters. In this case, to be on the safe side, we included the entire church. Then come the evidence technicians with their cameras and measurements. They ascertain distances, angles, trajectories. They look for trace evidence that may be helpful later. The secret, of course, is approaching the scene with a slow deliberation that disturbs nothing. This is one place where peons take precedence over rank. Sergeant Watkins paced in the background, observing the technicians' careful, unhurried efforts.

The medical examiner himself, the white-haired Dr. Baker, arrived before the technicians were finished. He made the official pronouncement of death. A double homicide was worthy of his visible, personal touch. Considering the accumulation of people, I was grateful Peters had gotten the chance to stash the recorder when he did.

A uniformed officer told Watkins that the church members were gathering outside and wanted to come in. What should he tell them? The sergeant directed him to assemble them in the fellowship hall, where we could once more begin the interviewing process.

I was a little puzzled when I saw the whole Faith Tabernacle group, as much as I remembered them, file into the room. After all, it was Tuesday morning and presumably some of them should have gone to work. It turned out that they had been scheduled to be there at five o'clock for a celebration breakfast. It was the traditional ending to a succesful Purification Ceremony, and would have marked the end of Suzanne Barstogi's ordeal of silence, fasting, and prayer.

Without Brodie's looming presence in the background to enforce silence, it was easier to get people to talk. It was plain that they were shocked by what had happened, and talking seemed to help. They were getting better at it.

The cook, a True Believer named Sarah Norris, had come to church at four to start preparing breakfast, which was due after a prayer session at five. Before early-morning services, she had been in the habit of taking a cup of coffee to Brodie in his study. It was when she took him his coffee that she had found first his body and then Suzanne's.

We were about finished with Sarah when the front-door cop came hurrying into the room. "You'd better come quick. Powell said to call him on a telephone, not the radio, and to make it snappy."

The only phone available at the church was in the study. If Powell didn't want us to use the radio for privacy reasons, the study was no better. We got in Peters' car and drove to the first available pay phone.

"What's up?" I asked as soon as Powell came on the line.

"The night clerk from the Warwick, that's what. He says Carstogi came back and tried to go to his room. He's got him down in the restaurant eating breakfast and wonders what he should do."

"Get a couple of uniformed officers over there to keep him there for as long as it takes us to drive from Ballard."

"They're on their way, but why do I have this sneaking suspicion that you've screwed up, Beaumont?"

"Experience," I told him, and slammed the phone receiver

down in his ear. I turned back to the car to see Maxwell Cole's rust-colored Volvo idling behind Peters' Datsun. "Shit."

I climbed into the car. "Sorry," Peters said. "He must have tailed us when we left the church. I didn't see him."

"It's too late now. Drive like hell to the Warwick. Carstogi's in the restaurant having breakfast."

Peters' jaw dropped in surprise. "No shit! Why would he go back there?"

"Beats me, but he did, and we'd better nab him before he gets away. Thank God the night clerk had brains enough to call and let us know." I glanced at Peters, who was looking in the rearview mirror. "Max still on our butt?" I asked.

"Yes."

"We'll just have to lump it. We don't have time to try to throw him off the trail. I don't want Carstogi to slip through our fingers."

"The gun has a way of equalizing things, doesn't it? Yesterday Carstogi was no match for Brodie when they were dealing with fists."

"You've already decided he's our man?"

"Haven't you?" Peters asked.

"No, I haven't. I like to think I'm a better judge of character than that. Carstogi wanted to kill Brodie, but he would have taken Suzanne back in a minute. You heard him yesterday."

"Well, who did it then?" Peters asked. It was a good question. We didn't have an answer by the time we stopped in front of the Warwick. Two patrol cars with flashing lights were outside the hotel, one parked in front of the garage on Fourth and the other at the front door on Lenora. We stopped by the front door.

The clerk met us at the car, the story bubbling out before Peters turned off the engine. "He came up to the desk, said he needed a wake-up call at ten. I didn't want him to go up to his room, so I told him we had a problem with the plumbing and that we'd buy his breakfast in the restaurant while we cleaned up the mess. I didn't know what else to do. I called right away, because you said it was important."

"Thanks," I said. "That was good thinking."

"Where is he now?" Peters asked.

The Volvo stopped across the street. I went back to an officer who was standing near the front door. "Don't let that yahoo in here," I said, pointing at Cole, who was just climbing out of the car.

The dining room at the Warwick is small and intimate. At that hour of the morning it was just filling up with tables of visiting businessmen and conventioneers. Andrew Carstogi had been placed at a small corner table. The hostess watched him nervously from her desk. Peters pulled his gun and put it in his jacket pocket. We approached the table warily.

Carstogi looked up and saw us coming toward him. He grinned and waved at us with an empty fork. "Hi, guys," he said.

"Where have you been?" Peters asked.

Carstogi's grin faded. "Out. Just got back. They told me there's a problem with the room and they're buying me breakfast while they fix it. Good deal."

"Out to where?" Peters continued.

"What is this?" Carstogi asked. "I went to a movie, and I met a girl. There's nothing the matter with that."

"What's her name?" I put in. "Where did you take her?"

"We went to her place. Jesus, how am I supposed to know where it is? What's going on? Why all the questions?"

"How did you get back here?"

"I caught a cab."

"Which one?"

Carstogi stood up. "Okay, I'm not saying another word until you tell me what's going on."

People around us were staring. We were creating a disturbance. "Sit," Peters hissed. We sat.

"We have two brand-new murders," Peters said. "Two homicides at Faith Tabernacle."

The color drained from Andrew Carstogi's face. "Not Suzanne," he whispered.

I nodded. "Suzanne and Brodie both. Sometime during the night. Now tell us, how'd you get back here from wherever you were."

Carstogi opened his mouth to say something and then shut it. Two gigantic tears rolled down his face. He brushed them away with his sleeve. "I caught a cab," he said.

"What kind? Yellow? Graytop?"

"I don't know. Just a cab. It picked me up at her house. I think it was the same cab as last night, but I'm not sure." He looked back and forth from one of us to the other. "It's not true, is it? Tell me it's not true."

"It's true," I said.

"Do you mind if we go through your room?" Peters asked.

Carstogi shook his head mutely. Peters signaled to an officer who had stationed himself next to the hostess's desk. "Have the desk clerk let you into his room to check it out," he instructed. "Let me know if you find anything." The officer hurried away. Carstogi's shoulders heaved with noisy sobs. Peters and I watched, saying nothing. Eventually, he regained control.

"Am I under arrest?" he asked.

"No, but as of now I'm afraid you're the sole suspect."

"But I never went near the church after we left there yesterday. I wouldn't know how to get there."

The officer returned to say that the room was clean. Carstogi looked from one of us to the other. "What's going to happen?" he asked.

I pushed back my chair. "Let's go up to your room and get a statement from you. Do you want an attorney present?"

"I don't need one," he said. "I didn't do it."

I believed him. I just wished that things were always that simple. We led him upstairs and took his statement. Carstogi answered all our questions willingly enough. According to him he had gone to a porno house and had been picked up by a prostitute after the movie.

I don't think Carstogi really grasped that the only thing between him and a first-degree murder charge was a prostitute whose name was Gloria, most assuredly not the name her mommy gave her. He couldn't remember her address, and the description he gave us would have fit half the females in the U.S. Average height, kind of light brown hair, lightish eyes, slim. Carstogi's life was hanging by a slender thread.

We turned off the recorder and stood up to leave. "Are you arresting me?" he asked.

"No, not now, but don't leave here. Stay in the room and don't talk to anyone."

"Okay," he said. "I just can't believe she's dead."

"Believe it," Peters said.

We left the room. "We should book him, Beau," Peters said to me in the hall. "Motive, opportunity. It all adds up. What if he splits?"

"Come on, Peters. We don't have a shred of solid evidence. Nothing more than the fact that he doesn't have an alibi for last night. The girl was probably some hooker off Aurora. You know how easy finding her will be."

"But you intend to look?" Peters regarded me wearily, shaking his head.

"That's right," I answered. We rode down in the elevator without saying anything more.

Maxwell Cole was in the lobby, arguing with the officer stationed at the registration desk, his walruslike face twitching with exasperation. "What's going on, J.P.? This asshole wouldn't spring with any information."

"Good," I said. "Neither will I. Pass the word."

Peters directed one of the uniformed officers to keep an eye on the seventh floor. He nodded and waved.

Cole blustered out of the lobby after us. "I want to know what's going on. Two innocent people have been slaughtered in cold blood. You owe the people of Seattle an explanation."

I turned on him. "I owe the people of Seattle a full day's work for a full day's pay. I don't owe you a fucking thing." The other cop heard this exchange with a poorly concealed grin. "If he gives you any trouble, lock him up," I said as I stalked away.

Peters moved his car to a parking meter and plugged it. We had decided to go up to my apartment and see what kind of fish our hidden recorder might have hooked.

Chapter 13

IT was only as we rounded the corner of Lenora onto Third that I remembered Anne was in my apartment. My mind had switched tracks completely, and now I didn't know what to do. I decided I'd better call her from the lobby and give her some warning of her impending company.

She seemed pleased to hear my voice. "I'm downstairs," I said. "I'm bringing Peters up with me."

"Who was that?" Peters asked with a conspiratorial grin as we got on the elevator. "Anybody I know?"

"As a matter of fact, you do know her. It's Anne, Anne Corley."

"Why you closemouthed son-of-a-bitch! I got the impression at lunch yesterday that you and she had just met. How long have you been holding out on me?"

The elevator door opened on eight. "Can it!" I snapped as Wanda Jamison got on, coffee cup in hand. She was on her way for a morning coffee klatch with Ida, my next-door neighbor. Wanda and I exchanged idle pleasantries while Peters continued to leer at me over her head.

If I thought Anne would have used the lead time to change out of my robe, I was sadly mistaken. She didn't. I was glad I waited until Ida's door was safely closed before I knocked on my own. Anne opened the door and gave Peters a gracious welcome, as though her being there in a state of relative undress were the most natural thing in the world. She was totally at ease, and Peters was getting a real charge out of my discomfort.

Peters made himself some tea while I paced the confines of my tiny kitchen. "What do you suggest we do with her while we listen to the tape?" he asked.

"I give up." I was long on embarrassment and short on ideas right then. I had told Anne she could stay as long as she liked, but I couldn't have her in the room while Peters and I listened to our illicit tape.

Peters carried his cup into the living room. He took my chair. I sat on the couch next to a cross-legged Anne. It disturbed me to be next to her. I wanted to touch her, but not in front of Peters. I didn't want to soften my image—whatever was left of it.

Peters looked at Anne. "Do you mind if we play a tape?"

Anne contemplated Peters with her direct, gray gaze. "Do you want me to leave? I can go in the other room."

Peters glanced in my direction, then nodded. "I'd appreciate it."

Obligingly, Anne rose. "I'll go get dressed then," she said. Much to my dismay, she leaned over and gave me a familiar peck on the cheek as she went by. The robe fell open, allowing me a fleeting glimpse of flesh and curve.

Once she was out of the room, Peters pointed an accusing finger at me. "You asshole," he said. "If you'd told me yesterday, I never would have tagged along with you to lunch."

I didn't feel like explaining that, yesterday at lunch, I hadn't known either. "Play the tape, Peters," I said wearily. "Just play the tape."

He did.

At first there were indistinguishable noises, openings and closings of doors that weren't followed by sufficient noise to keep the recorder running. Eventually, however, there was a murmur of voices punctuated by coughs and clearings of throats, the sounds of a fitful crowd settling itself. Then Pastor Michael Brodie's voice, stentorian and clear, filled my tiny living room.

"Brethren, we come together this evening as Believers in the one True Faith, as Partakers of the one True Life. We are the chosen generation, a royal priesthood. Are there any here who doubt that we are the People of God?" There was a pause with no answer. Brodie's voice was that of a born orator sounding a call to arms.

"We have come to this place as strangers and pilgrims. There are none of us here who did not once walk in lasciviousness and lust. Our Lord did not come to call the righteous. He came to call the sinners, and those of us who have seen and

heard are here, Brothers and Sisters. We are here! Praise God.''
A chorus of amens echoed on the tape.

"Are we going to have to listen to the whole fucking sermon?'' Peters asked.

"Looks that way," I told him.

"We have spoken many times how, in the early days, the Romans were the law of the land. In Romans 7:4 it says, 'Wherefore, my brethren, ye also are become dead to the law by the body of Christ.' Let there be no mistake about it. That means that once we are in Christ, once we have set ourselves firmly on His path, we are dead to the law of the land. We are apart from it. It has nothing to do with us. And when we return to the law of the Romans, the law of the flesh, we turn our backs on The Way, for it is impossible to live in the world of the flesh and the world of the spirit at the same time.

"The scripture goes on to say, 'For when we were in the flesh, the motions of sins, which were by the law, did work in our members to bring forth fruit unto death. But now we are delivered from the law, that being dead wherein we were held; that we should serve in newness of spirit, and not in the oldness of the letter.'

"Did you hear that, Brothers and Sisters? Did you hear that? It says we are delivered from the law. Delivered! Cut loose! Living under the Roman law shackles us, delivers us to death. It is only by living completely and totally in our newness of spirit that we find Life, Life Everlasting." Again we heard the echoing amens.

"He's really tuning up now. Getting into his act."

"Shut up, Peters. I'm trying to listen."

". . . was in this newness of spirit that we made the leap of faith that brought us here to this city. It took courage for each of us to leave the old ways behind. Each of us left friends and family and possessions. We all made sacrifices to be here, trusting that we had found the True Pathway to Christ. In doing so, each of us has taken a vow to lean not on our own understanding. We have sworn to be subject one to another, to submit ourselves to the elders, to humble ourselves under the mighty hand of God that He may exalt us in due time.

"We have found that there are those who would revile us for mortifying our members, who falsely accuse us of evil when in fact we who suffer for righteousness' sake are content and unafraid. There is one of our number here tonight who has brought herself to be purged of sin. In her hour of trial she turned from the teaching and cast herself back into the old ways, turning away from the Law of the Spirit to the carnal law. Sister Suzanne, will you rise and stand before the Brethren.''

There was a pause and some audible shuffling in the congregation. ''Last night, Sister Suzanne stood before you and confessed her sin, that when Angel, her worldly daughter, was missing, she secretly called the police, bringing the power of the Romans back into our midst.

''We know Jehovah has punished her for this act by taking Angel from her. We know, too, that for breaking her vows she could be Disavowed, cast away from the True Believers in disgrace. Last night she humbled herself before the elders and begged to be allowed to remain. Since yesterday morning at sunrise she has taken no food. She has prostrated herself in prayer at the altar of our Lord, begging His forgiveness, and ours as well.

''Last night, even as she prayed and wept, the elders met to consider her fate. I would like at this time for the elders to come forward.'' There was a shuffling noise and then quiet. ''. . . elders stand before you. Brother Benjamin? Sister Suzanne has submitted herself to the elders for punishment. Have you made a decision?''

I remembered Benjamin's work-hardened muscles. ''We have, Pastor Michael.'' I remembered his voice. It was Jeremiah's stepfather.

''And how do you judge?''

''By the stripes she shall be healed.'' The people in the room voiced their approval.

''Here it comes,'' Peters said.

''If our Lord who was without blemish or blame suffered the scourge for our sakes, then it is only right that we who are sinners should follow in His steps. Sister Suzanne, take comfort in the words given to the apostles who suffered and died in the service of our Lord. 'Beloved, think it not strange concerning the fiery trial which is to try you. But rejoice, inasmuch as ye are partakers of Christ's sufferings; that, when his glory shall be revealed, ye may be glad also with exceeding joy.' ''

Amens were more fervent now as people were caught up in

the spectacle. Even on the tape I could sense their excitement, the shuffling feet, the nervous coughs.

"It is written that 'the time is come that judgment must begin at the house of God: and if it first begin at us, what shall the end be of them that obey not the gospel of God? Wherefore let them that suffer according to the will of God commit the keeping of their souls to him.'

" 'Forasmuch then as Christ hath suffered for us in the flesh, arm yourself likewise with the same mind: for he that hath suffered in the flesh hath ceased from sin.'

"Sister Suzanne, cast all your care upon Him; for He careth for you. It says in First Peter 3:14, 'But and if ye suffer for righteousness' sake, happy are ye: and be not afraid of their terror, neither be troubled.'

"Do you come here willingly, Sister Suzanne?"

"I do."

"I'll just bet," Peters said.

Suzanne's response had been barely audible, but an exultant "Hallelujah" sprang from the crowd. Maybe if she had said no, that she had been forced, the ceremony would have been canceled and the True Believers would have been denied their blood lust. A baby cried somewhere in the background and was quickly hushed. So the children were there, watching, listening. I thought of Jeremiah. No wonder he was afraid.

Brodie continued now, his tone no longer that of an orator, but gentler, cajoling, not wanting to frighten Suzanne into backing out at the last minute. "Do you know, too, that those who will smite you do so only as tools of your salvation, bearing you no malice or ill will?"

"I do."

"I think I'm going to puke," Peters said. "She really let them do it to her."

This time there was no sound from the True Believers. They were holding their collective breath in anticipation. This was the sword Brodie wielded over his congregation. Not only had he inflicted bodily punishments, he had provided them for the vicarious enjoyment of his followers. Sickened, I resumed listening. Brodie was speaking again, his tone moving, hypnotic, molding her to his will. If Suzanne Barstogi would willingly hurt herself because Brodie asked, would she have resisted beating her own child?

" 'Being reviled we bless; being persecuted we suffer it.' Will you then, Sister, bless and forgive each of those who stand here tonight to be the instruments of your redemption?''

"Yes." Her answer was nothing more than a whisper. The recorder detected no shifting, no sound from the crowd. They were ready.

"Brother Amos and Brother Ezra, hold her wrists." There was the sound of people moving. "Brother Benjamin, rend her garment." We heard the sound of her dress tearing, the snap of her brassiere, and then, after a pause, the sharp crack of a lash biting into flesh. Reflex made me count the blows, seven in all, each one slow and deliberate. Suzanne made one involuntary cry at the outset. After that she was silent.

The tape went on. There had been an outpouring of amens and hallelujahs, but now that was silenced. Brodie was speaking. "Sister Suzanne will spend yet another night in prayer, not in the Penitent's Room, but here, at the altar, where she can feel our Lord's forgiveness. In the morning we shall come again to welcome her return to the fold. Go with God. It is finished."

I heard some murmur of talk as people filed out. The next sound was that of someone weeping. "Suzanne?" Brodie's voice.

She made no response, although the weeping subsided. "Suzanne. Look at me. I have something for you. It'll make it hurt less." A pause, then he continued, his voice soft and cajoling. "Don't try to cover yourself from me, Sister. I've come to minister to your wounds. It's a local anesthetic."

Again the silence. I could imagine him running a fleshy finger across her bleeding breasts, administering some kind of ointment.

"Thank you," Suzanne said softly.

"I want you," he said.

"No, please." There was no audible spoken answer although we heard the sound of the study door closing. I was taken aback. He had asked, and Suzanne had denied him. Even the pastor himself was subject to some rules and prohibitions. It was obvious what kind of additional comfort and forgiveness he had intended to offer.

The tape clicked on and off, running only when there was sufficient sound in the room to sustain it. There was no way to tell how much time elapsed each time the voices stopped and started.

". . . of-a-bitch" The voice was a man's, muffled and indistinct. It sounded as though it might have been coming through a closed door, maybe the study.

I strained to hear. "Turn it up," I said to Peters, and he did.

"Get out!" I could recognize Brodie's voice.

The other man was speaking now. ". . . her alone. She's my wife, not one of your whores."

I heard the familiar menacing tone in Brodie's voice. "You seem to forget, my word is law here." The door slammed. The visitor's hard-soled shoes stormed through the sanctuary. The front door slammed heavily behind him.

Now we could hear the mumble of Suzanne's voice alone. It rose and fell. It was a prayer of some kind, but the words themselves escaped us. It continued for some time, on and off, intermittently reactivating the machine.

Then suddenly, sharply, ". . . t do you want?"

A sharp report of a pistol answered her, followed by the sound of an opening door. We could hear Brodie's voice. "What happened? Suzanne?" A gunshot was his answer too, followed by silence as the machine shut itself off.

The next voice was that of Sarah, the cook: ". . . my God," and the sound of hurrying footsteps. Then came the sound of another door and more footsteps, followed by Peters' voice: "He didn't nickel-dime-around, did he?" The recorder was switched off before anything further was said.

"That was Carstogi!" said Peters, his voice tense with excitement. "It has to be."

"How can you be sure?" I asked. "I don't think it sounds like him at all."

Just then Anne asked permission to return to the living room. She was wearing the same blue suit she had worn the day before, only now her hair was pulled back and fastened in an elaborate knot at the base of her neck. She looked like a ballerina. The similarity wasn't just in looks. I knew that her external beauty concealed the finely tuned, well-conditioned body of a professional dancer.

"Beau, I'm going to take off now," she said, moving toward the door. She nodded to Peters. "Nice to see you again, Ron."

Peters stood up apologetically. "I hope you're not leaving on my account."

She smiled. "No. I have lots to do."

I followed her to the door. "Can you come back tonight? I don't know what time I'll be back, but I can give you a key so you can let yourself in."

"Do you think you can trust me?" She was laughing as she asked the question. I rummaged through the kitchen junk drawer to locate my spare keys.

I handed them to Anne, and she dropped it into her jacket pocket. "Thanks," she said, giving me a quick peck on the cheek.

I walked with her to the elevator lobby, where she turned and kissed me, a full-blown invitational kiss that sent my senses reeling. The elevator door opened. There stood three of my neighbors.

"That wasn't fair," I protested.

"It wasn't, was it?" she agreed. The elevator door closed, and she was gone.

Chapter 14

PETERS, still intent on the tape, was playing it again as I came back into the room. "So much of what Brodie says sounds like he's quoting directly from the Bible."

"Probably was. Taken out of context and given a forty-degree twist, you can use the Bible to justify almost anything."

Peters' tea was gone. I brought him another cup. We listened to the tape, not once but several times. "There's a clue in here somewhere, if we could just put our fingers on it," Peters said as he switched off the recorder for the last time. He stood up. "I guess we'd better get back over to Faith Tabernacle. The place is probably still crawling with people. Watty will be climbing the walls."

"What about Carstogi?" I asked.

"What about him? I'm sure the trail leads back to him one way or the other."

I remained unconvinced. I said, "Let's get a description of the hooker and put vice on it. Or maybe we could track down that cab."

"You're determined he didn't do it, aren't you? But you're right; we should check it out." Peters glanced down at the tiny machine in his hand. "What about this? Erase it?"

"No, don't. We'll want to listen to it again. If there's something in there that we're missing, maybe we'll catch it next time. Leave it here." I took the recorder from him and placed it in the top drawer of the occasional table beside my leather chair. "That way it won't leak into Cole's hands."

Back at Faith Tabernacle Sergeant Watkins was running the show, directing a small army of officers who scrutinized every inch of the church and took statements from anyone who looked remotely related to the case. At the moment we drove up, Watty was standing next to the front door, supervising a kneeling lab technician who was making a plaster cast of something behind a row of decorative bushes.

"What's up?" Peters asked him.

Watkins glowered at us. "Where the hell have you been?" He went on without waiting for an answer. "We found some tracks here. The footprints have been obliterated, but we should get good casts of the bicycle tires. Someone parked a bike here during the night."

"You think the killer used a bike for his getaway?" I asked, shaking my head.

"You have a better suggestion?" Watty snapped.

I had to admit I didn't have one. "Where's the father?" the sergeant asked.

"He's back at the Warwick. We've got a guard on him."

"A guard!" Watkins exploded. "What I want on him are cuffs and orange coveralls. We've got three people dead so far. We'd better arrest someone pretty goddamned soon."

"Carstogi didn't do it," I said.

"What? Are you his goddamned character witness? I understand he was out all night. Where was he?"

"He doesn't know."

"Doesn't know!"

"He went to the Palace for a sleazy, X-rated movie and got himself picked up by a hooker. He doesn't know where they went. He's from out of town."

Watkins examined my face as though he thought I was a raving lunatic. "That's the shakiest goddamned alibi I've heard this week!" He turned to Peters. "You agree with him, Detective Peters?"

Peters shifted uneasily under his gaze. "No," he said at last. "Beau and I differ on that score. I think Carstogi is our prime suspect."

Watty turned back to me, a look of smug satisfaction spreading over his face. "I'm glad somebody around here has some sense. Majority rules. Now I suggest you get off your ass and nail it down." He walked away.

Peters looked at me for a reaction. "He asked my opinion, Beau." It was part apology and part justification.

"That's why they have two detectives on this case, remember?" We went inside.

The bodies were gone and the crime lab folks were pretty much finished. One of them tossed Peters a bulging manila envelope. "You can cross robbery off the list of motives," he said. "There's seventeen thousand dollars in cash in that baby. It was in a bottom drawer in the study. We're taking it down to the department for safekeeping."

I went into the study. A well-thumbed and much-marked Bible lay open on the desk. I turned some of the pages. The marked passages were all of a vein similar to what we had heard on the tape. Nothing in Brodie's selections spoke of forgiveness or loving one's neighbor, to say nothing of one's enemies. Faith Tabernacle's leader had demanded retribution from his followers, had turned a blind eye on adultery. Someone had learned the lessons well and had given Brodie a taste of his own medicine. "Vengeance is mine" was the message. The Lord was excluded from the equation.

A halfhearted prayer service was continuing in the fellowship hall. The few True Believers who held jobs had not gone to work. Like bewildered sheep they huddled together for warmth, locked in a cell of interminable prayer, waiting for direction. Brodie had told them what to do and when to do it for a long time. Without him they had no idea how to function. I felt sorry for them. At the same time I felt repulsed. They had turned their lives and minds over to a monster masquerading as a messiah.

I saw Jeremiah. I tried to catch his eye in hopes I could get him to come talk to me. I think he saw me, but he studiously ignored me. Already someone had taken up Brodie's mantle and was pulling the strings.

Peters and I hit the street. We went back to Gay Avenue. Like the evidence techs before us, we found nothing. It looked as though no one had been in the house since we had come with Carstogi the day before. As we stepped off the porch to leave, Sophie Czirski hailed us from the concealed gate in her fence.

"Is it true?" she demanded as we approached. "They're both dead?"

"Yes," Peters responded.

"Serves 'em right," she muttered, "both of 'em." Her loose dentures clicked in satisfaction.

"You didn't do it, did you, Sophie?" Peters' question was a joke more than anything, but Sophie's face brightened.

"I didn't," she said. "Wish I had, though. I was right there in the house from "Little House on the Prairie" to the eleven o'clock news. Then I went to bed. No way to prove it, though. Nobody saw me. You want to take me in?"

Peters grinned. "That won't be necessary, but you call us if you see anything strange around here, will you?"

Her red hair bobbed up and down. "I will," she assured us, and we both knew it was true.

We questioned some of the other neighbors and then returned to Faith Tabernacle to canvass that area, looking for leads the whole time. We kept after it all day. For a while it looked as though we were going to come up empty-handed. We were still at it when yellow school buses started discharging passengers in late afternoon. Shortly after that a kid on a bike, probably junior high or so, rode up to where Peters and I were standing.

"You guys detectives?" he asked.

"That's right."

"I saw someone on a bike this morning when I was on my paper route. I usually cut through the church parking lot to get to the house across the street. It's the last one on my route. Someone was just leaving the front of the church. He was in a hurry."

"Did you get a good look at him?"

He shook his head. "It was too dark. I only saw the reflectors on the bike's wheels."

"What time was it?"

Again he shook his head. "I don't know. My dad gets home from work about two—he's a janitor—and he wakes me up. I deliver my papers and go back to bed. That way I can have breakfast with everybody else in the morning. I usually get home around three. This is my last house."

He couldn't give us much more than that. We took his name, address, and phone number and thanked him.

"Nice kid," Peters said as we watched him wheel his bike back down the street.

"He came within an inch of getting himself killed this morning. If he'd seen him, I don't think our killer would've hesitated pulling the trigger again."

About six-thirty we went back to the department to dictate

our reports. We finished about an hour later. Peters offered me a ride home, and I accepted. It had been a long day.

The lights were off in the apartment when I came in. I felt a jab of disappointment. I had hoped all day that Anne would be there when I came home. It had been years since someone had been at home waiting to welcome me. I fixed a drink and went to the bedroom to hang up my jacket. Anne was there in my bed, curled up and sound asleep. I beat a hasty retreat to the shower, overwhelmed with gratitude for my good fortune.

Clean-shaven and showered, I slipped into bed beside her. She snuggled against me. When I nuzzled her neck, she stirred. "Good evening, Sleeping Beauty."

She smiled contentedly as my fingers caressed her breast. "Does that make you Prince Charming?"

"Or his grandfather."

She laughed. "You're not that old, are you?"

"I feel that old," I replied. I studied her. She had to be over thirty, but she looked as young as twenty-five. I could feel my body hardening, wanting her, yet I held back, too. Her fingers trailed through the hair on my chest, drumming a tattoo that reverberated through my head.

"You don't feel old to me," she said. The texture of her nipple changed beneath my hand. She pulled her hair to one side, exposing the smooth skin of her bare neck. I kissed her there, feeling her body go taut, her response immediate and palpable. There was an urgency in her kisses, a hungry need that overtook us both. In responding to that need, age was no longer an issue.

Her lovemaking taxed my skill and knowledge, taking me far beyond the gradual experiments Karen and I had evolved together. Anne required nothing less than full satisfaction and gave it as well, her body an exquisitely tuned instrument responding vibrantly to the slightest touch.

It pains me to admit that in things sexual, Anne just flat knew more than I did. Later, as she lay in my arms, satiated and content, I remembered how much she knew and it began to bother me. I began to wonder how she had come to know so much. I began to want to piece together Anne's romantic past. I was rational enough to know it was none of my business, but that didn't stop me. It's a kind of inquisitor mentality that makes me think I've been in this business too long. It also makes me realize what a prude I am. I guess deep down, like most men, I wanted the woman I loved to be a virgin. An adept virgin.

Eventually Anne slipped out of bed. "What do you eat around here?" she asked. "I've seen better-stocked refrigerators in motel rooms."

"I don't cook. I eat out."

"When? I'm starved."

"For what?"

"For food. Any kind."

I thought about the Porsche and the fur jacket. I thought about the Doghouse. I thought about age and sex and money. We were worlds apart, yet I wanted us to end up in the same orbit. "Well, if you're tough enough, I'll introduce you to one of my favorite hangouts. Believe me, reservations won't be necessary."

She took a red sweatsuit out of her Adidas bag. I watched her pull it on, marveling at her sleek, firm body. I drew her to me and zipped up the top. "How do you do that?" I asked.

"Do what?"

"Stay in shape."

"Oh, that," she said laughing. "I jog, I ride, do aerobics, lift weights. Anything else you'd like to know? Measurements, weight?"

"As a matter of fact, I want to know everything."

"For instance," she teased.

"I wrapped my arms around her. "For instance, tell me about your sister, Patty. What happened to her?"

She stiffened in my arms. "No," she said quietly. She moved away. I caught a glimpse of her face as she turned. A curtain had come down over her gray eyes. They were suddenly solemn and distant. "Don't ask me that again." It was a statement, not a request.

I had blundered onto dangerous ground, and I would do well to be more wary in the future. I see that in cops all the time, had seen it in Peters and myself. We can talk about crime in the abstract; just don't bring it too close to home.

Anne reached into her bag, pulling out a brand-new pair of jogging shoes. She held them up for my approval. "I went shopping today," she said in a halfhearted attempt at gaiety. It didn't take.

We walked to dinner. I tried to recapture the evening's

earlier, lighter mood without success. Anne had crossed over her solitary bridge and left me alone on the other side. What exactly had she told me about Patty? I wondered. That she had died when Anne was eight? Why, then, did the mere mention of Patty more than twenty years later cause such a reaction?

Connie welcomed us with a knowing wink that set my teeth on edge. It got worse when she brought the menus. She gave Anne an appraising once-over. "I heard you were pretty, honey, but that don't hardly do you justice."

I bit. "How'd you hear that?"

She grinned. "I've got me some confidential sources. The clam strips are good tonight, and we've got liver and onions on the special."

I watched for any hint of disdain as Anne perused the menu. There was none, no hint of snobbishness. She ordered the special, then waited, oblivious to her surroundings, still far removed from me and from the present.

"Hello," I said at length, trying to get her attention. "Where are you?"

"Sorry, I didn't mean to do that."

"It wouldn't be so bad if you'd take me along when you go."

She gave me a searching look. "How did you know I was somewhere else?"

"For one thing, I asked you twice if you wanted a glass of wine."

Connie slung a cup of coffee in my direction and returned with one for Anne when I gave her the high sign. We were halfway through dinner when Maxwell Cole showed up. I thought it was an unfortunate coincidence. I found out later he had been in and out three times earlier in the evening looking for me.

He favored Anne with a deep bow. "What a pleasure to see you again," he oozed, as his cigarette smoke invaded the end of our booth.

Connie came over with an ashtray, which she held out to Max. "This is the no-smoking section, Mr. Cole. If you want to keep that cigarette, you'll have to go over to the next section." Cole ground out the stub.

"I've been on a wild-goose chase," Max said, addressing Anne. "That little Porsche of yours shouldn't be so hard to find, but it seems to have fallen off the face of the earth."

"Why are you looking for my car?" Anne asked.

"I'm not, actually. I've been looking for you. I wanted to ask you some questions abut Angela Barstogi's funeral. Are you a relative of hers?"

"Go fuck yourself, Mr. Cole." She said it in such a sweet-tempered tone that at first Max didn't believe his ears. He flushed as he tried to recover his dignity.

"I don't think I said anything offensive," he said.

"Your very presence offends me, Mr. Cole. If you can't stand the heat, you know where they say you can go."

"I could offer a suggestion or two," I added helpfully.

The tips of his walrus mustache shook with rage. "You're going to regret this, J. P. Beaumont. That's the second time today you've taken a hunk out of my skin. I'm gunning for you."

"Sounds like business as usual to me."

Max would have taken a swing at me, but the bartender, who doubles as bouncer, turned up right then. Connie had summoned him soon enough for him to be there when the trouble started. "I wouldn't do that if I were you, Mr. Cole. I think maybe you'd better go in the other room to cool off." The bartender didn't brook any arguments. He took Cole's upper arm and bodily led him away.

"What's the problem?" Anne asked when they were out of earshot.

"He doesn't like me."

"That's pretty obvious. It's also obvious the feeling's mutual. Why does he call you J. P.?"

I sighed. If we were going to end up in the same orbit, it was time to drag out some of the old war stories, the stuff that made me what I am, and let her take a look at it, warts and all. If that didn't drive her away, maybe she'd return the favor.

"Which do you want first, J. P. or Maxwell Cole?"

"Let's try for J. P."

"I'll have to tell you about my mother first. She was a beauty growing up, but headstrong as they come. She would sneak out of the house at night to date my father. He was a sailor, the first man who asked her out. She was only sixteen. They planned to run away and get married, but he was killed in a motorcycle accident on the navy base over in Bremerton. She didn't know she was pregnant until after he was dead.

"Her parents threw her out, told her they no longer had a daughter. My mother went to the Salvation Army Home for

Unwed Mothers in Portland and signed in under the name of Beaumont, my father's hometown in Texas. My first names are Jonas Piedmont, after her two grandfathers. None of her family ever lifted a finger to help us. When she told me where my first and middle names came from, I hated them. I still do. I've gone by Beau most of my life. The initials came up during college. Some of my fraternity brothers figured out it bugged me to be called that. Max never got over it."

"Where's your mother now?"

"She died of breast cancer when I was twenty. She never made up with her parents. They lived here in Seattle the whole time, but I never met them. Didn't want to."

"You loved her very much, didn't you?" Anne commented gently.

It was becoming a very personal conversation. Anne seemed to bring out the lonely side of me, the part that needed to chew over my life with another human being.

"Yes," I said at last, meeting Anne's steady, level gaze. "I loved her. She could have taken an easy way out, given me up for adoption or had an abortion. She didn't though. She never married, either. She said that being in love once was enough for her."

"What about you?" she asked.

"What do you mean?"

"Is once enough for you?"

"Maybe not," I said. It was more a declaration of susceptibility than one of intent.

Anne looked away. "Tell me about Maxwell Cole."

I wasn't quite ready to talk about Karen, but Maxwell Cole led inevitably in that direction. "As I said, we were fraternity brothers together. He started out being Karen's boyfriend. We met at a dance he brought her to, a Christmas formal, and the sparks flew. She broke up with him right after New Year's and started dating me."

"He's a pretty sore loser. Is that the only grudge he's got against you?"

"It's gone beyond the grudge stage," I said grimly. "He's deliberately torpedoed me. When I was a rookie, he almost got me thrown off the force."

"How?"

"There was a kid, a young crazy up on Capitol Hill. He was

up there taking potshots at people with a gun. I was the first on the scene. I called to him and told him I was coming in. I thought we could talk it out. As soon as I came around the corner into the alley, he fired at me, hit me in the arm, my left one. The bullet knocked me to the ground. He evidently thought I was dead, because he got up and started walking toward me. I shot him, killed him on the spot.

"Max was just starting on the *P.I.* then. He was a cub reporter, so he wasn't assigned to front-page stuff, but he did a feature on the kid and his family, how the kid had been an emotionally troubled boy who had been shot down in cold blood by a trigger-happy cop with a bullet in his arm. I'm still a killer cop as far as Max is concerned. He brings it up again whenever he has a chance."

"And are you a killer cop?"

"I don't think so. It took months to come to terms with it. I've never had to do it again."

"Would you?"

"Would I what?" I had gotten carried away with the story. Her question brought me back to earth in a hurry. Her eyes were fixed on mine, searching, questioning.

"Would you do it again, given the same circumstance?"

Her gray eyes were serious, her face still and waiting. Here it comes, I thought. The answer to this question is going to blow it. There was no sense in lying. If we were going to be together, I would have to be able to be the real J. P. Beaumont.

"Yes," I said. "Given the same circumstance, where it was either him or me, I would kill again."

Anne stood up abruptly. "Let's go," she said.

Chapter 15

THE bike washed up with the tide on Wednesday morning. I was still in bed sampling the sensations Anne Corley's body had to offer when Watkins called for me to hit the bricks. He said Peters was on his way from Kirkland. I turned back to Anne. "I have to go," I said.

"Do you have to? Again?" she whispered, her lips moving across the top of my shoulder to the base of my neck. She pulled me to her, guiding me smoothly back into her moist warmth. It would have been easy to stay.

"Yes, goddamnit," I said, pulling away. "I have to. That's what I get for being a cop."

"All right for you," she said, petulantly. She smiled and sat up in bed, the sheets drawn across her naked breasts, watching me as I dressed. It made me feel self-conscious. My body's not that bad for someone my age, but it suffered in comparison to her lithe figure.

"What are you thinking?" I asked, sitting on the bed and leaning over to pull on my shoes and socks.

A man should never ask that kind of question unless he's prepared for the answer. She ran her fingers absentmindedly across my back. "Do you believe in love at first sight?" she asked.

I almost fell off the bed. I turned and looked at her. "Maybe," I said.

She smiled and planted a firm kiss on my shoulder. "I hoped you'd say that," she murmured. I finished tying my shoe and bolted from the room. I was still trying to regain my equilibrium when the bus dropped me at Myrtle Edwards Park, eight blocks from my building.

In Seattle, if you want something named after you, you have

to die first. Myrtle Edwards Park is no exception. Myrtle Edwards was a dynamo of a city councilwoman, and the park named in her honor, after she went to the great city council in the sky, trails along the waterfront from Pier Seventy to Pier Ninety-one. It consists of a narrow strip of grass, bicycle and jogging trails, some blackberry bushes, and a rocky shoreline. There is no sandy beach. The waves crash onto a seawall made up of chunks of concrete and rocks, carrying a deadly cargo of stray logs and timbers. Nobody swims in Myrtle Edwards Park, although it is a popular gathering place for noontime joggers and other fitness fanatics.

A squad car was there before me. A park maintenance worker had read a morning newspaper account of the Faith Tabernacle murders. When he saw the bike, a sturdy English three-speed, smashed beyond repair but still a relatively new and fairly expensive one, he called the department. Someone had put him through to Watkins. Not only did he talk to the right person, it even turned out to be the right bike. The tire treads matched the plaster casts taken at Faith Tabernacle.

So how do you find the owner of a bike? It's not like an automobile where everyone has to register and license it. The few who do are mostly those unfortunates who have already been ripped off once and who know there's no other way for them to identify and reclaim a bike if the department happens to get lucky and recover it. In other words, bicycle registration in Seattle is a long way from 100 percent.

Peters and I started at the other end of the question, going to the manufacturer and tracing the serial number to the retail outlet that sold it. The actual store was in my neighborhood, which isn't that unlikely since my neighborhood is a big part of downtown Seattle. The store was a Schuck's, right across the street from the Doghouse. It took Peters and me the better part of two hours of letting our fingers do the walking before we got that far. We ambled into the store about eleven-fifteen, feeling a little smug. A clerk searched through some files before he found what we needed, but twenty minutes later we walked away with a name and address on Queen Anne Hill.

It sounds simple, doesn't it? You apply a little logic, a little common sense, and everything falls right into place. We should have known. Things were going far too smoothly. The house on Galer Street was vacant and had been long enough that weeds were pushing up through a once pristine lawn. There was a For Sale sign with a telephone number on it in the front yard. We took down the number and the address.

We called from a pay phone and were directed to a real estate office on the back side of Queen Anne. Our good fortune continued. The listing agent happened to be in. She remembered the owner well. He had been transferred to London with Western Electric. He had been in a hurry to pack and move. His company bought up the equity in his house, and he had held a gigantic moving sale early in March, unloading everything but the bare essentials. It had been a good sale. A bike might have been one of the items sold. Dead end.

This job is like that. You take a slender lead and do your best with it. Sometimes it pays off, sometimes not. You have to take the good with the bad. We called Watkins to let him know we had come up empty-handed. He told us the preliminary report had come in on the Faith Tabernacle murders. Ballistics tests showed the weapon to be a .38. It was hardly a quantum leap toward identifying the killer. Watkins also said Carstogi had called and wanted to see us.

We went to the Warwick. A detective sat at the end of the seventh-floor hallway. Powell and Watkins were making sure Carstogi didn't go anywhere without an escort.

We knocked. Carstogi opened the door. He looked a little shaken. "Have you seen the paper?" he asked.

"I don't read papers," I said.

Peters shook his head. "I didn't have time."

"Look," Carstogi said bleakly.

Peters read aloud. " 'Police have sequestered the father of Friday's slain child in connection with the subsequent double murder of the child's mother and minister.

" 'Andrew M. Carstogi, being detained in an undisclosed downtown location, arrived in town Sunday evening and was involved in a confrontation at Faith Tabernacle in Ballard during the day on Monday.

" 'The church in the Loyal Heights area was the scene of two gangland-style murders that occurred later that night. Dead are Pastor Michael Brodie, age forty-nine, and his parishioner, Suzanne Barstogi, Carstogi's estranged wife. The woman's age has not been released.

" 'Arlo Hamilton, Seattle Police public information officer, said that detectives are searching for a bicycle that may have been used by the killer in making his escape.

" 'Barstogi and Carstogi, whose exact marital status is unclear, lost their only child, Angela, on Friday. She was the victim of a brutal homicide that occurred in Discovery Park. That incident is still under investigation. No arrests have been made in that slaying and police officials refuse to say whether or not Carstogi is a suspect in either the church murders or the death of the child.

" 'Inquiries in Chicago, former location of Faith Tabernacle, revealed that the group, a fundamentalist sect, left Illinois under a cloud after accusations of physical violence and alleged child abuse. At least one of the violent incidents involved Carstogi, but none of the alleged charges against the group were subsequently proven.

" 'Interviews with Suzanne Barstogi prior to her death gave no hint of any dissatisfaction or disagreement within the Faith Tabernacle organization. She expressed gratitude that the entire congregation had stood by her during the period of the loss of her child.

" 'An unidentified airline employee revealed that Carstogi was a passenger on a flight that arrived at Seattle's Sea-Tac International Airport Sunday night, where he was reported to have been inebriated. He was overheard making threatening statements regarding Brodie. Carstogi allegedly held the minister responsible for the loss of his wife and child.

" 'He reportedly left the airport in the company of two homicide investigators, Detectives Ronald A. Peters and J. P. Beaumont, who are assigned to the murder investigation of Carstogi's daughter.

" 'Funeral arrangements for Brodie and Barstogi are pending with the Mount Pleasant Mortuary, where a spokesman indicated the bodies will probably be returned to Chicago for burial.' "

Peters folded the paper when he finished.

"There's more," said Carstogi. "Look on page seventeen."

Obligingly Peters reopened the paper. "The top corner," Carstogi said.

Peters glanced at me over the top of the paper. "It's Cole's column," he said.

"Read it."

" 'Who is the Lady in Red? The mysterious lady, although that may be a title she doesn't deserve, first appeared in a red dress, driving a red Porsche, and carrying a red rose at the funeral of Angela Barstogi, Seattle's five-year-old murder victim. The lady has since been seen several times in the company of Detective J. P. Beaumont, the homicide investigator assigned to the case.

" 'Seen last in a red sweatsuit in an area restaurant, she became verbally abusive when questioned about her connection to the case. She was accompanied by Detective Beaumont at the time.

" 'Because you, my faithful readers, are the eyes and ears of Seattle, I would appreciate knowing about this lady and why Seattle's finest are keeping her under wraps.' '' Peters handed me the paper. Next to the column was a picture of Anne Corley as she had appeared at the funeral, tears streaming unchecked down her face.

"Who is she?" Carstogi asked. "What does she have to do with all this?"

"Nothing," I said. "We've checked her out. She's collecting data for a book on violent crimes with young victims."

"But he says you've been seen together."

"We happened to hit it off, just like you and that girl did the other night, except she's not a professional. Understand?"

Carstogi looked chagrined. "Yeah, I understand."

I was furious at Maxwell Cole. It was one thing to keep my professional life under the bright light of public scrutiny. It was another to expose my personal life, to make my relationship with Anne a topic of casual breakfast conversation.

"I think you'd better hurry up and remember anything you can about that date you had the other night," Peters was saying to Carstogi. "We're looking for a needle in a haystack, but with what you've given us, we don't know what kind of needle or which county the haystack's in." He shook the folded newspaper in Carstogi's direction for emphasis. "Detective Beaumont may not think you're the one who killed Brodie and Suzanne, but he's going to have one hell of a time convincing the us."

"I already told you. Her name was Gloria. That's all I know," Carstogi said, caving in under Peters' implied threat.

"Try to remember where you went." Peters pressed his advantage, finally getting through Carstogi's reluctance to a bed-rock of fear beneath.

"I was kind of drunk. I think we drove over a long bridge."

"In a cab, a car?"

"A cab. I think I came back in the same one the next morning."

"Pickup-and-delivery prostitution," Peters muttered. "Where did you go?" he continued. "A motel? A house?"

"It was a house, I guess. I didn't pay much attention. A man came out to the cab and took my money, then Gloria and I went inside, into a bedroom."

"What about the cab?" I asked. "Do you remember anything about it?"

"No. It was blue or maybe gray. The guy chewed gum. He was a big guy, dark hair, kinda oily. That's all I remember."

"Nothing other than that?"

"No." Carstogi shook his head.

I looked at Peters. "What say we take him for a spin and see if he can lead us back to the little love nest?"

"You do that," Peters said. "Drop me at the department. I'll see if vice has been able to dig anything up."

Carstogi came with us reluctantly. There had been some pho-tographers outside the hotel when we went in, and we attempted to avoid them by leaving through the garage. We weren't en-tirely successful. Maxwell Cole's sidekick from the funeral caught us as Carstogi climbed into the backseat.

Once in the car Carstogi seemed more dazed than anything. "Why does everyone think I did it?" he asked.

"For one thing, your alibi isn't worth a shit," Peters told him. "And the place where the bike was found is well within walking distance of the Warwick. But most important, you're the guy with the motive. Our finding your friend Gloria is prob-ably your one chance to avoid a murder indictment. You'd better hope to God we can find her."

"Oh," Carstogi said. From the look on his face, Carstogi was beginning to grasp the seriousness of his situation.

After dropping Peters off, Carstogi and I headed north on Highway 99. Aurora Avenue, as it is called in the city, has its share of flophouses and late-night recreational facilities. Car-stogi recognized the Aurora Bridge, but that was all. He had no idea where they had turned off. He and Gloria had apparently played kissyface in the backseat. He said he dozed on the way back, that he didn't remember any landmarks. We wound through the narrow streets around Phinney Ridge and Fremont, to no avail.

"If I could just remember something about that cab," Carstogi said, more to himself than to me.

"I wouldn't count too heavily on that," I countered.

"Why not?"

"Prostitution is illegal in this state. If they say you were with them, they'll blow their little business wide open. I'd guess, from the sound of it, that they're probably a group of freelancers, independents. If we don't get them, the Mafia will."

"You mean they'd lie and say I wasn't with them?"

I looked at Andrew Carstogi with some sympathy. The young man seemed ill-equipped to deal with the real world. "That's exactly what I mean."

Carstogi hunched miserably in the front seat. "But I didn't do it. I would have taken her back. I wanted to kill Brodie, but never Suzanne. I still loved her."

I shook my head at my own stubbornness. "Alibi or no, I believe you."

"Thanks," Carstogi said, his voice crackling over the word.

"It's cold comfort," I acknowledged. "That and fifty cents will get you a cup of coffee."

"Not at the Warwick."

I laughed at his small joke, and he did too. I think he felt a little better when I dropped him off, but I didn't. I figured it wouldn't be long before the room at the Warwick would be traded for somewhat plainer accommodations in the city jail.

Chapter 16

I STOPPED by the Doghouse and had a cup of coffee after I dropped Carstogi at the hotel. I talked with the waitresses, the cashier, the bartender. I asked them all the same thing. Did they know of a gum-chewing cabbie who might be involved in a prostitution ring? No one mentioned anybody right off, but then I didn't expect them to. I had at least gotten the word out. That was worth something.

The apartment was close by. I went up just in case Anne was there. She wasn't, although the subtle fragrance of her perfume lingered in the room. I lingered too, drinking it in. Anne Corley secondhand was better than no Anne Corley at all.

I went back to the department. There was a message on my desk saying that Peters, Watkins, and Powell were having a meeting in Powell's office. I was expected to join them as soon as I returned. I looked at my watch. It was four-forty on Wednesday afternoon. It didn't take a Philadelphia lawyer to figure out what the topic of discussion might be. If we arrested Carstogi right then, he wouldn't stand a chance of getting out before Monday. By the time his seventy-two hours were up, it would be right in the middle of the weekend.

"Where've you been?" Powell growled as I came into the room.

"With Carstogi. We were looking for the place he went night before last."

"I've checked with vice, Beau," Peters said. "Gloria seems to be a popular professional name these days. At least ten have been booked for soliciting in the past three months. How about bringing Carstogi in to look at our pinup collection? Of course, all of them will just jump at the chance to have the book thrown at them one more time."

"I'll bet they will," I said.

"Look," Watkins interjected. "This Gloria story won't hold water and you know it. Why're you so dead set against Carstogi being our suspect?"

"He didn't do it," I insisted.

"Oh, for Chrissakes!" Powell was exasperated. "Whose side are you on, Beaumont? He's got motive, no alibi, physical proximity. What more do you want? I say book him. We'll never get a confession out of him while he's down at the Warwick living in the fucking lap of luxury. What if he blows town while we're standing around arguing about it? Let's get him in here and ask him some bare bones questions."

"What about Brother Benjamin?" I countered. "He lives nearby. Did we get anything back from Illinois on him? What if he had the same kind of beef with Brodie that Carstogi did?"

Watkins shuffled through a sheaf of papers. "Benjamin Mason alias Clinton Jason. Wonderful guy. Ex-junkie, ex-small-time hood. According to this, he stopped being in trouble about the time he hooked up with Brodie. At least there haven't been any arrests since then."

"Is that when he stopped renewing his driver's license?" Peters asked.

Watkins consulted the paper. "Looks that way. How'd you know that?"

Peters shrugged. "Lucky guess," he said.

Powell had been sitting quietly. "Now wait a minute. What's all this about Brother Benjamin? You got anything solid that points to him?"

"We've got as much on him as we do on Carstogi," I said.

"Brother Benjamin didn't have a plane reservation to leave town yesterday. Carstogi did. I want him in here for questioning. Is that clear?" Powell was in no mood for argument.

"It's clear, all right." I could see I was outgunned. "But I think you're making a hell of a mistake."

A newspaper had been lying open on Powell's desk. He picked it up. "Talk about mistakes. Since when do investigators become personally involved with someone from a current case? Maxwell Cole is having a field day. Who is this broad anyway?"

"She's an author," I said maybe a tad too quickly. "She's collecting material for a book. That's why she was at the funeral. It has nothing to do with the investigation."

"Right," Powell said, dragging the word out sarcastically. "If you're going to have a little roll in the hay, I'd suggest you do it a little less publicly."

Peters rose to his feet, placing himself between Powell's words and my flaring temper. "All right, we'll go down and bring him in," he said.

We waited for an elevator. I was still fuming. "You know, Powell does have a point," Peters said. "Maybe you should cool it for a while."

"Mind your own fucking business," I muttered.

We started for the Warwick in silence. In my fifteen years on homicide, I've developed a gut instinct. I know when it's right, and when it isn't. This wasn't. Carstogi wasn't a killer. He didn't have the killer instinct, the solid steel core it takes to pull the trigger. I knew I did. I had done it once. Maybe it takes one to know one.

"Wait," I said. "I want to go see Jeremiah. Before we pick up Carstogi."

Peters clicked his tongue. "You are one stubborn son-of-a-bitch, Beaumont. I'll say that for you." But he headed for Ballard.

The traffic was snarled on Fifteenth. We had to wait for the drawbridge. "You almost blew it on the driver's license thing," I said. "The only way you could have put that together was from the sermon on the tape."

"Sorry," Peters said.

I had written Jeremiah's address in my notebook. We found it without difficulty. Jeremiah was sitting on the front steps of a tiny bungalow. He watched us get out of the car.

"Your folks in there?" I asked, approaching the steps where he was sitting.

He shook his head without getting up. I sat down beside him. "I'm here alone," he said.

"How are things?"

He shrugged. "Okay, I guess."

"You been in any more hot water?"

"Probably am now," he said. I knew he meant for talking to us.

"Were your folks both home Monday night?"

"You mean after we left the church?"

I nodded. He continued. "Someone asked me that yesterday. I already told him."

"Tell me, Jeremiah."

"We were maybe the last ones to leave. Mom and I waited in the car for a long time."

"Was your stepfather upset when he came to the car?"

Jeremiah nodded gravely. "He and Mom had a big fight. They yelled at each other."

"What did they fight about?"

"Someone at church."

"What did they say?"

He called one of the ladies a . . ." He groped for the word. "A whore."

"Which one, do you know?"

"Sister Suzanne."

"Do you know if he left the house again? Later?"

"I don't know. I went to sleep."

Peters had been listening to this exchange. Now he became a part of it. "Does anyone call Benjamin Uncle Charlie? Have you ever heard that?"

Jeremiah shook his head.

"You ever hear of an Uncle Charlie?"

"Only Angel's."

"Does he belong to Faith Tabernacle? Is he a member?"

"No. I never saw him. Angel said he lived far away from here. She said he was nice, that he promised sometime he'd take her for a ride in his van. Some of the other kids thought she made him up."

We asked Jeremiah for more details, but he clammed up. He kept watching the street nervously, as though afraid his folks might drive up any minute. We beat a hasty retreat so they wouldn't see us talking to him. I didn't want them to know we had been there. I didn't want Jeremiah to have to suffer any consequences.

When we got in the car, Peters asked, "Where to?"

"I guess we go pick up Carstogi."

Peters started the motor. "You think Benjamin's voice is the one we heard, not Carstogi's?"

"I don't know what to think," I replied.

Carstogi wasn't surprised to see us. I think he knew it was inevitable. When we came into the room he was sitting on the side of the bed, shoulders hunched, face buried in his hands.

"You'll have to come with us," I said.

Peters brought out the cuffs. Carstogi stood up and pulled away. It was reflex. I caught him by the shoulder and swung him around. "Don't do anything stupid," I warned him. "Things are bad enough for you already."

Carstogi came with us quietly. Peters read him his rights. I didn't have the stomach for it. The public wanted a fall guy, and it was Peters' and my job to provide them with one. We herded him through the booking process. He reminded me of a steer being driven to slaughter, numb with fear and unable or unwilling to help himself. He didn't ask for an attorney.

Once he was dressed in the bright orange jail coveralls, we began to question him. First Peters would grill him and then I would. He sat at the table in the tiny interview room, gazing at the floor while we asked him our questions. His story never varied, but it didn't improve, either. He stuck to it like glue. The questioning process went on for hours. We finally sent him to his cell about nine o'clock. I left right after he did, without saying good night to anyone, including Peters. There was nothing good about it.

I walked my usual path down Fourth. I needed to think, to separate myself from the stifling closeness of the interview room. I didn't like the feeling that I was part of a railroading gang. What we had on Carstogi was totally circumstantial, but I was afraid it might stick. After all, any port in a storm, and Carstogi didn't have much of a cheering section in this part of the world.

What about Brother Benjamin? According to Jeremiah, he wasn't the mysterious Uncle Charlie, but he was certainly a likely suspect with Brodie and Suzanne. The questions circled in my head, but I was too tired to draw any conclusions.

I opened the door to my apartment hoping Anne would be there. I more than half expected that she would be, but she wasn't. I tried calling the Four Seasons and was told Mrs. Corley wasn't taking any calls. That pissed me off. I poured myself a MacNaughton's and settled down to wait. And sulk.

It must have been three drinks later before she called me

back. By then I was pretty crabby. "I just now got your message," she said. "Would you like me to come over?"

I felt like saying, Suit yourself. What actually came out of my mouth was, "Sure."

She was there within minutes, greeting me with a quick kiss. I had drunk enough that I resented her lighthearted manner. "What are you so chipper about?" I groused.

"I got a lot done today, that's all. How about you?"

"Same old grind."

We were standing in the entryway. She took the glass from my hand, reached around the corner, and set it on the kitchen counter. Then she took both my hands in hers and placed them behind her back. "Kiss me," she demanded.

I did, reluctantly at first, still trying to hang on to being mad at her. It didn't work. My hunger for her reawakened. I crushed her to my chest as the touch of her lips sent me reeling.

"Marry me," she whispered.

"What?" I asked, thinking I couldn't possibly have heard her right. I pushed her away and held her at arm's length.

"Marry me," she repeated. "Now. We can get the license tomorrow and get married on Sunday."

I examined her face, trying to tell if she was kidding. No hint of merriment twinkled in her gray eyes.

"You mean it, don't you!"

She nodded.

"So soon? We hardly know each other."

"I've just now gotten up my courage. If I give myself any time to think about it, I might back out. Besides, I know all I need to know."

I made the transition from being half drunk to being totally sober in the space of a few seconds. She moved away from me and settled on the couch. I stood for a long time in the doorway, thunderstruck. It was one thing to ask if someone believed in love at first sight, but proposing marriage was something else again.

I come from the old school where men make the first move, do the asking. Not that the thought hadn't crossed my mind. Eventually. After a suitable interval.

"I take it that means no?" she asked softly, misinterpreting my silence for refusal.

Hurrying to her, I sat down next to her and put my arm around her shoulders. "It's just that . . ."

"Please, Beau." She looked up at me, her eyes dark and pleading. "I've never wanted anything more."

We had known each other for barely three days, yet I couldn't conceive of life without her, couldn't imagine denying giving her anything she wanted, including me. I leaned down and kissed her. "Why not? What have I got to lose?"

A smile of gratitude flashed across her face, followed by an impish grin. "Your tie, for starters," she responded airily, kissing me back and fumbling with the knot on my tie. "Your tie and your virtue."

Chapter 17

WHEN I woke up, Anne's fingers were tracing a pattern through the hair on my chest. It was morning, and rare Seattle sun streamed in the bedroom window, glinting off the auburn flecks in her dark hair. She was sitting on the bed, fully dressed and smiling.

"It's about time you woke up. Coffee's almost done."

I pulled her to me. "Did I dream it?" I asked, burying my face in a mass of fragrant hair.

"Dream what?" she countered.

"That you asked me to marry you."

"And that you accepted. No, you didn't dream it." She pushed me away. "And now you'd better get up because we're about to have company."

"Company?" I protested, glancing at the clock. "It's only a quarter to seven."

"I told him to be here at seven so we could go to breakfast."

"Told who?"

"Ralph Ames, my attorney. You talked to him on the phone, remember?"

She went to the kitchen, and I ducked into the bathroom, ashamed that she knew I'd been checking on her.

I was shaving when Anne tapped on the bathroom door and brought me a steaming mug of strong coffee. She set it on the counter, then perched on the closed toilet seat to visit in the custom of long married couples. She watched me scrape the stubborn stubble from my chin. "No second thoughts?" I asked, peering at her reflection in the mirror.

She shook her head. "None," she replied. "How about you?"

"I'm not scared if you're not."

A pensive smile touched the corners of her mouth. "I was just like your mother, you know."

I paused, holding the razor next to my jaw. "What do you mean?"

"I thought once was enough."

The phone rang just then. She hurried to answer it, and I heard her direct Ralph Ames into the building. She came back to the bathroom as I was drying my face. She put her arms around my waist, resting her cheek on the back of my shoulder. "I love you, J. P. Beaumont," she said.

Turning to face her, I took her chin in my hands and kissed her. "I love you, too." It was the first time since Karen that I had uttered those words or experienced the feelings that go with them. It amazed me that they came out so easily and felt so right. I kissed her again. A thrill of desire caught me as her lips clung to mine. There was a knock on the door, and she pushed me away.

"Hurry," she said.

When I walked into the living room a few minutes later, a man with a trench coat draped over one arm stood with his back to the room, gazing out at the city. I felt a twinge of jealousy when he turned. He was younger than I by a good ten years, well built, handsome in a dapper sort of way. He was wearing a natty three-piece pinstripe. He extended his hand, and his grip was unexpectedly firm.

"Beau," Anne said, "I'd like you to meet Ralph Ames, my attorney."

I managed a polite enough greeting. "Care for some coffee?" I asked.

Ralph's eyes swung from Anne back to me. "Do we have time? You said we'd grab some breakfast on our way to the courthouse. Then I have a plane to catch."

Seeing my look of consternation, Ames glanced quickly at Anne, who smiled brightly. "We have time."

"But you did say we're going to get the marriage license this morning, didn't you?"

She nodded. "Ralph has agreed to be our witness down at the courthouse."

That brought me up short. When had Ralph Ames been scheduled to serve as a witness? Before Anne had popped the question? Before I had accepted? Or had she called him that morning while I was still asleep?

"Great," I said, trying to sound casual.

Anne handed Ames a cup of coffee and motioned him into my leather recliner. "We've got time," she said, returning to the kitchen for two more cups. I settled grudgingly on the couch, determined to be civil. My first halting attempt at conversation wasn't much help.

"What brings you up here, Ralph?" I asked.

His eyes flicked from me to Anne, who curled up on the couch beside me. She shook her head slightly in his direction, and Ames turned back to me. "Anne had some legal matters she wanted me to straighten out for her before the weekend. When she calls, I drop everything and go. I got here yesterday afternoon."

"It must be nice." A trace of sarcasm leaked into my voice. It offended me that Ralph Ames and Anne Corley shared secrets to which J. P. Beaumont was not privy. Theirs was obviously a long-standing relationship, although I could detect nothing overt to indicate it was anything other than one between a client and a trusted attorney. Trusted retainer, actually. Ames asked a series of pointed, proprietary questions that gave me the distinct impression he was doing a quick background check to see if I measured up.

When it was time to go to breakfast, I led them to the Doghouse. That was pure cussedness on my part. I wanted to drag Ralph Ames someplace where his pinstripe suit would be just a tad out of place. Ames, however, continued to be absolutely amiable. Good-naturedly, he wolfed down the Doghouse's plain breakfast fare.

Throughout the meal, I couldn't shake the sense that I was being examined by some sort of future in-law. It irked me to realize that Ralph Ames knew far more about Anne Corley than I did—that she liked her bacon crisp, for example, or that she preferred hotcakes to toast. J. P. Beaumont was very much the outsider, but I decided I could afford to play catch-up ball.

After breakfast we caught a cab down to the courthouse. I guess I should have been nervous or had some sense of being railroaded, but I didn't. Anne's hand found mine and squeezed it. The radiant happiness on her face was directed at me alone, and it made my heart swell with pride.

We were first in line when the licensing bureau doors opened. I had no idea King County wouldn't take a check for the twenty-six-dollar marriage license fee. Luckily, Ralph had enough cash on him, and he came up with the money. That, combined with his picking up the check for breakfast, made me more than a little testy. As far as I was concerned, he was being far too accommodating.

Ames took a cab to the airport from the courthouse. "Will you be here for the wedding?" Anne asked, as he climbed into the cab.

"That depends on how much work I get done tomorrow," he replied.

Once again the little snippet of private conversation between them made me feel like an interloper. When the cab pulled away, Anne turned back to me. "What are you frowning about?"

"Who, me?" I asked stupidly.

"Yes, you. Who else would I mean?"

"How long have you known him?"

"A long time," she answered. "You're not jealous of him, are you?"

"Maybe a little."

She laughed aloud. "Don't be silly. Ralph is the last person you should be jealous of. He's a good friend, that's all. I wanted him to meet you."

"To check me out? Did I pass inspection?" Even I could hear the annoyance in my voice.

"You wouldn't have a marriage license in your pocket if you hadn't passed. What's the matter with you?"

I shrugged, unwilling to invite further teasing about my jealousy, but making a mental note to remember crisp bacon and pancakes. Anne walked me as far as the department, then struck off on her own up Third Avenue, while I headed for my desk on the fifth floor. There was a note on my desk saying that Peters was in the interview room with Andrew Carstogi, that I should follow suit.

I guess his fellow inmates convinced Carstogi of the error of his ways and had him run up the flag to the public defender's office. By the time I got into the interview room on the fifth floor, Peters and Watkins were there along with a tough-looking female defense attorney. She nodded or shook her head whenever we asked Carstogi a question. Usually I look at this process as a game where we try to get at the truth and the lawyers try to hide it.

Sitting in jail overnight, Carstogi had come up with one additional detail that he had forgotten before. He said he thought the cab company had something to do with the Civil War. After we sent Carstogi back to his cell, we returned to our desks, and I hauled out the yellow pages.

"What's with you today?" Peters asked, thumping into his own chair. "You were late."

I decided to put all my cards on the table at once and get it over with. There's something to be said for shock value. I tossed him the envelope with the marriage license in it. He removed the license, read it, than looked at me incredulously. "You've got to be kidding!"

"Why?"

"Beau, for Chrissakes, what do you know about her? You only met last Sunday."

"She wants me; I want her. What's to know?"

"This is crazy."

"We're getting married Sunday."

"In one week? What's the big hurry? Is she pregnant or something?"

"Look, if you want to come, you're invited. Otherwise, lay off."

Peters was still shaking his head when I turned back to the yellow pages. Halfway through the taxi listings, I found it—the General Grant Cab Company.

We checked out a car from the motor pool and went looking. We found the faded blue cab in a lineup waiting for passengers at Sea-Tac Airport. The driver was chewing a wad of gum when we showed him our badges. His hair looked like he still used Brylcreem. He rolled down the window. "What's up?" he asked.

He didn't want to lose his place in line, so we sat in the cab to ask him our questions. He knew nothing about some hooker named Gloria. He'd never seen Carstogi. We showed him Carstogi's mug shot. Well, maybe he had seen someone like him, but he couldn't remember where or when. We made a note to check out his trip sheets later, but I had an idea that if the driver had been the one who gave Carstogi a ride, it was as a sideline the cab company knew nothing about.

Carstogi's flimsy alibi had just gotten a whole lot flimsier. Peters and I headed back into town. "Where do you want to go? The office?" Peters asked.

"No. Let's go back to my place. I want to listen to that tape."

"Why? Because you still don't think Carstogi did it?"

"Why do you think he did?" I answered Peters' question with a question of my own.

Peters looked thoughtful. "Maybe because I think I would have in his place," he said solemnly. From his tone of voice, it was readily apparent that he wasn't making a joke.

"So you're layering in your own motivations and convicting him? He's innocent until proven guilty, you asshole. That's the way the law works, remember?"

"Who did it, then?" Peters asked. "If Carstogi didn't, who did? The tape shows that whoever the guy was, he'd been around the True Believers long enough to know the rules."

"The guy we heard on the tape knew the ropes, but we don't know for sure he was the one who killed them." We drove silently for a time while I retraced the conversation.

"Maybe we need to go back to Angela Barstogi," I mused aloud. "What I just said about Carstogi is true about Brodie and Suzanne as well."

"What do you mean?"

"We never convicted them, either. Just because they're dead doesn't automatically make them guilty. We never proved anything other than the fact that they had some pretty weird ideas."

Peters clicked his tongue thoughtfully. "I see where you're going. You think the same person may have killed all three of them."

"Having Carstogi here makes it too simple, too easy."

"Maybe so," Peters agreed.

We hurried to my place. I wondered if Anne would be there, but she wasn't. Peters dragged the recorder out of the drawer and turned it on. Personal considerations were forgotten in the charged tension between us. We were ready to listen to the tape from a different point of view.

It was the third time through when it hit me. "Stop," I said. "Run it back just a few turns."

Peters did. For a few moments we heard Suzanne Barstogi's voice raised in solitary prayer, then her abrupt "What do you want?"

"That's it! It can't be Carstogi. She spoke to him."

Peters looked at me, puzzled.

"Remember Monday?" I asked. "She didn't speak to Carstogi, not since he was Disavowed. I don't think she would have broken that rule even if he was holding a gun to her head. She'd be a lot more likely to speak to Benjamin."

"I'll be damned. You could be right, Beau. We'd better take this thing downtown and show it to Watty."

"He's not going to like it. Illegal listening devices are frowned on by the brass."

"We'd better tell him just the same."

A key turned in the lock. Anne Corley hurried into the apartment just as were were getting up to leave. Peters guiltily shoved the recorder into his pocket like a kid caught stealing candy.

"I'm sorry," she said. "I didn't mean to interrupt. I left my watch in the bedroom. I forgot to put it on this morning."

She went into the bedroom and came out fastening the watch. "What about lunch later?" she asked. "We've got lots to talk over."

"We're on our way back to the department right now. Maybe about one-thirty or two."

"Great," she said enthusiastically. "I'll stop by about then."

Anne walked out the lobby door with us. The red Porsche was parked on the street. "Do you need a ride?" she asked, opening the door.

I waved her away. "No thanks."

Peters whistled as the Porsche rounded the corner onto Blanchard. "That's her car?"

"Nice, isn't it."

"Beau, who the hell is she?" I gave him a warning look, just one, and he let it drop.

We took the recording to Sergeant Watkins. As predicted, he was not pleased. He listened to the tape in stolid silence and heard our analysis without comment. "Play it again," he ordered. We went over Monday's confrontation in great detail and heard the tape yet again.

"Taking everything into consideration, you might be right," he allowed reluctantly. "But you're drawing conclusions. None of this has any basis as evidence. It's a damn shame this state can't even spring for voiceprint equipment. So what are you going to do now?"

"Go looking for someone else."

"So look," he said. "Nobody's stopping you. We've got Carstogi locked up until Monday afternoon with what we've got so far. What have you got to lose?"

Peters and I went back to the drawing board. We went over the previous Thursday in minute detail, listening to the initial recorded report of Angela's disappearance, as well as the statements taken later. We learned nothing new.

We tried Sophie's house. We wanted to know if she had seen a van, the one Jeremiah had told us about. Nobody was home but Henry Aldrich, the cat, and he wasn't talking.

At one-twenty Anne showed up for lunch. We invited Peters, but he claimed to be busy. We left him at his desk and ate in a little Mexican dive at the foot of Cherry. Anne was brimming over with infectious happiness. She had found a minister to marry us and had made arrangements for the ceremony to be held at six a.m. in Myrtle Edwards Park.

"Why there?" I asked. "And why so early?"

She shrugged. "I like it there," she replied, "especially in the morning when it's quiet."

Anne walked me back to the Public Safety Building and kissed me good-bye on the sidewalk, much to the enjoyment of a group of street people gathered around the hot bagel stand outside the front door. "I'll see you when you get off work," she said. "I'll be at your place."

I went up to the fifth floor to find Peters pacing impatiently beside my desk. "Come on," he snapped. "We just hit the jackpot. A grit-truck driver from the Westside Treatment Center saw a black van parked near where Angela was found. He saw it about nine-thirty the morning she died."

"No shit!" We were already on our way to the elevator. "So where has he been all this time?"

"He just got back in town from a fishing trip. He hadn't seen anything about the murder on the news, but someone was talking about it when he went out to pick up a load this afternoon. He called about ten minutes after you left for lunch."

As usual, we had to wait for an elevator, and as usual too, it would have been faster to take the stairs.

Dick Aubrey, the grit-truck driver, turned out to be a wiry, tough little man with a fiery temper and an ever-present cigarette. He had been fishing in Idaho since the previous Friday afternoon.

"I came down the hill around nine-thirty or so, and here's this big black van parked almost in the middle of the friggin' road. I blew my horn at him a couple of times to get his attention."

"Him?" Peters asked. "You could tell it was a him?"

"Oh, sure. He was just starting to climb out of the van. I almost took the door off."

"What did he look like?"

"Big. Straight yellow hair, long. Overweight."

"Would you recognize him if you saw him again?"

"Sure. I got a pretty good look at his face. He was an ugly son-of-a-bitch."

I brought out some glossies of both Pastor Brodie and Brother Benjamin, taken at the funeral. We had purchased them from the *P.I.* We also showed him Carstogi's mug shots. "Any of these?" I asked.

Aubrey stroked his chin. "Naw. None of these guys. I'm sure of that. This guy was built like a tank. About six-five. Neck like a bull."

"What happened next?" Peters urged.

"Well, I went down to get loaded. You haul two things out of sewage plants, sludge and grit. I do grit. I figured if he was still there when I got ready to leave, I'd call and have him towed away, but by then he was gone. It's a pain in the ass having cars parked on that road. It's too narrow."

We picked Dick Aubrey's brain. He came down to the Public Safety Building and did a composite sketch. With the Identikit sketch in hand, Peters and I went over the names of everyone we had questioned in connection with the case. We were able to put names and faces with every person but one. Angela Barstogi's Uncle Charlie had to be the wild card in the deck.

We took the sketch and went to see Sophie. This time she was home. We walked up to her front door and could hear the television set blaring through the wood. Peters knocked, twice.

"Oh," she said, "are you coming to arrest me?"

Peters laughed. "No, we're here for some help."

We went inside. The cat, inside now, was already on the couch. He took a dim view of sharing it with company.

Peters brought out the sketch Aubrey had made and handed it to Sophie. She held it close to her face, examining it first with the pointed glasses in place and then with them lowered so she could peer over them. She handed it back to Peters.

"Maybe," she said.

"What about a van? Do you remember seeing one of those in the neighborhood?"

She furrowed her brow. "I do, now that you mention it, a black one, but not the last few days. I thought it was part of the group. I saw it a few times, usually in the morning."

"Will you call us if you see it again?" I asked. "Try to get the license number and call us right away."

"I most certainly will, young man," she said. I got the distinct impression Sophie Czirski still didn't approve of me.

We escaped without having tea. We went back to the department and reported to Watkins. We felt like we were making progress. We sent for motor vehicle reports on a list of known sexual offenders in the state of Washington. It's the grunt work, routine things, an expired vehicle license or an unpaid traffic ticket, that often break a case. We left the computer folks to pull together the information we needed.

"Ready to call it a day?" I asked Peters.

"How about stopping by for a drink on the way home. I'll buy."

I glanced surreptitiously at the clock, trying to remember exactly when I had told Anne I'd be home.

"Come on," Peters insisted. "You're not married yet."

I took the bait. "All right," I agreed. "I guess I can stop off for a while."

Chapter 18

WE went down to F. X. McRory's on Occidental Street. Peters got off on the right foot by buying a bottle of champagne. "All right, you closemouthed bastard," he said, raising his glass, "now that I'm a party to this little romance, you'd better tell me about her."

I didn't need to be asked twice. I hadn't had a chance to tell anyone about Anne. I'm afraid I waxed eloquent. I told him how she had looked at the funeral and about our first dinner at Snoqualmie Falls afterward. I told him about the Porsche and the fur jacket and the Doghouse and the depth and the laughter and the wit and the sudden darknesses, all the things that seemed so contradictory in Anne, and all the things that made me love her.

About that time Captain Powell showed up and, uninvited, took a chair at our table. "What's this I hear about you getting married?"

I looked to Peters for help, but he stared off into space, as innocent as the day is long. "Who is she?" Powell continued.

Taking a deep breath, I said, "her name's Anne Corley. She's the Lady in Red from Maxwell Cole's column."

"Are you shitting me? You said you met her at Angela Barstogi's funeral, last Sunday. What is this, love at first sight? That only happens in the movies."

"It's a shotgun wedding," Peters interjected snidely. I aimed a swift kick at him under the table, but I missed. He grinned at me and motioned to the waitress for what I thought would be our bill. Instead, a second bottle of champagne was delivered, Eastern Onion Style.

It consisted of a singing telegram complete with a down-and-dirty stripper. Only afterward, amid hoots of laughter, did I realize that while we'd been talking, the bar had quietly filled with people from the department. They were all there. Not only Powell, whose frown of disapproval had been replaced by a wide grin, but also the rest of the guys from homicide, Hamilton from public information, and the women from word-processing.

They had a wild assortment of off-color cards, congratulating me for lechery despite my advanced years. It was a rowdy party by any standards. I don't know how Peters managed to arrange it. He must have done it while Anne and I were having lunch.

I had a good time. It was getting late, though, and no one seemed to be in any hurry to leave. I was trying to think of a polite way to abandon ship, when there was a flurry of activity near the front door. My reason for going home early strode toward me, a dazzling smile on her lips. Anne's very presence brightened the room, and it became an engagement party to remember.

Captain Powell came up to be introduced. "Now that I see the lady in question," he grinned, "maybe love at first sight isn't out of the question after all."

Well-wishers came forward for introductions and congratulations. The guests milled around for some time before they gradually began to disappear. At last only the three of us remained —Anne, Peters, and me. Peters looked enormously pleased with himself.

"You sure put one over on me," I said to him. "Thanks."

Anne added her thanks to mine and gave him a peck on the cheek.

"You're welcome," Peters replied.

We left Pioneer Square on foot. Peters said he was going back to the department, while Anne, after producing her pair of Nikes from the ubiquitous Adidas bag, set a swift pace up First Avenue. I found myself hurrying to keep up, wanting to shield her from the human debris around us. "Couldn't we take our constitutional in a better part of town?" I suggested. "First Avenue tends to get a little rough."

"The bums don't bother me," she said, and they didn't. Panhandlers pick out soft touches from blocks away. It's as if they have a radar connection. None of them approached Anne as she marched through them. Something in her carriage, her bearing, moved them away from her. Like the crush of people in Snoqualmie Lodge, the groups of bums opened before and shut behind her while she moved forward unimpeded.

Driving in a car you're not as aware of it, but from Pioneer Square to Seattle Center there's a long, steep grade that tops out at Stewart Street. By the time we reached that point, I was about half winded. Anne set a stiff pace.

"I didn't know I was so far out of shape," I grunted.

Anne was clearly enjoying herself. "You'll just have to get out and walk more," she said.

We walked in silence for a block or two. "Is Ron coming to the wedding?" she asked suddenly.

"Ron? Oh, you mean Peters? I don't know. I invited him."

"I don't think he likes me particularly."

"What makes you say that?"

"During the party I caught him staring at me several times."

"I think he'd like to believe you're after my money, although seeing your car should have taken care of any suspicions on that score. I guess he thinks we're rushing into something. Leaping without looking, that kind of thing."

I caught her by the hand and pulled her back to me. "Why *are* you marrying me? Everybody knows cops make lousy husbands."

She reached up and kissed me on the cheek. "But great lovers. I'm marrying you for your body."

"Anne, you could have any body you wanted. Why me?"

Her eyes, which had been bright and teasing a moment before, softened. "Because you made me remember what it's like to be a woman, Beau. I had forgotten."

I pulled her to me, and we stood clasped in an embrace for a long moment at the corner of First and Virginia. Her answer may not have been good enough for Peters or Powell, but it was for me. At last we resumed walking, both of us quiet and lost in our own private thoughts.

We ran into Ida Newell, my neighbor in the lobby. It was a moment I had been dreading. I was sure by now Ida had monitored Anne's comings and goings on the closed-circuit channel. It was time to make an honest woman of her, I decided. "I'd like you to meet my fiancée, Ida. This is Anne Corley. Ida Newell."

"Fiancée," Ida sniffed. "I'm surprised. I haven't met you before."

"I'm from Arizona," Anne said with an easy smile. "It's been one of those long-distance affairs. I'm very happy to meet you."

That seemed to satisfy Ida. At least she entered her own apartment without further comment. "That was masterful," I murmured gratefully. "You saved my bacon on that one."

Anne smiled. "It'll cost you," she said.

Safety deposit boxes have never been high on my list of priorities. What few trinkets I've kept over the years, I've stowed in various nooks and crannies around my house. I left Anne in the living room and rummaged in my bottom dresser drawer. I found the faded velvet box in its place in the left-hand corner. I felt a lump in my throat as I opened it.

My father was a sailor, a wartime enlistee who probably hadn't learned one end of a ship from the other before he died. The ring he had given to my mother wasn't much, but I'm sure it was the most he could offer his sixteen-year-old sweetheart. I could imagine him proudly making the purchase at some low-life pawnshop in Bremerton. My mother had kept the ring, treasured it. It came to me when she died, and I kept it too. It was my only link with a father whose face I never saw.

I slipped the tiny box into my pocket and returned to Anne. She was sitting on the couch, her head resting on the back of it. "Tired?" I asked.

"A little," she said.

I sat down next to her with my hand on her shoulder, rubbing a knot of stiffness from between her shoulder blades. I cleared my throat. "You know, we had a wonderful engagement party. It's a shame we didn't have a ring."

"We don't need a ring—" she began.

I lay my finger across her lips and silenced her. "Then as we walked, or rather, as we ran home, I remembered that I did have a ring buried among my treasures." I pulled the box from my pocket and opened it. The tiny chip of diamond caught the light and sparkled gamely. "My mother was never married," I explained; "she was always engaged. And now, from one of the longest engagements in history, this ring is going to be part of one of the shortest."

Anne took the ring from the box and held it up to the light. "This was your mother's?"

"Yes."

She gave the ring back to me and held out her hand so I could place it on her finger. It slipped on as easily as if it had been made for her. "Thank you," she said. "You couldn't have given me anything I would have liked more."

We sat on the couch for a long time without speaking or moving. It was enough to be together, my arm around her shoulder, her hand touching mine. That night there was no need in the touching, no desire. We sat side by side, together and content.

"Happy?" I asked.

"Ummmhm," was the answer.

"Let's go to bed," I said, "before we both fall asleep on the couch."

"But it's early," she objected. It was a mild protest, easily overruled.

We undressed quickly but without urgency. Our bodies met beneath the sheets, her skin cool against my greater warmth. I eased her onto her side so her body nestled like a stacked saucer in my own, my hand resting comfortably on the curve of her breast. "Just let me hold you," I murmured into her hair.

It couldn't have been more than eight o'clock, but the previous days of frenetic activity had worn us, fatigued us. Within minutes we both slept. For all the ease of it, we might have been sleeping together like that for years.

Chapter 19

MAYBE I should start reading the newspapers first thing in the morning. That way I wouldn't get caught flat-footed quite so often. Peters brought me a copy and I read it at my desk with him watching from a few feet away. Maxwell Cole's column pronounced Anne Corley to be a dilettante copper heiress from Arizona.

Max had done some homework. He had dug up a good deal of information. Had Anne Corley not been linked to J. P. Beaumont, I think she would have been pictured sympathetically. Colored by his antipathy for me, however, she became something quite different. Rich, and consequently suspect, Anne Corley was depicted as a character out of a macabre, second-rate movie.

Cole reported as fact that for eleven years, between the ages of eight and nineteen, Anne Corley had been a patient in a mental institution in Arizona. She had been released, only to marry one of the staff psychiatrists, Dr. Milton Corley, a few weeks later. The marriage had caused a storm of controversy and had resulted in Corley's losing his job, in his being virtually discredited. He had committed suicide three years later, leaving a fortune in life insurance to his twenty-two-year-old widow.

Corley's money, combined with that already held in trust for Anne as a result of being her parents' only surviving child, created a formidable wealth. Cole touched on her book, but focused mainly on her wandering the country dropping roses on the caskets of murdered children. It could have been touching. In Cole's hands, Anne became a morbid eccentric, one whose continued sanity was very much in question.

Trembling with rage, I set the newspaper aside. Anne Corley was not a public figure. What Max had written seemed clearly an invasion of privacy, libelous journalism at its worst. My first thought was for Anne. What if she had purchased a paper and was even now reading it alone? How would she feel, seeing her painful past dragged out to be viewed and discussed by a scandal-hungry audience? That was what Cole was pandering to. He was selling newspapers with lurid entertainment rather than information, and he was doing it at Anne's expense.

"How much of it is true?" Peters asked.

It took a couple of seconds to comprehend the implications behind Peters' question. "How the hell should I know?" Angrily I shoved my chair away from the desk, banging it into the divider behind me. I stalked out the door with Peters hot on my heels. We said nothing in the lobby or in the crowded elevator. A couple of people made comment about the previous day's engagement party. It was all I could do to give their greeting a polite acknowledgment.

Once on the street I struck out for the waterfront. Peters picked up the conversation exactly where we'd left off. "You mean she hasn't talked about any of it, at least not to you."

"What's that supposed to mean? That she told all this to Cole and not to me?"

"Seems to me that she would have told you. After all, you are engaged, remember?"

I stopped and turned on him. "Get off my back, will you? I'm your partner. You're not my father confessor."

"But why hasn't she told you? If you had spent eleven years in a mental institution, wouldn't you give your bride-to-be a hint about it, so that if it came up later she wouldn't be surprised?"

"I don't know why she didn't tell me, but it doesn't matter. It's history, Peters. It has nothing to do with now, with the present or with us. Her past is none of my business."

"Why the big rush, then?"

"What's it to you? Why the hell is it any concern of yours?"

"It looks as though she thought if you found out, you'd drop her." He was silent for a minute, backing off a little. He came back at it from another direction. "Did you know she had that much money?"

We resumed walking, our pace a little less furious. "I knew she had some money," I allowed, "quite a bit of it. You don't stay at the Four Seasons on welfare. She said having too much money made it hard to know who her friends were."

"And you think that's why she didn't tell you how much?"

"Maybe," I said, "but I didn't ask her how much, Peters. Don't you understand? I don't have to know everything about her. She doesn't know that much about me, either. That takes time. There'll be time enough for that later."

"Has she shown you any of her book or have you personally seen her working on it?"

"Well, we've discussed it, but . . . No."

"Tell me again why she came to Angela's Barstogi's funeral."

Peters is single-minded. I have to respect that; I am too, usually. The only way to get him to drop it was to tell him what I knew. So I told him about Patty, about how much Anne had loved her, how Patty's death had upset and hurt her, how being unable to attend her sister's funeral as a child was something Anne Corley was doing penance for as an adult. It was a sketchy story at best, lacking the depth of details that would give the story credibility.

"How did she die?"

"I don't know."

We were walking north along the waterfront with a fresh wind blowing in across a gunmetal harbor. Peters listened thoughtfully as I told him what I could. Even as I told the story, I didn't need Peters' help to plug it full of holes.

"Just supposing," Peters suggested, "that she did have something to do with Angela Barstogi's death."

I stopped dead in my tracks. "Now wait a fucking minute."

"You wait a minute, Beaumont. You're too embroiled to see the forest for the trees, but that doesn't mean the rest of us are. All I'm doing is asking questions. If Anne Corley isn't hiding something, it's not going to hurt anything but your pride. Maybe there's a connection between Anne Corley and Uncle Charlie."

"Peters, Anne Corley had nothing to do with Angela Barstogi's death. She wasn't even in town until after the wire services had the story."

"It shouldn't be hard to prove, one way or the other. You owe it to yourself to get to the bottom of this. You can't afford to accept her presence at face value, particularly if she's not being up-front with you. You're a better cop than that."

Unerringly Peters hit the nerve where I was most vulnerable. Cops want to be right, one way or the other. They have to prove themselves over and over. Usually it's less personally important to them. Conflict of interest walked up and smacked me right in the face.

"I'd better ask Powell to pull me from the case," I said.

"Don't be an asshole. That's not necessary, not yet. If we come up with something definite, then it'll be time to bring Watkins and Powell into it. In the meantime, I think some discreet questions to your old friend Maxwell Cole are in order."

"Me talk to Cole?"

"No." Peters laughed. "Not you. I will."

"And what am I supposed to do while you do that?"

"Go back over every shred of information we have so far to see if you can find anything new."

We had reached the Hillclimb, a steep flight of stairs that leads from the waterfront up through the Public Market and back into the heart of the city. I felt beaten, defeated. I had turned on her, given tacit approval to Peters to go ahead and scrutinize Anne's past. Suddenly I was more than a little afraid of what he might find there.

We climbed the stairs without speaking. The market was jammed with vegetable and fish merchants setting out their wares. The boisterous activity was totally at odds with how I felt. We came out of the market at First and Pike. Peters turned right and started back toward the Public Safety Building.

I stopped. "I'm going to go talk to her," I called after him.

Peters came back. "Why?"

"I have to. I have to give her a chance to tell me. I want to hear it from her."

"Suit yourself," Peters said with a shrug.

I didn't go directly back to the Royal Crest. Peters' questions hadn't fallen on deaf ears. Why hadn't she told me? More to the point, what *had* she told me? Very little, I decided. She had said she had been married once, but she hadn't mentioned her husband's profession or his subsequent suicide. That's not surprising. Suicide is something that hangs around forever, dropping load after load of guilt on the living.

Anne had divulged little of her family background, other than bits and pieces about Patty. And she certainly hadn't mentioned being institutionalized; but then, that's hardly something you go around advertising. I know I wouldn't.

Come to think of it, there was a lot I hadn't told her, either, gory details in the life and times of J. P. Beaumont. I had touched briefly on my relationship with Karen, but that was all. It was as if Anne and I had an unspoken agreement not to let the past taint our present or our future. On the one hand, I could rationalize and justify her not telling me her life story. On the other hand, I was angry about it.

I walked for a long time, trying to think what I would say to her. There wasn't the smallest part of me that accepted the idea she might have been responsible for Angela Barstogi's death. I finally turned my steps homeward. I stopped and bought a *P.I.* from a vending machine on the corner. I remembered her reaction when I had asked her about Patty. I had an obligation to be there when she read the article. After all, it was because of me that she was drawing Maxwell Cole's fire.

The halls in high-rises are less well soundproofed than the apartments. As I approached my door, I could hear Anne's voice from inside the unit. That surprised me because I expected her to be there alone. I paused before fitting my key in the lock. Listening through the door, I could hear she was on the telephone, that she was finishing a conversation. I turned my key in the lock and pushed the door open.

I expected to find her on the couch next to the phone. Instead, she was halfway across the living room, eyes frantic, face ashen. She looked at my face blankly, with no sign of recognition. All I could think was that she had laid hands on the article before I got there.

I moved across the room quickly and grasped her by the shoulders. She was shaking, quivering all over like someone chilled to the bone. "Anne, Anne. What's wrong? Are you all right?"

For a long second we stood there like that, with me holding her. I don't think my words registered at all. "What are you doing here?" she asked.

"I came to check on you. I was afraid you'd read it by yourself. Have you read it?" She was struggling, trying to escape my grasp. Her eyes stared blindly into mine. She didn't answer.

"Who was that on the phone?" I demanded. "Who were you talking to?"

My words finally penetrated and she seemed to focus on my face, to hear what I said. "No one," she stammered. "It was a wrong number."

I shoved her away from me, sending her reeling into the leather chair. "Don't lie to me, Anne; for God's sake don't lie to me!" I wanted to shake her, force her to tell me the truth. I started toward the chair, but the look on her face stopped me. In seconds her face had been transformed. She might have put on a mask. A calm, cold mask.

"It was business," she said, her voice flat and toneless.

"Yours or mine?"

"Mine," she said.

"Why did you tell me it was a wrong number?"

"I was upset."

I turned back to the couch and sat heavily, the weight of the world crushing my shoulders. When I looked at her again, she was under control and so was I, but something was dreadfully wrong. I forced my tone to be gentle, made the words come slowly, the way you might if you were speaking to someone who didn't know the language. "Was it about the newspaper article?"

She blinked, puzzled. "What article?"

"Maxwell Cole's. In today's paper. It talks about Milton Corley. Tell me about him." I handed her the paper, open to Maxwell Cole's column. She read it quickly, then dropped it in her lap. She looked up at me.

"Why didn't you tell me, Anne? You left me wide open to attack."

Her eyes, fixed on mine, didn't waver. "I didn't think it mattered," she said.

"But it does matter. You should have told me. Yourself."

"What do you want to know?"

"Tell me about Milton Corley. Why did you marry him?" It was not a question I had expected to ask. It was the wounded cry of a jealous suitor, not a professional cop with his mind on his job.

"Because I loved him," she answered.

"Loved him or used him?"

"Used him first, loved him later."

Maybe she was being honest with me after all. "What about J. P. Beaumont? Is it the same with him?"

She raised her hands in a helpless gesture, then dropped them back in her lap. She nodded slowly. "At first I only wanted information."

I felt my heart constrict. "And now?"

"I love you." They were the words I wanted to hear, but I couldn't afford to believe them.

"Why?" The word exploded in the room. "Why do you love me?"

"Because you found the part of me that died when Milton did. I told you that last night."

"You expect me to believe that?"

"Yes. It's the truth."

My gaze faltered under her unblinking one. "Tell me about your book. I want to read it."

"All right," she said. "After I get it back from Ralph. I sent it to Phoenix with him. He's having it typed for me. I have to revise the last chapter."

"Why?"

"I made a mistake."

"What kind of mistake?"

She looked at me as if puzzled. "The kind that shouldn't be made if you're any kind of writer. Why all the questions?"

"I wanted to hear this from you, Anne. You should have told me. I shouldn't have had to read it in the newspaper. It makes you look suspicious."

For several long minutes we sat without speaking. "What about us?" she asked.

"I don't know," I said. "I'll have to give it some thought." I got up to leave. I had touched the personal issue and skirted the basic one. I had to ask. I had to have the answer from Anne Corley's own lips. "Did you have anything to do with Angela Barstogi's death?"

She heard the question without flinching. "So that's what's

bothering you,'' she said in a monotone. She dropped her head in her hands. ''No, Beau, I didn't. I was in Arizona. Check with United. Check with anybody.''

''Do you know someone named Uncle Charlie?''

She shook her head. I went to the door and stood there uncertainly, my hand on the doorknob. I didn't know whether to leave or apologize. ''I didn't think you did, but I'm getting some heat thanks to Maxey. I'd better go back to the office,'' I said at last. ''I've got work to do.''

Chapter 20

WORK was a tonic for me that day. I worked like a fiend. I dove into every statement and every file with absolute concentration, finding comfort in the necessary discipline. Anne had said she had nothing to do with Angela Barstogi. I wanted to prove it to the world and to myself. There was nothing I wanted more than for Peters' suspicions to be dead wrong.

I put in a call to United. They said they'd call back with the information I needed. They did eventually, confirming Anne's arrival in Seattle. It proved the point as far as I was concerned, but the rest of the world needed more convincing. I had to lay hands on Angela Barstogi's killer. That was the only way to clear Anne once and for all. Who the hell was Uncle Charlie, and where was he? How could I find him?

It had been just over a week, but already Angela Barstogi's file was voluminous. I read through it all—statements, medical examiner's report, crime lab report—searching for some key piece that would pull the entire puzzle into focus. I had moved on to the Faith Tabernacle file when Peters came back about four o'clock.

"How's it going?" I asked. It was a natural enough question, but I felt strange after I asked it. I didn't know whether or not Peters would answer me. I didn't know if I wanted him to.

"Maxwell Cole is a jerk," he said. That was no surprise. It was something that found us in wholehearted agreement. Peters peered over my shoulder at the files. "Any luck?"

"Yeah. All bad."

He waited, expectantly, but I didn't volunteer any information. I wanted to see if he would ask. "What did she say?" he inquired finally.

"That she didn't have anything to do with it."

He shook his head. "And that's good enough for you, I suppose?"

"As a matter of fact, it isn't. If it were, I wouldn't be going blind reading these reports, and I wouldn't have called the airlines."

Peters settled on the corner of my desk. "Did you say you met Ralph Ames?" he asked.

"The attorney. Yes, I met him."

"How did he strike you, hotheaded maybe? Prone to fly off the handle?"

"No, just the opposite. Of course, he could be schizo. Who knows?"

"I put a little pressure on Cole. He gave me the name of the girl he talked to in Ames' office. I called right after I left Cole. Ames fired her fifteen minutes before that, for talking to Cole. That surprise you?"

"No. When I tried calling there I went through a screening process. It strikes me that Anne is a valued client."

"Valuable, certainly. The lady's loaded." He paused. "I'm going down there, Beau, to Arizona."

"Why?"

"I've picked up some information, enough to warrant the trip."

I stifled the desire to demand the information, to get Peters in a hammerlock until he came clean. But I knew he was doing his job, holding out on me until he had something concrete. He was right, of course.

"You've told Watty, then?" I could feel my heart pounding in my chest.

"No. I'm going on my own nickel. It's the weekend, and I want to get away from this drizzle. I'm feeling a yen for sunshine."

It took a second or two for me to understand the implication behind what he was saying. Gratitude washed over me like a flood. "Peters, I—"

"Don't thank me, Beau. You may not like what I find."

There was more than a hint of warning in his tone, but I ignored it. I chose to ignore it because I didn't want to hear it. "When's your plane?"

He glanced at his watch. "A little over an hour and a half.

Want to take me down and keep the car?'' He thought better of it. ''Wait a minute. My plane gets in late Sunday evening. That's probably a bad time for you to come pick me up.''

''If you're thinking about the wedding, we may go for a stay of execution.''

He grinned and tossed me the keys. ''Good,'' he said. ''Let's go.''

Late Friday afternoon traffic taxed my limited current driving skills. I had gotten out of the habit of fighting the freeway jungle. I had forgotten what it was like. Living downtown had liberated me from the tyranny of Detroit and Japan as well, to say nothing of Standard Oil. Peters winced at a tentative lane change.

''I don't get much practice driving anymore,'' I explained.

''That's obvious.''

I dropped Peters in the departing-passenger lane and drove straight back to town. I didn't know what to think. There was no way to anticipate what I might find at the Royal Crest. My best possible guess was an empty apartment with or without a note.

If Anne Corley did nothing else, she consistently surprised me. She was waiting in the leather chair. A glass of wine was in her hand. A MacNaughton's and water sat on the coffee table awaiting my arrival. Anne was wearing a gown, a filmy red gown.

''Hello,'' she said. ''You look surprised to see me.''

''I am,'' I admitted. I examined the gown. I was sure I had seen it before, but I couldn't imagine where. At last it came to me—the hallway dream with Anne disappearing in a maze of corridors. I had dreamed the gown exactly, I realized as the odd sensation of déjà vu settled around me.

''I'm a very determined lady,'' she said softly. ''Anybody else would have thrown in the towel after this morning. You didn't want me to go, did you?''

I sat down on the couch cautiously, tentatively. I tested my drink. ''No, I didn't want you to go.''

She took a sip of her wine. ''You asked me this morning if I'd had anything to do with Angel's death. Does that mean I'm under suspicion?'' I nodded. ''And I'm being investigated?'' I nodded again.

''That first afternoon we were together you said something

that made me think Brodie was responsible. Yesterday the newspaper mentioned a man in a black van. Today you seem to think I did it. It reminds me of a game of tag with you standing in the center of a circle and pointing at people, telling them they're it."

"I have to prove they're it," I interjected. "In a court of law, beyond a shadow of doubt. That's a little different from pointing a finger."

"What if you make a mistake?"

"The court decides if they're guilty or innocent. That's not up to me. Where's all this going, Anne?"

She held up a hand to silence me. She was working her way toward something, gradually, circuitously. "How do you feel about those people afterward?"

I laughed, not a laugh so much as a mirthless chuckle. "In the best of all possible worlds, the innocent would go free and the guilty would be punished. In the real world, it doesn't always work that way."

"Supposing . . .," she started. She paused as if weighing her words. For the first time I noticed a tightness around her mouth. Whatever she was working up to, it was costing her. She had been looking out the window as she spoke, uncharacteristically avoiding my eyes. Now, she turned away from the window, settling her gaze on my face. "Supposing someone was guilty of something but the court set them free. How would you feel about that?"

"If the court sets them free, I have no choice but to respect the court's decision. My feelings have nothing to do with it."

"That's not true, they do!" She jumped up quickly and hurried to the kitchen to replenish the drinks. I watched in fascination. Her movements were jerky, as though she changed her mind several times in the course of the smallest gesture. Where was her purposeful manner, her fluid grace? She came back with the drinks.

"Have you ever been around someone who's retarded?" she asked?

The question was from way out in left field. "No," I replied, "I never have."

"Patty was retarded. I loved her and I didn't mind taking care of her, but she didn't have any control over her bowels. My father hated her for it." Anne stopped abruptly and stood by the coffee table, staring at me as though she expected me to say something. I didn't know what. I reached out and took her hand, drawing her toward the couch.

"I'm sorry," I said. Her body was like a strung bow. I pulled her down beside me, a question formulating itself as I did so. "Who killed Patty?" I asked. I expected her to rebel, to shy away from my hand.

"My father," she whispered. "I saw him do it, but no one would believe me. The coroner ruled it an accident. I tried to tell people, but that's when they started saying I was crazy."

"Who said that, the people you told?"

"Yes," she said quietly. "My mother, her friends."

"And that's when they wouldn't let you go to the funeral?"

A single tear brimmed over the top of her lower lash and started down her cheek. "Yes," she answered. "She wouldn't let me go."

She turned to me for comfort from an old but open wound, burying her head in my chest. Wracking sobs filled the room, the kind of sobs that leave you exhausted without bringing relief. I held her, imagining a helpless eight- or nine-year-old battling alone against injustices perpetrated by adults. Injustice is hard enough to handle as a full-grown man, as a homicide detective. To a child it must have been overwhelming.

I let her cry. There was no point in my saying anything or in attempting to stop her tears before the pent-up emotion had run its course.

At last the sobs subsided and she pulled herself away from me. "I'm sorry," she said. "I never can talk about it without that happening."

"Don't apologize. It's not necessary."

She leaned her head back against my arm and closed her eyes. "I wanted to tell you this morning, but I couldn't. It took me all afternoon to work up to it."

"Thank you," I said, and meant it. I looked at her as she lay with her head thrown back, the strain of the last few hours and moments still painfully etched on her face. She had opened the door a crack and let me see what was inside. It helped me understand her complexity a little and her reticence. I leaned down and kissed away a smudge of tear-stained mascara from her cheek. "Stick with me, kid. We'll make it."

She lifted her head and looked at me. "What makes you say that?"

"I love you, Anne. That's what makes me say it."

The kiss I gave her then was not a brotherly, comforting kind of kiss. I felt the exhilaration you feel after you step off a roller coaster and know you haven't died of it. I wanted to affirm our loving and our living. I wanted to put the ghosts from her past to rest once and for all, and she did too. She responded willingly, hungrily.

The gown was fastened by a single tie. She was naked beneath it, naked, supple, and ready. I slipped out of my own clothes and fell to my knees before her, letting my hands roam freely across her body, letting my tongue pleasure her with promise and torment her with denial. I reveled in the power of control, the feel of her body's aching need awakened at my touch. Several times I brought her to the brink, only to back off, pulling away before she crossed the edge, leaving her writhing, pleading for satisfaction.

"Please, Beau," she begged. "Please."

I drew her to the floor and onto me, my own need no longer held at bay. Her body folded around me and I was home. She gave a muffled moan of pleasure and release. I was complete and so was she.

Chapter 21

WE napped. There on the floor. Much later, nearly ten, she stirred and awakened me. She snuggled close to me for warmth. "Hungry?" I asked.

"Of course."

"Where would you like to go?" I asked. "I have Peters' car parked downstairs. For a change, wheels come with the invitation."

She laughed. "Uptown, huh?"

"Not exactly, it's a Datsun." She laughed again and got up, picking up the gown from where it had fallen on the couch and tying it deftly around her. It was lovely, but I preferred her without it. I too scrambled to my feet. She stood looking up at me, her eyes momentarily uncertain. I held her close, hoping to stifle all doubt. "Don't worry," I told her. "It'll be all right."

That seemed to give her the reassurance she needed. I followed her into the bedroom. A set of suitcases sat in one corner. She lifted one onto the bed and opened it. "I didn't know if I was moving in or moving out."

The suitcase was filled with clothes on hangers. I picked them up, all of them, and swept them into one end of the closet. "Moving in," I said.

She unpacked quickly with the practiced hand of one who has done it many times. I had never learned to use all the drawers in the obligatory six-drawer dresser, so there was room for her to unpack without my having to shove things around. It seemed as though I had been saving a place for her in my life.

While she showered, I took a lesson from the lady and called for a dinner reservation. Most people who live in Seattle regard the Space Needle as a place visited only by tourists. Not me.

It's special enough for a meal there to be an occasion, and it has the added attraction of being within walking distance. I take my kids there for Christmas dinner when they're home for the holidays. The Emerald Suite, the gourmet part of the restaurant on top of the Space Needle, had a last-minute cancellation, so they were able to take us.

When Anne emerged from the shower, I was tying my tie and humming a little tune. I was starting to feel as though the two of us might be on somewhat equal footing. I was conscious of being terrifically happy, and for right then, at least, I was wise enough not to question it.

I had dressed while she unpacked. Now it was my turn to lie on the bed and watch her. She stood indecisively at the closet door for a moment. "What should I wear?"

"We're not going to the Doghouse," I replied.

She chose a muted red dress of delicate silk. Red was her color on any occasion, in any light. Before I met her I had no idea red came in so many different shades. Maxwell Cole had been more correct than he knew when he called her the Lady in Red.

Carefully she selected underwear and put it on. It was a quiet, intimate time together, with her doing things she would usually do alone. She didn't seem disturbed by my presence or by my watching her. In the short period we had been together a bonding had occurred. I had experienced that bonding only once before, with Karen, and then I'd lost it. I was grateful to have it back. I hadn't realized how much I'd missed it.

Anne came to me to zip the dress and to fasten the diamond pendant. "From Milton?" I asked, surprised that there was no pang of jealousy as I asked the question.

"Yes," she said, turning to kiss me. "Thanks."

"Where's your car?" I asked. "Did you bring it along with your clothes?"

She nodded. "It's down on the street."

"We'll have to move it to a lot in the morning, or we'll spend all day feeding parking meters."

"Would you like to take it?" she asked.

I tossed Peters' Datsun keys into the air. "Not on a bet. I don't think I'd better press my luck. I'm just barely qualified for a Datsun. A Porsche would be overkill."

Of course we could have walked, but I drove up to the valet

parking attendant. He opened the door with a slight bow in Anne's direction, diplomatically concealing most of his disdain for the battered Datsun.

The old Anne Corley was back. She was delighted and delightful. Everything about the evening pleased her. As the restaurant rotated she asked questions about various landmarks. She ate like a famished puppy and joked with the waiter, who regarded her with a certain awe. We drank champagne and toasted our future. It was a festive, joyous occasion.

The conversation was light, fun-filled nonsense. It was only when the coffee came and we were working our way through two final glasses of wine that she turned serious on me. I knew enough to be wary by now, to tread softly and not force her beyond her own speed.

"Do you want me to tell you about Milton?" she asked softly.

"Only if you want to, only if you think I need to know."

"It's the same version they wrote years ago. He sounds like a monster who took advantage of a young female patient, doesn't he?"

"That's why he lost his job, isn't it?"

"People were only interested in how things looked. No one cared how things really were. It's too much trouble to look beneath the surface."

"But he committed suicide."

"He didn't do it because of his job," she said. "He was dying of cancer. He didn't want to go on. He didn't want to face what was coming. I understand that a lot more now than I did then." She paused. "How old are you, Beau?"

"Forty-two, going on sixty."

"Milton was sixty-three when I married him." She made the statement quietly and waited for my reaction.

"Sixty-three!" I choked on a sip of coffee.

Anne smiled. "I've always gone for older men," she teased. The smile faded from her face, her eyes. "He was the first person who believed me."

I struggled to follow her train of thought. "You mean about Patty?"

She nodded. "I had been locked up in that place for five years when I met him, and he was the very first person who believed me."

"How is that possible?"

"You told me yourself. This isn't the best of all possible worlds, remember? I stayed because my mother had enough money to pay to keep me there. I'd have been pronounced cured and turned loose if we'd been poor."

She watched in silence as the waiter refilled her cup with coffee. "Doctors become omnipotent in places like that. They have the power of life and death over you. The smallest kindness becomes an incredible gift. He took an interest in me. He promised he'd take care of me if I'd have sex with him."

Outrage came boiling to the surface. "When you were thirteen and he was fifty-seven?"

"No. I said I met him then. I was seventeen when it started." She was holding her cup in both hands, looking at me through the steam, using it as a screen to protect her from my sudden flare of anger. "There's no need to be angry," she said. "He kept his part of the bargain, and I kept mine. He saw to it that I got an education, that I had books to read, that I learned things. On weekends he would get me a pass and take me places. He bought me clothes, taught me how to dress, how to wear my hair. I don't have any complaints."

"But Anne . . ."

"When my mother died, I was nineteen. He hired Ancell Ames, Ralph's father, to lay hands on the moneys left in trust for me, money my mother had been appropriating over the years. He got me out of the hospital, and we got married. Everyone believed he married me because of the money. Nobody cared that he had plenty himself. It made a better scandal the other way around." For the first time I heard a trace of bitterness in her voice.

"Did you love him when you married him?"

She shook her head. "That came later. I loved him when he died."

She set down her coffee cup, gray eyes searching mine. "Do you want to know about the money?"

I reached across the table and took her hand. "No," I said, laughing. "I don't want to know about the money. Maybe you should get Ralph to draw up a prenuptial agreement. Would that make you feel better?"

"What's mine is yours," she said.

"Me too," I grinned, "but I think you're getting the short end of the stick."

She sat there looking beautiful and troubled. A lifetime of tragedy had swirled around her and brought her to me. I wanted to free her from all that had gone before, to set her feet firmly on present, solid ground. I took her hand and held it with both my massive paws around her slender fingers. "Considering what you've been through, you have every right to be totally screwed up."

"Maybe you haven't noticed," she replied. "I am totally screwed up."

"So where does all this leave us?" I asked.

"I've talked to Ralph. He's coming back up tomorrow night. I want him to be a witness. What about Peters?

"He's out of town," I told her, guiltily remembering that I had assured Peters the wedding would be postponed. It was too late to do anything about that, however.

Anne must have seen my hesitation. "You do still want to get married, don't you?"

She sat waiting for my answer; both pain and doubt visible in her face, her eyes. I succumbed.

"I think all my objections have just been overruled," I said. "Would you like to dance?"

She nodded. There was a piano player in the bar, the music soft, old and danceable. I'm a reasonably capable dancer, and Anne flowed with my body. The admiration of those watching was obvious, and I enjoyed it. I wanted to be seen with her; I wanted to be the one who brought Anne Corley to Seattle and kept her there.

We danced until one. I was sleepy when we got back to the apartment. Anne said she was wide-awake and wanted to stay up and rework the last chapter. She wanted to send it with Ralph on Sunday. She also said she planned to jog early in the morning. I kissed her good night in the living room.

"Thanks for a wonderful evening, Anne. All of it."

"It was good, wasn't it?" she agreed.

"Promise we'll have a lifetime of evenings like this."

She didn't answer; she kissed me. "Good night," she murmured with her lips still on mine.

"Good night yourself."

I went to bed and slept the sleep of the just. Peters wouldn't be bringing me any surprises when he came back from Arizona. Anne had finally told me everything.

Chapter 22

FRESHLY shampooed hair, newly dried and fragrant, awakened me on Saturday morning. Anne slipped into bed beside me, her body still warm from a steamy bathroom. "Been out running?" I asked.

"Yes."

She rested her head in the curve of my neck and ran her fingers along the stiff stubble on my jaw.

"What time is it?" I asked, not wanting to turn to see the clock.

"Six," she replied.

"In the morning?" I groaned. "On Saturday? You get up and run at this ungodly hour on Saturday?"

She closed her teeth gently over the muscle on the side of my neck, sending involuntary chills through my body. "What's the matter with being up at this hour?"

"Nothing at all," I said, "now that you put it that way." I rolled over on top of her, pinning her beneath me. "You shouldn't start something you can't finish."

"I can finish it," she replied, placing her hands around the back of my neck and pulling my lips to hers.

What she said actually turned out to be a gross understatement. She was a wild woman, frenzied in her demands for gratification. Had I not known better, firsthand, I might have thought she had gone without for years. She crouched naked astraddle me, plunging herself down on my body with wild abandon, her head thrown back, her face reflecting a fleeting mixture of pain and pleasure. I held back as long as I could, wanting to prolong her enjoyment, but that wasn't enough.

She came back again for more, kissing me, touching me, renewing me until I was able once more to probe inside her, to touch that part of her that had gone for far too long untouched. This time she collapsed on my chest afterward, breath coming in short gasps, her heart thumping wildly from exertion. "Not bad for an old man," I managed.

"Not bad at all," she agreed.

We lay together for a long time, our legs entwined, her head pillowed on my chest. She dozed. We both did. The next thing we knew it was almost eight o'clock. I woke up first, and gave her a gentle slap on the rump. "All right, now it's time to rise and shine," I told her. "We've got to go shopping, and I suppose you're starved. You always are."

"You called that shot," she replied.

I got up and wandered over to the window. The first thing I saw was a diligent meter maid making her way down Third Avenue. "Oops," I gulped. "I'd better run and feed the meter. Where's you car?"

"I already moved it to a lot," she said.

I hurried down to the Datsun and got there as the parking cart was pulling to a stop. "You just made it," the driver said.

Happily I hurried back to Anne. "Saved us ten bucks just now, which I intend to blow on breakfast. I only put half an hour in the meter."

"Where are we going?"

"I've got a friend who left the force to run a jewelry store in Northgate. We're going there for wedding rings. All we have right now is an engagement ring. I'm the old-fashioned type."

"I never would have guessed."

I took her arm and pulled her to me. "Look, young lady, just because we've been having the honeymoon before the wedding, doesn't mean I approve."

She laughed. "I haven't heard any strenuous objections."

We had breakfast before the jewelry store opened and made what plans we could for the day. Ralph Ames' plane was due in at eight fifty-seven, and I thought it only reasonable that we pick him up. I found myself wondering if he was coming as a guest or if his attendance was an official function for which Anne would be billed later. It was none of my business, however, and I didn't ask.

I wished Peters would call. He had left the name of a hotel in Phoenix, and I tried reaching him there but was told he had checked out. I wanted to invite him to the wedding, now that it was on again. He was the only guest from the department I wanted to be there.

The jeweler, Jackson Hall, was a cop until he got ulcers. A partial disability had made him take a second look at the family jewelry business. He had accepted the Northgate branch with good grace if not enthusiasm. He was happy to help us choose matching gold bands, and threw in a set of crystal cocktail glasses as a wedding present.

Jackson sent us to a friend of his in the travel business. In all the rush we had neglected to discuss a honeymoon. Now, with Ralph's plane schedule in hand, we decided on a wedding trip to Victoria on Monday morning. I had plenty of vacation time available, and I figured Powell wouldn't squawk too loud if I used some of it. Through a fluke, a split-level suite with a fireplace was available in the Empress Hotel. We booked it on the spot for Monday and Tuesday nights. We also got a reservation for Monday afternoon's ritual High Tea.

Anne and I gave ourselves a shower that morning and afternoon, not the rubadubdub variety, but the bridal kind. We went from one department store to another, splurging on new sheets, towels, kitchen linens. Anne, long a nomad, had seldom purchased household items. She did it beautifully, her choices impeccable, but also with a childlike wonder and glee that made it seem a springtime Christmas shopping spree. Sometimes I paid, and sometimes she did, but there was no point in quibbling over money. Obviously, we weren't in a position that we would have to worry about the bills.

We dragged our last load of purchases to the car, laughing and cutting up like a couple of kids. The trunk was full and the backseat was rapidly disappearing. "What now?" I asked.

"I'd like you to choose my dress," she said.

For some reason, that touched me, put a lump in my throat. "All right, but you do so at your own risk. I know what I like. I don't know anything about fashion."

"Whatever you like will be fine."

We hopscotched from store to store, with Anne gamely trying on first one dress and then another. Spring dictated pastels, which looked washed out and pale against her strikingly dark hair and tawny complexion. I was going to give it up and marry her in her red jogging suit when a saleswoman brought out a vivid turquoise suit. There was a hint of the Far East in the cut, and the material was a burnished silk. I knew it was right before she ever put it on.

The clerk, pleased to be making some progress, located a delicately feminine blouse and a suitable pair of shoes. When Anne came out of the dressing room, she had fastened her hair on top of her head, with a few tendrils dangling here and there. She was breathtakingly beautiful, and she was mine.

To give the store time to press it, we made arrangements to pick the dress up in an hour. Then we went in search of flowers. I can see how planning for a wedding can take a lifetime. We made decisions together, quickly, and in perfect agreement.

Last but not least, I too was decked out in a new outfit—a suit plucked right off the rack with a matching shirt and tie. It was late afternoon before we finished shopping and staggered back to the apartment. We unloaded the car and left again, this time in search of groceries. Anne had decided to cook a prewedding supper to be served after Ralph's late-evening arrival.

Anne bustled happily in the kitchen while I refrigerated her corsage and two boutonnieres—one for Ames and one for me. By the time I unpacked the rest of our purchases, my linen closet bulged with new additions, and I bagged excess castoffs to take to the Children's Orthopedic Thrift Store on Third Avenue. Already the apartment was showing signs of Anne's presence, her blues and greens softening and diluting the masculine "statement" my decorator had undeniably achieved.

By seven my part of the job was under control. I sat in the living room waiting until it was time to go to the airport. It was then I remembered Andrew Carstogi for the first time that day. He had been so far from my thoughts that his jail cell might have been in Timbuktu. I had been too full of my own plans and concerns to give his problems any consideration.

He came to mind, and I felt a twinge of guilt. It was his pain that was directly responsible for my newfound happiness. I was sorry he was locked up. Our investigation had found nothing that would justify holding him beyond Monday. He would go free that afternoon and return to Chicago and pick up the shattered remnants of his life, having lost a wife, a child, and a week from his life, while I had gained Anne Corley. Life is not fair.

Anne came in from the kitchen, untying the apron we had

purchased that afternoon. Already it was soiled with a variety of
culinary debris. Stuffed Cornish game hens had gone into the
oven along with some scalloped potatoes. A complex salad
lurked in the refrigerator. We had chosen an exotic Häagen-
Dazs ice cream for dessert.

"Ready to go get Ralph?" she asked.

"Do we have to? Can't I just have you all to myself?"

"Let's go," she said. "If I followed the directions right, the
oven will turn off and the food will still be hot when we get
back."

"Slave driver," I said, but we headed for the airport.

A magnificent sunset was in progress as we drove south
along the Viaduct. The snowcapped Olympics reached skyward
over a mirrored sound, while the sky ranged from lavender to
orange above us. "I don't know when I've been this happy,
Anne. Not for years."

"No second thoughts?"

"Nope."

"I don't have any either."

I laughed. "Do you realize we're getting married on our an-
niversary? We will have known one another for one whole
week tomorrow."

"I think I've known you forever," Anne said softly.

I glanced across the front seat at her, took her hand in mine,
and squeezed it. "I think maybe you're right."

I had the usual hassle with airport security over the .38 Smith
and Wesson under my jacket. I stuck out like a sore thumb
while they verified that I really did have a permit to carry it.
Once that was squared away, Anne and I wandered the airport
hand in hand, watching planes take off and land, eating caramel
corn we bought from the airport candy shop, and griping at one
another about ruining our dinner. The passage of time was
magic. It seemed to lengthen, but without a sense of waiting.
Happiness can do that to you. So can grief.

When Ralph got off the plane, he had a huge box under one
arm. It contained long-stemmed red roses, two dozen of them to
be exact. I looked at Ralph as a brother-in-law of sorts, which is
to say somewhat critically. I watched Anne open the box and
wondered crabbily where the hell we would put two dozen roses
once we got them home. A mayonnaise jar? Masculine decor
isn't long on vases.

I need not have worried, however. In the car Ralph produced another box from a suitcase. He gave it to Anne, with orders that I was to open it when we got to the apartment. The flowers were from him to Anne, but the box was a wedding present to both of us from the firm.

Inside the box was a tall, slender crystal vase. Anne arranged the roses in it and set it on the stereo. Dinner was festive. Ralph was interested in our plans and, to all appearances, more than happy with Anne's decision to marry me.

"She's a wonderful lady," he said to me later in the evening when we were alone in the living room for a few minutes. "She deserves a little happiness out of life, and I've never seen her happier than she is right now."

I felt as though someone had just placed the Good Housekeeping Seal of Approval square in the middle of my forehead. "Thanks, Ralph," I said. "I'm pretty happy myself."

Chapter 23

SOME days are forever etched in your memory. Three of them come to mind right off the bat—the day my mother died, the day I married Karen, and the day I married Anne Corley. Anne had assured me there was no need to set an alarm, that she would be awake long before five o'clock, and she was. She kissed me and set a cup of coffee on the table beside my bed.

There was no question of fooling around. She was all business. She had finished in the bathroom, leaving it clear for me. I showered and shaved carefully, critically examining myself in the mirror. I hadn't thought about my looks in years, but I was reasonably happy with what I saw. There was a sprinkle of gray around the temples. Anne liked it, said it gave me an air of authority, liked a seasoned anchorman. I managed to put aside my antimedia prejudices long enough to accept that as a compliment. There would have been a lot of gray in the beard if I'd let it grow. The point was, if all the gray didn't matter to Anne, it didn't matter to me.

I wrapped a towel around me and went into the bedroom. Anne stood before the dresser in her slip and bra, piling her hair on top of her head. The result was a gentle framing of her face that reminded me of the late 1890s. It was old-fashioned and attractive.

"You look lovely," I said, running my finger along the soft curve at the top of her lacy slip.

She caught my finger and held it to her lips. "Thank you," she said. "You're not so bad yourself."

I lifted her chin and looked at her. Her eyes were quiet, subdued. "Are you all right?" I asked.

"I'm fine. Just a little nervous."

"I'm a lot more than a little," I told her. That brought a trace of a smile.

Ralph Ames came by the Royal Crest and drove the Datsun. Anne and I took the Porsche. She drove. The minister arrived in a pea green Volkswagen bus. Those were the only three cars in the parking lot at Myrtle Edwards Park when we got there about ten to six. The sun was just putting in an appearance over the hills behind us, while a fresh breeze blew off the water. I worried that Anne might not be warm enough in the shimmering blue suit with its flimsy blouse.

Anne introduced me to the minister. I don't know where she found him. He didn't push any creed, and it may well be that marrying people was his whole ministry. That was okay by me. When the minister asked, "Who giveth this woman?" Ralph stepped forward and said he did. I thought he had a hell of a lot of nerve, but since he was giving her to me, I didn't complain. The ceremony took exactly six minutes. We were in the Four Seasons for breakfast by six-fifteen.

Anne was radiant. I could have slit my throat for not having a camera along, but once more Ralph rode to the rescue. He took pictures of both of us together, and each of us separately. He had even made last-minute arrangements with the hotel for them to produce a tiny three-tiered wedding cake with all the trimmings. It was a nice gesture. It pissed me off. I would have preferred him to be not quite so thoughtful or indispensable.

It was time for Ralph's plane before we finished breakfast. I told Anne I'd take him to the airport in the Datsun. She could take the Porsche back to the apartment, and I'd meet her there later. We rode down the escalator together. The parking attendant brought the Porsche first. I could hardly blame him for that. I opened the door and gave her a hand inside. I leaned down so our heads were even. "I love you, Anne Corley Beaumont,'" I said.

She smiled. "I love you too." With that, she drove away.

Ralph Ames was standing beside me when I straightened up. "Ready?" he asked. We said little as we drove to the airport. We had nothing in common but Anne. "Did she give you the last chapter to her manuscript?" I asked as we pulled under the airport awning.

He patted his briefcase. "Last chapter? I've got the whole

book right here. She's been working on it for so long I can't believe I'm finally going to get a look at it."

"You mean you've never read any of it before? I thought she had already given you everything but the revised last chapter."

"Not before today. I'm planning to take a peek at it on the plane." He dragged his luggage out of the backseat and hustled off toward a waiting skycap with a brief salute to me from beside the car. "Best of luck to you," he said.

I drove back out to the freeway, a little edge of worry gnawing at me. I could have sworn Anne had said the manuscript was already in Phoenix, that was why she couldn't show it to me. Had I somehow misunderstood?

I was halfway back to Seattle when a state patrolman pulled me over. I got out of the car in a huff, ready to show him my I.D. and give him a piece of my mind. I knew damned good and well I hadn't been speeding.

"You J. P. Beaumont?" he asked as he reached the car.

"What of it?"

"We've got an APB out for you. Captain Powell has been trying to get you at home since seven o'clock this morning. Get in. I'll patch you through to Seattle P.D."

I got in, and the patrolman made a connection to the Seattle dispatcher. "Get down here right away. Powell is waiting. He's hot!"

"What the hell do you mean, get down there? I just got married. I'm supposed to be off duty."

"He said to tell you your leave is canceled. He needs you now."

I got out of the patrol car and slammed the door. "Sorry I pulled you over," the patrolman said. "If I'da known the circumstances, I never would have seen you."

"Thanks," I said. "For nothing," I added under my breath.

I drove to the Public Safety Building. Powell was in the fishbowl on the phone as I came in. "What the fuck is going on?" I growled as he hung up.

"We've got another homocide. This one's down in Auburn. It was in the paper this morning."

"I hate to mention this, but I don't work in Auburn. I work for the city of Seattle."

Powell went on as though he hadn't heard me. "A guy came

tearing in here at seven o'clock looking for you. He says it's about the Auburn case. He refuses to talk to anyone but you."

"Where is he?"

Powell nodded in the direction of one of the interview rooms. "He's in there. His name is Tom Stahl."

I didn't recognize the name right off the bat, and the slightly built, crewcut young man who paced nervously back and forth in the tiny interview room didn't ring any bells either. From the delicate sway of his hips, I guessed he was a little light in his loafers, one of Seattle's more obvious gays. I let the door slam shut behind me. "I'm Detective Beaumont," I said. "What can I do for you?"

"Everybody connected with this case is getting killed. I'm sure I'm next. When I read the newspaper this morning, I almost had a heart attack. I knew right away it was the same man; I mean, how many Charles Murray Kincaids can there be?" His words came in a breathless lisp.

"What the hell are you talking about?" Stahl had been clutching a newspaper in his hand. Now he dropped it on the table like a hot potato.

"It happened right after I tried to call you, the night before last or yesterday morning, too late to make it into the paper until today. I always read the paper early, before I go to church."

"What happened? For God's sake, make some sense, man." Without meaning to, I was yelling at him. He pushed the paper in my direction and scurried to the far side of the room.

"Read it yourself. I demand some protection."

I read the article. It was simple enough. An Auburn resident, Charles Murray Kincaid, had been found shot to death in an automobile outside his home early Saturday morning. Police were investigating. He had been shot once in the back of the head. There was nothing in the article to explain Tom Stahl's extreme agitation. "So what?" I asked.

"Look at the address." I looked. "It's the same address I gave your wife."

"Now wait a minute," I said, trying to modify my tone. He was obviously frightened. "Let's get this straight. I didn't have a wife until six-fifteen this morning. Why don't you tell me the whole story, from the beginning."

He took a deep breath. "It's about Angela Barstogi," he said. "She ran up a big long-distance bill talking to some guy down in Auburn. Her mother called to complain about the bill. Said she wouldn't pay it because she didn't make the calls. I did some checking. Kincaid had an easy telephone number, 234-5678. It's long-distance from Seattle. Kids called him all the time. As soon as they learned their numbers on "Sesame Street," they'd string numbers together and call him: 1-234-5678. We tried to get him to change his number, vacate it so it would be a disconnect. But he wouldn't. Claimed he loved talking to little kids.

"Anyway, I called one morning to talk to the mother, Mrs. Barstogi. She was asleep, so I ended up talking to Angela. I told her she shouldn't call him anymore, that her mother would have to pay the bill. She said she liked talking to Uncle Charlie on the phone, so when—"

"Wait a minute," I interrupted. "Did you say Uncle Charlie?"

He nodded. "So after I heard she was dead, I tried to call you and tell you, just in case it was important. I only wanted to give you his name and phone number. It's illegal for me to do that, you know. I could be fined and lose my job, but I didn't want to go through security when it was probably nothing. The guys in security don't like me."

"You work for the phone company?" The name came back to me, the messages I had ignored and thrown away. He nodded again.

"When I couldn't reach you at the office, I finally got your unlisted number and called your house. I could be fired for that too."

"My house?"

"Yeah. I called Friday morning. I went to a two-day training session out in Bellevue on Wednesday and Thursday, so I didn't try calling again until I got back to the office on Friday. The woman I talked to said she was your wife, said she'd give you the message. I left Kincaid's name and address with her."

My stomach turned to lead. Just then Powell tapped on the door. "A detective from Auburn is here with their preliminary report. I thought you'd like to talk to him. He says Kincaid drove a black van. You think maybe there's a connection?"

"I'd bet money on it," I said grimly. "Where's the detective?"

"He's taking some stuff down to the crime lab."

I picked up the phone in Powell's office. Some numbers you know by heart. I dialed the crime lab. Janice Morraine answered. I recognized her voice. "Hi, Jan," I said, trying to sound casual. "Beaumont here. Did they bring you a slug from that Auburn case?"

"I think so," she replied.

"Run a comparison with the Faith Tabernacle slugs and call me back." I put down the phone, fighting the urge to heave it across the room.

Powell was looking at me, puzzled. "What have you got, Beaumont?"

"Just a hunch, nothing more."

Tom Stahl came to the door of the interview room. "What next? Protective custody? Do I go, or stay, or what?"

"First we'll need to get a statement. Hang on a minute. You want a cup of coffee?" I couldn't handle being locked up in a small room taking a statement, not when my mind was flying in a dozen different directions.

"Coffee would be fine," he said. "Black."

I walked past my desk on the way to the coffeepot. I stopped and dialed my home number. I got a busy signal. There was a stack of messages on the desk, too. The top one was from Peters, clocked in at seven-twenty that morning. The number was different from the hotel I had tried the previous day.

I dialed and was connected to Peters' room. "Thank God you caught me. I was just heading out to catch a plane. I've booked an earlier flight from Tucson. Where'd they find you?" he asked. "When the operator said your phone was out of order, I took a chance and called the department. They were looking for you. I told them you might be driving the Datsun."

"It worked," I said. "They found me. What have you got?"

There was a distinct pause. "It's not pretty, Beau," he began. "I hope it's not too late. Has she told you about her father?"

"Some," I replied.

"Coroner ruled it a suicide, but Anne swore she'd shot him for killing her sister. That's when her mother had her committed."

My mind scrambled to make sense from what Peters was saying. "Shot him? Anne said she shot her father?" I felt like I was stumbling in the dark.

Peters heard my disbelief. "I came down to Bisbee to check it out. According to records here, Anne's father fell carrying Patty down some stairs. He felt so bad about it he put a bullet in his head two weeks later. Anne insisted she shot him, and she claimed that Patty's death was no accident, that her father had murdered her. Her mother had Anne committed. That's why she spent eleven years in the state hospital."

I could hear the sound of Peters' breathing on the other end of the phone. For the life of me, I couldn't think of anything to say.

"Beau, are you all right?"

After being in the dark, sudden light blinded me. "I've gotta go, Peters," I said. I slammed the phone down in his ear. Powell was coming toward me. I almost knocked him over. "Get somebody to take Stahl's statement," I said over my shoulder.

"Hey, wait a minute. Janice Morraine from the lab tried to get you while you were on your phone," he called after me. "Says to tell you it's a match."

And the rest of my world tumbled down around my ears.

Chapter 24

My hands were shaking so badly I could hardly get the key in the ignition. Truths and half-truths chased each other in dizzying circles in my head. Milton Corley had been the first to believe her. That's what she had said. So he was the first to understand that Anne had told the truth about killing her father. The realization sickened me, but I feared the past far less than I did the present.

It was not yet ten o'clock on Sunday morning, and downtown Seattle was virtually deserted. I made short work of the trip to the Royal Crest. She wasn't there. I knew she wouldn't be. The telephone in the bedroom was slightly off the hook. When I hung it up properly, it started working again. How long had the phone been disabled? I wondered. Since last night?

I looked in the closets, in the drawers. The clothes were there; nothing was missing. Then I checked the corner on the other side of the dresser. The Adidas bag was gone. I poured myself a shot of MacNaughton's and sat down in my leather chair. I needed to think.

I tried to remember Friday night. When had we gotten home? What had been said? I remembered going to bed, her saying she wanted to stay up and work on the last chapter so she could send it down to Phoenix with Ralph.

The next thing I remembered was her crawling into bed with me Saturday morning, telling me she had been out for a jog. I had no way of knowing whether or not she had come to bed before that. It had seemed reasonable to assume she had. There had been no cause to question it, but there was no way to prove it, either. There would have been plenty of time for her to drive to Auburn and back between the time I went to sleep and the time I woke up. When had she moved the Porsche to a parking lot?

I waited for the phone to ring, knowing it was unreasonable, knowing she wouldn't call. Where could she be? What was she thinking? Didn't she know I loved her, that I'd find help for her whatever the cost? I waited.

I thought about Pastor Michael Brodie and Suzanne Barstogi blown away in Faith Tabernacle by the same weapon that had killed Charles Murray Kincaid. The same .38. Christ. She must have done that, too. What night was that? Monday? I tried to remember Monday night. She had been here; we had made love. We had made love Saturday morning, too. My stomach rebelled at the thought of her excitement, her need for satisfaction. Had she come to me on the crest of murderous heat that I had misread as passion? I battled to keep breakfast and the MacNaughton's in place. The breakfast, the liquor, and the wedding cake. Jesus.

Had she thought she could get away with it forever, that I would never find out? Or was I next on her list? How long was the list, for that matter? Her father, Brodie, Suzanne, Kincaid? How many more were there? What about Corley? Had Milton Corley really committed suicide, or had he been given a helping hand along the way?

I waited. Peters would be home by four or so. At that point Powell would know and Watkins and the world. An all-points bulletin would go out for Anne Corley Beaumont, wanted for murder, beautiful and highly dangerous. I had to find her before then. I had to be the one to bring her in. The thought of Anne in handcuffs, tossed in the back of a patrol car, was anathema to me.

I waited, watching the time slip by, watching the minute hand move inexorably. I sat for a long, long time, letting my mind wander through the last few days, searching for some hope, some consolation. There was none. I watched the clock without thinking about it, without internalizing the information it was trying to give me. It was two o'clock when I got the message, two o'clock when I realized that at that time one week ago, Angela Barstogi's funeral was just getting under way, and Anne Corley was about to walk into my life.

I jumped to my feet, remembering. She had said she intended to have a standing reservation for Sunday dinner at Snoqualmie

Lodge. My nerves were too shot to tackle the phone book my-self. I placed a call to the lodge and a hostess answered. "Does Anne Corley have a reservation there for this afternoon?"

There was a pause while she looked. "Yes she does, a reser-vation for two at three o'clock." I had been holding my breath. I let it out in a long sigh.

"Would you like to leave a message? I'll be glad to give it to her."

"No. No, thank you. I'll catch her later."

I put down the phone. Either she wouldn't show or she was expecting me. It was one or the other. The hostess had said the reservation was for two, not one. I went into the bathroom and splashed cold water on my face. I buried my face in a towel, a soft new towel Anne Corley herself had chosen. I flung it away from me, sending it sailing down the hall. How dare she buy me towels!

I went to the hall closet for my shoulder holster and .38. The holster was there. The gun wasn't.

There was no point in searching the apartment. I knew I had put it away. I always put it away. Anne had taken it. Anne Cor-ley Beaumont, armed, beautiful, and exceedingly dangerous.

I'm qualified to carry a .357 magnum. You get qualified by being an excellent shot. It's a macho symbol I don't need to pack around the department. I keep one, though, in the same bottom drawer where I had kept my mother's engagement ring all those years. I got it out and checked it to make sure it was loaded. I put it in my jacket pocket. A .357 is only good for one thing—killing. I prayed I wouldn't have to use it.

My body ran on automatic pilot. I don't remember getting into the car or driving up Interstate 90 to Fall City. I was doing what I had to do, what was inevitable. It was too painful to do it consciously, so I did it like a sleepwalker. It was like that last night with my mother, wanting her to die and not wanting her to die, wishing her suffering over yet not wanting to lose her. I didn't know whether I should hope for the red Porsche to be there or not. It would hurt either way.

I was trying to readjust my thinking, to turn Anne Corley Beaumont my love into Anne Corley Beaumont my enemy. She would have to be that if I was going to confront her and win. Afterward I could try to salvage what could be salvaged, once she was safe. Locked up and safe.

As it turned out, the Porsche was there, parked directly in front of the restaurant. There was no attempt to conceal her presence. She wanted me to know where she was. I was expected.

I grappled with the realization that Anne had called every shot since I met her. This was no exception. My hand dropped unconsciously to my pocket, checking the .357, making sure it was available. She had outwitted me at every turn. I would have to be wary. She was Mrs. J. P. Beaumont in name only. She was also a ruthless, savvy killer.

The vestibule was crowded. Of course it would be. This was Sunday afternoon. For the first time I realized how foolhardy I had been to attempt this without calling for help, without having a backup. The restuarant was full of innocent bystanders, any one of whom could suffer dire consequences for my going off half-cocked. I eased my way through the crowd to the hostess desk and peered through the dining room.

Anne was there, at a corner table. Our eyes met and held above the heads of the other diners. She motioned for me to come to her.

The hostess appeared then. "Oh," she said, "are you Mr. Beaumont? Mrs. Corley has been expecting you."

"I see her," I said stiffly. "I can find my way."

There was a glass of wine on the table in front of her, and a MacNaughton's and water at the place on the other side of the table. She was still wearing the blue suit. The Adidas bag lay in her lap. A lump rose in my throat. It was all I could do to speak. "Hello," I managed.

"Hello, Beau. I'm glad you came."

A thousand questions should have tumbled out one after another. Instead I looked around the room, J. P. Beaumont, the cop, looking over the lay of the land, looking for cover, for trajectories, for who would be hurt in a hail of bullets. "Let me help you, Anne," I pleaded.

"You already have."

My anger blazed to the surface. "I've helped you, all right, led you to three more victims."

She had held my gaze steadily. For the first time she looked down. My hand sought the safety of the .357 in case she reached into the bag. She raised her eyes. "I made a mistake with Brodie and the woman. Even so, they deserved to die."

"Anne! You had no right to judge them. You're not a jury. They were innocent of a capital crime. Child abuse is a felony, but it's not premeditated murder."

"I was evening the score, an eye for an eye." She looked at me defiantly, daring me to take exception to what she said. "I listened to the tape," she continued. "I found it in the table drawer after you and Peters left. It was strange hearing it. Athletes must feel that way when they see an instant replay. I thought there would be something in it that would point to me."

"We'd have been better off if there had been," I said.

It was all coming together now, all the missing pieces. "And the phone call I overheard was from Tom Stahl at the phone company? That's when you discovered your mistake?"

"Yes, but I'm not sorry I killed them, if that's what you mean." There was no hint of remorse about her.

"What did you put in the last chapter, Anne? You told me I couldn't read the book because you had given it to Ralph, but he didn't get the manuscript until this morning. He was planning to read it on the plane."

"I wasn't sure how it would end. I wasn't sure until I saw you walk through the door. I didn't know if you'd come."

"And now you know?"

"Yes, don't you?"

It was like we were playing a game, some private guessing game that had nothing to do with life and death. The people sitting around us had no idea that the attractive couple chatting earnestly in the corner near the window had enough firepower between them to lay waste a roomful of people.

I knew how I was afraid it would end. She was absolutely without fear or compunction. I couldn't let that happen, not at such close quarters, not in a crowd of defenseless Sunday afternoon diners. "Come with me, Anne. Let me take you in. No jury in the country would convict you."

"An insanity plea?" Her voice was full of bitter derision. "You know where they'd send me, don't you? Have you ever been in one of those places? Do you know what goes on?"

"Anne, I'll stick by you. I'll see that you get the help you need. In sickness and in health, remember? That's what we said. This is sickness." I was pleading for my life as well as hers.

"You wouldn't be there at night when the orderlies came.

Even Milton couldn't stop that. I had to have an abortion, you know. He paid for it. He didn't cause it, but he couldn't prevent it either.''

"What about Milton, Anne? Did he commit suicide?"

"He was scared of what the cancer was doing to him."

"You didn't answer the question."

"No," she said softly. "He didn't commit suicide."

I heard the words and knew they were the truth. "My God, Anne, you told me you loved him."

"I did."

The toll kept rising. I didn't want to know any more, but I was unable to stop the questions. They are too much a part of me, waking and sleeping. "Why your father?"

"The things he did to Patty were terrible, not once, but over and over. I tried to stop him, but my mother wouldn't let me. I should have killed her too, but I never got a chance. I think she knew it. That's why she never let me out. It was only after she died that Milton was able to get me released."

"What about the book?"

"It's a collection. Until now, I was the only one who knew the rest of the story, things that happened after the fact."

"All over the country?"

She nodded. "It happens everywhere," she said.

"How long have you been doing this, Anne? How long have you been a one-woman avenger? How many J. P. Beaumont suckers are there in this world?"

"I've been a widow for ten years," she said.

"And no one's ever caught you?"

"I never wanted to be caught."

The waitress came to take our order. "The gentleman isn't feeling well. We won't be eating after all. If I could just have the bill." She laid a twenty on the table as a tip.

Until she saw the size of the tip, I think the waitress was prepared to be upset. She pocketed the twenty. "Thank you very much," she said, smiling.

The interruption allowed a new train of thought. "Where'd you get the bike? The owner left town in March."

"St. Vincent de Paul's over on Fairview."

"Where'd you keep it?"

"In the parking garage of the building right behind the Royal Crest. It was just one night."

"And you got it out after I fell asleep?"

She nodded.

"What about Kincaid?"

"After the man from the phone company called, I went to Auburn and found his house. He had a black van."

"It could have been the wrong man."

"He wasn't. He confessed. I didn't want to make the same mistake twice." She paused. "Is that all you wanted to know?" she asked.

"Yes," I said. There was nothing else. I knew far more than I wanted to.

"Let's finish this outside, Beau. It's too crowded in here."

With catlike grace, she picked up the Adidas bag and walked outside.

Chapter 25

I KNOW how Pharoah felt trying to catch Moses as he disappeared into the Red Sea. Anne Corley Beaumont melted through the vestibule crowd the same way, leaving me pushing and shoving, trying to catch up. When I finally hit the outside door, I made a dash for the Porsche, expecting to see her speeding away. The Porsche sat empty, untouched.

The roar of the falls filled my head. I kept my hand on the gun without drawing it. This could be a trap, I reminded myself. I was dealing with Anne Corley the enemy. She had enough of a head start that she could easily have hidden herself away and be lying in wait. Even then I could have gone back inside and called for help, for a backup, but I didn't. Stubborn, stupid, I thought I could talk to her, persuade her to turn herself in.

Cautiously I made my way around the restaurant. In a heap near one corner of the building I found the blouse, suit, shoes, and discarded Adidas bag. Up the path, heading toward the observation area, I caught a glimpse of red. She had changed into the jogging suit. Any advantage I had because of dress was instantly nullified. With me in my suit and slick-bottomed shoes, she now had an edge. I started running too.

I didn't try for speed. I don't do wind sprints, but I can keep a steady pace for a fair distance. She was running up the path, away from the lodge, toward the hordes of tourists filling the viewpoint and picnic area. I kept my hand on the concealed .357 as I passed a group of picnickers. I didn't want them to raise an alarm, to cause a panic.

I saw her turn down a trail, one that veers steeply down the basalt canyon wall to the pool at the bottom of the falls. I had never been on it. I was sure it was the only way down and the only way back up. Three different times I pushed my way around huffing sets of climbers. Two of them were large groups. The last was a couple, a retired couple, walking by themselves.

"Did you see a woman?" I gasped. "A woman in a red jogging suit?"

"She almost knocked Mabel here down," he said.

I stopped, trying to catch my breath. "Are there any other people down there?"

The man shook his head. "There weren't when we left."

I reached in my pocket and pulled out my badge. "Stand at the head of the trail," I said to him. "Don't let anyone else come down." He looked at me questioningly. I wanted to shock him, galvanize him to action. "She's dangerous, armed and dangerous." I took the .357 from my pocket then, for emphasis, to get his attention. It worked. He grabbed his wife's arm and they hurried up the trail.

I stood for a few moments after they left, slowing my breathing, steadying my nerves. It was more than I could have hoped. We were isolated from the crowd above. I had bought some time. Maybe I could lay hands on her, shake some sense into her, talk her into surrendering. Before reinforcements arrived. Before someone called in a SWAT team.

I stood immobile, listening. Except for the roar of the water, the forest was silent. It was the eye of the hurricane. I was standing like that when the bullet hit me. It caught me full in the left shoulder and spun me into a tree.

The tree kept me from plunging headlong down the side of the canyon. I clung to it for support, my left side numb from shock. The .357 had fallen from my hand. Desperately I looked for it, expecting the next bullet to hit before I could find it. I saw it finally, lying out of reach to one side of the trail.

I looked up to see if I should make a grab for it. Anne was standing in the trail, my short-barreled .38 still pointing in my direction. We looked at one another, both lives hanging in the balance. It couldn't have been more than a second or two in time, but I aged an eternity. Then, with agonizing slowness, she lowered the gun, turned, and disappeared around a curve in the trail.

I let myself slip to the ground. I hoped shock would last a

little longer, staving off the pain. I crawled to where the gun had fallen. Once my fingers closed over the butt, I dared breathe again. Slowly I pulled myself to my feet, the world spinning crazily as I did so. I took a tentative step. The movement jarred me, starting shocks of pain pulsing through my body. I gritted my teeth and took another step.

Each movement was excruciating. The bullet, lodged against my broken collarbone, scraped along a nerve at every step. I walked. Slowly and painfully, but I walked. The descent was steep and slippery, the ground wet with slick green moss. Mist from the falls swirled around me like thickening fog. I strained to see. How much of the difficulty in vision was mist? How much was losing consciousness?

My subconscious framed the questions. I answered them aloud. "No. If I pass out, she'll kill me." Pain of realization dulled the pain in my body. I struggled through the last of the trees. There in a clearing, a flat, perpetually wet clearing on the bank of the river, stood Anne Corley Beaumont, her back to the water. The gun was still in her hand, aimed straight at me. She was waiting.

"Drop it," I yelled.

She didn't move. I heard the explosion. A bullet smacked into a tree behind me. I don't know if she thought she heard something off to her left or if some movement caught her eye. She turned slightly, pointing the .38 in that direction. I raised the .357, aimed it, and fired.

I'm a crack shot. I aimed at the .38. I should have hit it, but just as I fired, she lost her footing on the slick moss and fell. I saw the look of surprise and hurt as the slug crashed into her body. The force of the bullet lifted her and spun her to the left, sending her sprawling into the turbulent water. I dropped the .357 and raced toward her, my own pain forgotten.

I reached the bank and saw the torrent fling her against a rock, then pull her away, sending her toward the bank, toward me. I had one chance to catch her before the water dragged her under. I threw myself lengthwise on the bank and grabbed. I caught one leg of the jogging suit. Barely. The force of the current, the deadweight, should have swept her from my grasp. There should have been no strength in my injured shoulder, but fueled by adrenaline, I worked her toward the bank. Inch by inch. At last, shaking with exertion, I dragged her out of the water.

She was coughing and gasping. Blood foamed in the water that erupted from her mouth. I cradled her head in my lap, willing her to live. The coppery smell of death was all around her. I tried to wipe the hair from her mouth, from her eyes. I was crying by then. "Anne, Anne, why?"

She tried to say something. I could barely hear her; the roaring of the water was too loud, the roaring in my ears. I leaned toward her, her lips brushing my ear. "You said . . .," she whispered, ". . . said given the same . . . the same circumstances . . ." And that was all.

I was still holding her when a Snoqualmie City officer charged into the clearing from the bottom of the path. He was young but his instincts were good. He came on strong, ready to haul me in single-handed. He held his .38 Colt on me and picked up my .357 with his other hand. I tossed him my I.D., letting it fall at his feet.

"Call Captain Powell at homicide, Seattle P.D.," I told him. "Tell him I got her. Don't let anyone who isn't a cop come down that trail."

He left without argument. I lay Anne Corley Beaumont down, closing her eyes, stroking the hair from her forehead one last time. I stood up, feeling the aching chill from my sodden clothes. It was nothing compared to the glacial chill inside. Sudden weakness robbed my legs of strength, forcing me to sit once more. I didn't sit next to Anne. There was nothing more I could do for her.

The officer returned with a couple of blankets. He wrapped one around my shoulders and covered Anne with the other. "Powell says to tell you he's on his way." He looked at me closely. "You need an ambulance."

"No," I said. "I'll wait."

I have no idea how much time passed before I heard the wail of sirens. Peters loped down the trail ahead of Powell and Watkins. How he managed to make connections back from Arizona that fast I'll never know. I was glad to see him. Powell and Watty went to the blanket-covered figure on the edge of the river. Peters came to me. "I'm sorry, Beau," he said.

I felt a sob rising in my throat. It took me by surprise. Peters put his arm on my good shoulder and left it there.

"A week," I said when I could talk again. "I only knew her a week."

"I know," he said.

Powell came over to me then. "The officer says you're hurt." He lifted the blanket and looked for himself; then turned to Watkins. "Get those ambulance people down here now," he ordered. "Have 'em bring a stretcher."

Peters came with me. I was glad to be taken away. I didn't want to be there for the ritual pictures and the measurements. I didn't want to watch as the search for evidence started, as people who knew nothing about Anne Corley or J. P. Beaumont started trying to learn everything about us. They would. That's a homicide detective's job.

Peters pretty much took over. He directed the ambulance to Harborview. The doctors put me under while they removed the slug. When I came back around, Peters was there. I thought he had been there the whole time. It turned out he had gone back to Snoqualmie in the meantime and picked up the Datsun. The city of Snoqualmie had impounded the Porsche, pending completion of its investigation.

The doctor wanted to keep me overnight. I wouldn't hear of it. I wanted to be home. Like an old snakebit hound wanting his own cave under a house, I wanted to go home to lick my wounds. The doctor finally relented only because Peters assured him he would stay with me.

Watkins was waiting in the lobby of the Royal Crest. The building manager had let him in along with someone I didn't know, an eager young man Watty identified as the Snoqualmie homicide detective, Detective Means. Means could hardly restrain himself. He wanted to get started. This was his moment of glory, his first big case. He almost panted with enthusiasm. The whole idea made me weary beyond words.

The doctor had given me the slug. I handed it to Watty, who in turn gave it to Detective Means. "It'll match the ones from Brodie, Suzanne Barstogi, and Kincaid," I said. "It's from my departmental-issue thirty-eight."

We went up to the apartment. I was thirsty. I went to the refrigerator for something to drink. That was how I found the leftover wedding cake, neatly covered in plastic wrap, sitting on the bottom shelf. Peters saw me sag against the cupboard for support. He came and peered over my shoulder. "Jesus," he said.

He scraped it off the plate and ran the garbage disposal. Everybody needs a friend like Ron Peters, especially at a time like that.

We went back into the living room. Means asked the questions. Watkins was there to handle administrative procedures. I was a little surprised Means let Peters and Watkins stay. I expected him to throw his weight around.

He turned on a recorder and read me my rights. "I understand the deceased, Anne Corley, was your fiancée?" he asked.

"No," I said softly. "She was my wife."

Chapter 26

WATKINS and Means left hours later. I don't know when. Peters walked them down to their cars. He came back and poured a MacNaughton's for me and a gin and tonic for himself. He handed me my drink and an envelope.

"I found it under the front seat of the Datsun."

I held the envelope up and looked at it. My name was written in bold letters on the outside. A small piece of paper fluttered out of it. I caught it in midair. "You'll have to write the last chapter yourself," it said.

I crushed the paper in my fist. "Goddamn her! She knew! She forced my hand!" Peters sat on the couch. "Did you look at it?" I asked.

He nodded. "You probably shouldn't have read it right now." Peters had pulled the plug on both phones in the house, effectively shutting out all unwanted intruders.

I gazed at Seattle's downtown skyline, the golden lights Anne Corley had loved. Or at least seemed to have loved—but then, she seemed to have loved me too. That showed how much I knew. Peters waited quietly, not prying, ready to listen when I was ready to talk. He had gotten a hell of a lot older and wiser in the last few days.

I tossed the wad of paper to Peters. He opened it and reread it.

"We talked about it once, you know," I told him. "She asked me if, given the same circumstances, I'd do it again. When I got her out of the water, that was the last thing she said to me. She repeated what I said, that I'd do it again."

"Do what?"

"Kill. Kill someone in self-defense. I told her I thought I

would." My voice broke, tears blurred my vision. Peters got up and took my empty glass to the kitchen. He returned with a full one.

"You were right," he said. "Don't you think Anne knew you would? Don't you think she counted on it?"

"But why? And if she knew, knew it was coming, why the fuck did she marry me?"

Peters shook his head. "I don't know," he said.

For the first time I thought of Ralph Ames. I closed my eyes and shook my head. "What?" Peters asked.

"Ames, her attorney. He'll be back in Phoenix by now. Someone should call him, I guess."

Peters stood up. "What's his number? I'll call."

"Thanks," I said. "I'd better do it myself." The bandage on my chest made it difficult for me to move. Peters reattached the cord to the wall plug and handed me the phone. I got Ames' home number from information. I dialed direct, hoping like hell he wouldn't answer. He did, on the third ring.

"Ralph Ames speaking," he said in his best three-piece-suit diction.

I cleared my throat. "It's Beau, J. P. Beaumont, calling from Seattle. It's about Anne."

"Thank God, I've been trying to call—"

"She's dead, Ralph, I . . ." I interrupted, but I couldn't go on. There was stark silence on the other end of the line.

"Are you all right?" he asked.

I could hear sympathy in his voice, sympathy and concern. "It wasn't a car wreck, Ralph, nothing like that. I shot her. She was trying to kill me."

"There's a plane from Phoenix that gets into Sea-Tac tomorrow morning at ten. Have someone out there to meet me."

"But . . .," I started to object. He didn't hear me. The receiver clicked in my ear.

I put down the phone. "He's coming up," I told Peters. "He wants someone to meet him at the airport at ten in the morning."

Peters took my glass and gave me a mock salute. "Aye aye, sir," he said. "I'll be there."

The phone rang. I had forgotten to unplug the cord. It was Karen, calling from Cucamonga. "Katy Powell called me an hour ago. I'm sorry, Beau. Are you all right?"

Surprised to hear her voice, I mumbled something unintelligible. I was touched that she had bothered to call.

"The kids don't know what to say. They're sorry too. Do you have someone there with you?"

I looked at Peters. "Yes, I do. My partner. He's staying over."

The conversation fumbled along for another minute or two. When I hung up, Peters looked at me quizzically. "Your ex?"

I nodded.

"It was nice of her to call."

We pulled the plug on the phone before it had a chance to ring again. Peters and I proceeded to get shit-faced drunk. We ran out of gin and MacNaughton's about the same time. I passed out in the leather chair. When I woke up the next morning, there was nothing left in the liquor cabinet but a half jug of vermouth. I had a terrible hangover. Anne Corley Beaumont was still dead.

Peters went down to stuff some money in the Datsun's parking meter. I told him I'd break his face if he brought up a newspaper. I didn't want to see what they'd print about Anne and me. Talk is cheap, though, and I don't know if I would have been able to carry out my threat. I was in a good deal of pain. I was grateful the doctor had insisted on giving me a prescription of painkillers. I helped myself to a generous dosage, not only for my shoulder but also for my head. Nothing helped the ache in my heart.

Peters called in sick for the day. It wasn't a lie. Neither of us is a very capable drinker. Without the haze of bourbon, I worried about Ames' arrival. I was sure he meant trouble, that he was flying in to bird-dog the investigation. If the coroner called it justifiable homicide, Ames would still try to see to it that I lost my job. After all, Anne had been one of his prime clients. It was the least he could do.

Peters tried to talk me out of going to the airport, but I insisted. I wanted to get it over with as quickly as possible, like a kid who'd rather have his licking sooner than later. We went down to the lobby. The Datsun was parked across the street. Behind it sat a rust-colored Volvo.

"Goddamn! What the hell is he doing here?"

"Come on, Peters, you didn't expect Max to miss a sideshow like this, did you? I'm surprised he didn't turn up in the emergency room yesterday.''

Max crawled out of the Volvo as we crossed the street. "Did you marry her so you wouldn't have to testify against her?''

My fist caught him full in the mouth. A front tooth gave way under my knuckle. Cole fell like a stunned ox. He lay partially on the curb and partially in the street. Hitting him was pure gut reflex. I couldn't help myself. Then I stepped on his glasses. That was deliberate malice. We left him lying there without a second glance.

"Drive like hell," I told Peters. He did. My knuckles bled. I could feel a warm ooze under the bandage on my shoulder.

"You landed a pretty good punch for an invalid," Peters commented. "Remind me not to make you mad when you're not all shot up.''

The United flight got in early. We met Ames at the baggage carousel in the basement. He hurried up to me, hand outstretched. "Did you read the last chapter?" he asked without greeting.

"No," I said. "There is no last chapter. She said I'd have to write it myself.''

Ames noticed Peters, realizing we weren't alone. His manner changed abruptly, stiffened, withdrew. "I brought the rest of the manuscript back with me," he said. "You'd better read it first. Then we'll talk.''

Peters and I read it in the Royal Crest that afternoon. Ames sat to one side, watching us, saying nothing. I had given him the envelope with Anne's note. He looked at it without comment.

We didn't speak as we read. Words could not have lessened the horror. One city after another, one case after another, dates, times, weapons. Anne Corley had been a one-woman avenging angel, striking before the law could, the cases so far-flung, so widely scattered, that no one had ever put the pattern together. The manuscript ended with the death of Charles Murray "Uncle Charlie" Kincaid. There was a handwritten postscript. "I know Beau will keep his word. Love, Anne.''

Peters read the note, then got up, took out three glasses, and poured three slugs of vermouth, dividing it evenly three ways.

"Did you know?" I asked Ames, looking at him over my empty glass as the vermouth scorched my throat.

"My job was just to pay the bills as they came in. I never had a clue. Not until I was on the plane going home yesterday," he said. "I tried to call as soon as I got home. There was no answer. I left messages for you at the department. I wanted to warn you, but, as her attorney, I couldn't tell anyone else. I never thought this would happen. She seemed so happy that morning." He ran his hand across his forehead. "It was too late when I left Seattle, Beau. It was too late when you met her."

"Why did she let herself get caught? Why here? Why now?" They were haunting questions, ones I had asked myself over and over all day long.

"She must have wanted to be caught. That's the only thing that makes sense. You were her first connection to the real world since Milton Corley. You made her realize what she'd become."

The room was suddenly too small. I couldn't breathe. I walked to the balcony door, opened it, and went outside. It was late afternoon. The roar of rush hour was just tuning up.

Ames continued, his voice carrying above the noise of the traffic. "Her mother was right to have her committed. She was right, but for the wrong reason. Anne Corley was two different people, Beau. The one is here, on these pages, cold-blooded and ruthless. The other Anne Corley loved you very much." He reached down and pulled a legal-sized packet from his briefcase, the same briefcase from which he had removed the manuscript hours earlier.

"The other Anne Corley is here, in these pages. It's her will, Beaumont. She left you everything. That's why she had me come up on Wednesday. She wanted her will redrawn."

I heard what he said. I drew only one conclusion. I strode back into the room and hauled him to his feet. "Then you did know, you sorry son-of-a-bitch. You knew she was planning something like this."

"No, Beau. Honest to God I didn't. Not until yesterday on the plane, and even then she seemed so happy I never dreamed—"

I shoved him back onto the couch. His head whacked the wall behind him. "Goddamn you," I bellowed. I had to vent my rage on someone. Ralph Ames and Peters were the only ones there.

''If I just could have convinced her to turn herself in, she could have pleaded insanity.''

Ames' voice came to me from a long way off. ''She had already spent a third of her life in one of those hellholes,'' he said gently. ''She's better off dead.''

I made it to the bedroom before the sob rocked me. I couldn't argue the point. I knew he was right.

Epilogue

WE buried Anne Corley Beaumont in her blue silk suit on the bluff of Mount Pleasant Cemetery, as close as we could to Angela Barstogi. She wore the gold wedding band. I put mine in the velvet box along with the engagement ring and put the box back in my bottom drawer.

Ames handled everything. He managed to track down the minister in the pea green Volkswagen to conduct the funeral service. Ralph is nothing if not thoughtful. He squelched the assault charge Maxwell Cole was getting ready to file and handled all the details of both the Snoqualmie investigation and the departmental review. He saw them through to completion, when all charges were dropped and my record at the department had been cleared. He contacted all other jurisdictions, closing the books on other cases involving Anne Corley.

Ralph took me down to the Four Seasons and showed me Anne's suite. Those elegant rooms and I were kindred spirits. Once we had both been full of Anne Corley. Now we were empty. Vacant. There was a difference, though. The rooms were made up, awaiting someone else's arrival. I wasn't. I made Ames take me home.

Peters continued working on the Angela Barstogi case, tying up loose ends. When the final count came in, he discovered Angela had been Kincaid's third victim, all of them picked up by his unusual telephone number. He had a notebook with the names and numbers of children all over the state of Washington. Speaking as a cop, it was lucky for those other kids that Anne killed Kincaid when she did.

I operated in a haze. I developed an infection. For the better part of two weeks, I wasn't connected to what went on around me. It was probably better that way. By the time I rejoined the world, the worst of the difficulties seemed to be over except for figuring out how to go on living without Anne. I wasn't sure I wanted to.

The day I came out of the fog was the day Ames announced we needed to go pick out Anne's headstone. "Where do we have to go?" I asked, thinking about bus schedules.

"I checked on the map," he said. "It's somewhere up Aurora."

We got in the elevator. I pressed Lobby, and he pressed Garage. He led the way. The Porsche was parked in a space on the second level. "I rented it with an option to buy," he explained.

"I can't afford to buy a parking place," I said.

He handed me the keys to the Porsche. "I think we need to have a little talk about your financial position." The results dumbfounded me, the details were staggering. There was something called a marital deduction. The fact that we had been married at the time of Anne's death meant that most of the money went to me without anything going to estate taxes. I had more money than I'd ever know what to do with.

The night before Ames was supposed to fly back to Phoenix, the three of us went to the Doghouse for dinner—Peters, Ames, and me. I was beginning to like the idea of having Ames around, to appreciate being able to ask his advice. A couple came in with two little girls, pretty little things with long brunette hair. I saw Peters' heart go to his sleeve. That's when the idea hit me.

"How are you at interstate custody cases?" I asked Ames.

"I don't usually handle those personally," he said, "but our firm has won more than we've lost."

"And deprogramming?"

"We've handled a couple of those, too," he said.

Peters looked at me then. He was beginning to get my drift. I winked at him. "You know, Ames, unless you've got something really pressing, I think I'd like you to stop by Broken

Springs, Oregon, and see if you can pull Peters' two kids out of there.''

Ames shrugged. "You're the boss," he said.

I think Anne Corley Beaumont—the Anne I loved—would have approved.